DARK TIDES

AN ALLISON HART NOVEL
BOOK 5

ROBIN MAHLE

HARP House Publishing, LLC.

Published by HARP House Publishing
October 2021 (1st edition)

1

The morning line odds were set, and the races were about to begin. It was the best part of Terry Hart's Day, and the only part that mattered. The 72-year-old shuffled in white sneakers atop a stained concrete floor toward the betting desks. He gazed up at the screens mounted to painted steel columns and reached into his khaki shorts to retrieve his wallet. Easy money was the lure. The excitement of watching the racehorses was the apex.

Terry patted down his blue Hawaiian shirt and stepped up to the desk. He laid a twenty on the counter. "20 for a trifecta key, 3 to win with 5 and 6, with 1,4,5, and 6."

"Good to see you, Mr. Hart." The young, lanky man behind the counter took the cash and printed the ticket. "Here you go. Good luck to you, sir."

Terry winked and with his right hand, smoothed his thick salt and pepper hair. "Luck's got nothing to do with it, kid. It's all skill." And that was what he believed, though the meager contents of his wallet might suggest differently. A veteran gambler, Terry spent just about every day at the Bayside Downs in Tampa. He loved his horses, even if they hadn't always loved him back.

Large air coolers were installed on each floor of the grandstands, but they only brought relief to those nearby. The sun beat down on the rest of the stands and was relentless in these Florida summer months, so was the dense, sticky air.

Terry, a retired welder, had nothing better to do in any case. His grandkids were grown, and he hardly saw them anymore. Ever since his son, Leo, got divorced from his wife, Allison, Terry had become persona non grata. The two had never been close, but it was still nice to see his grandkids during the holidays. Now they were both in college, or something like that. In all honesty, Terry wasn't a model grandfather, or father, for that matter, so he tended not to keep up on all the latest. The last time he talked to Leo, he had mentioned his grandson playing minor league baseball. Terry recalled how Leo had also played but it hadn't ended well for him.

"The race is about to begin..."

Terry heard the race caller over the loudspeaker and took his seat. "Come on, Grandpa needs to pay the electric bill."

The gates opened and horses shot out, moving faster than freight trains. Beautiful, elegant, they appeared to merely canter were it not for the wafts of dust that billowed beneath them on the dirt track. Their thunderous tremors rattled the lower stands.

Terry listened as the caller offered commentary while his deeply lined brown eyes remained fixed on the lanes. This was going to be his day. "Number 3. Let's do this, number 3." The third horse, Pale Ale, had to win first place for Terry to get the big payout, doubling his money. It wasn't much, but the day was young, and he could build on a winning streak. Down to his last twenty, and his next Social Security check not due to arrive for two more weeks, Terry needed the wins.

"Son of a..." Terry shot up from the bench as Pale Ale fell back. "No."

"And it's My Gal Sal for the win..."

Pale Ale needed to finish in the top three. He didn't, and Terry struck out. The so-called exotic bets were the riskiest but paid out the most. He shuffled inside and headed toward the escalator, his head low, and mumbling under his breath.

A stocky, middle-aged man in a short-sleeved button-down shirt and dress pants seemed to appear out of thin air. "Hey, Terry."

He stopped and raised his sights. "Oh. Hey, Lou, how's it hanging, man?"

"Same as ever, Ter. Same as ever. Leaving so soon?" he asked.

"Struck out early today. No worries. I'll be back on my game again. Always am," Terry replied. "Listen, I gotta..."

"Why don't you come sit down in my office for a minute? Want to talk to you about a few things."

"Now?" Terry checked his watch and searched his mind for any excuse. "I don't know..."

"Sure you do. Come on back. I won't keep you for long." He turned on his heel and started on.

Terry regretted not slipping out sooner, already keenly aware of what this conversation would entail. It wasn't the first time he'd been summoned to Lou Santos's office. The track manager was responsible for a lot of things, including collecting on customers' debts. He followed Lou inside and sat down. "Boy, I wouldn't mind a bottle of water if you got one to spare."

"Sure thing, Ter." Santos turned around to the small fridge behind his desk and retrieved a bottle. "Here you go, buddy. It's a hot one already, am I right?"

"Yes, sir." Terry opened it and took his time with a nice long drink.

Santos rubbed his balding head as he watched with obvious impatience. When Terry finished the last of it, he peered at him. "You enjoyed that, did you?"

"Very much. Thank you."

Santos folded his arms over his broad chest. His high forehead creased as he regarded Terry. "I know you know why I asked you in here."

"I have an inkling," Terry replied. "Like I said before, I'm working on a solution, Lou. I promise you that. I just need a little more time."

"You're ten grand in the hole, man. I've given you enough time to find a solution. You think I don't have a boss? Someone who's not breathing down my neck? And you come in here making more bets with whose money, huh?"

Terry lowered his gaze. "That race should've panned out."

"It didn't." Santos pressed his back against his chair. "Listen, I don't want to see you back here unless you come to pay your debt, you understand me, Terry? I see your old wrinkly face in here placing bets with money you should be giving me, we're going to have ourselves a situation. Don't make me have to take this upstairs. We've known each other a long time, Ter, you know I'm not playing. Now get the hell out of my office."

Terry slowly pushed off the chair with a noticeable groan and shuffled out of the office. If there was one thing he hated worse than losing a bet, it was tucking his tail between his legs like a damn dog. He was at Santos's mercy and was lucky he'd let him off again, but if today was any example, his luck would run out sooner rather than later.

———

THE CONCRETE STAIRS outside Terry's apartment building were only feet away from his front door. Everyone who trotted up and down those steps sounded like a herd of elephants and it was usually at all hours too. But when he rented the place, it had been the only first floor unit available. No way could Terry's knees handle an upstairs unit. He keyed the lock and opened his door to the musty smell that never went away no matter how often he opened the windows. It wasn't often this time of year in any case. The carpet inside looked like it had never been replaced and certainly not since he moved in a few years ago. That was when Sue died. Cancer at 65. It hadn't been fair. Sue took care of herself. Hardly drank, ate fairly well. So why her and not him? Because God wanted him to realize how good he had it for a while, even if he hadn't known it at the time. He had been a lucky son of a bitch to land Sue. She passed on shortly after Leo got divorced. Maybe it was Leo's fault.

Terry walked to the fridge and grabbed a can of Coors. It was barely noon and he had zero items on his agenda, so why not have a beer for lunch? He lived off the government now, and it was his right to collect from a system he spent his life paying into. If only he had something to show for that life of work besides a shitty one-bedroom apartment and worn, outdated furniture. Now Santos wanted to collect on the line of credit extended to him. Okay, so Terry had gotten out over his skis. So what? Everyone did once in a while. Still, not everyone owed 10k to someone like Lou Santos. If only the track owners knew what their manager had been up to.

Terry sat down on his recliner and scratched at his stubbled, leathery face. If he thought his son had the money, he'd ask. Then again, it was pretty damn unlikely Leo would fork over that kind of dough and least of all, to his father. Not to mention, Leo was getting married again. What a crock. Could he have been any more of a walking cliché? Marrying a younger woman after getting divorced from his first wife of 20 years. And it wasn't like Allison had let herself go either. He should've slapped Leo around a little to knock some sense into the kid. He was never going to do better than Allison. Guess he thought he'd try anyway. That reminded him, he'd better get his suit cleaned.

As Terry stared at his old, boxy television, which broadcast absolutely nothing of interest, his gaze shifted to the knick-knack on the side table. It was a ceramic owl with the paint chipped off one eye and stood about 6 inches tall. He'd put it on the side table after he moved in as a reminder of his dead wife. Sue had been a collector of all things crap, or so Terry believed. He had gotten used to all of it laying around their old house before she died. Since then, he'd packed up most of it, the owl was an exception. It was one of her favorites, mostly because she'd bought it after their son was born. The rest of her collection sat in the closet of his apartment. Five boxes, if he recalled correctly. As he peered into the hall near the closet, his brow creased. "Huh, I wonder."

———

THE SOUND of the front door opening drew Allison's attention. She glanced through the breakfast window from the kitchen sink. "You're here." With a wide smile, Allison set down the dishtowel and hurried to the foyer when the door opened. "Micah!" She pulled her daughter into an embrace.

"Can I step inside first, Mom?"

"Oh, sorry, honey. I'm just so excited you're here." Allison stepped back. "Let me look at you." Her gaze roamed over her. "You look well. Maybe a little thin, but otherwise, well." She patted Micah's shoulders. "Come on. Leave your bag, we'll get it later. I made sandwiches. I thought you might be hungry, and it'll be late by the time we eat anyway since your brother won't be here for a while." Allison walked into the kitchen. "You want a soda or some tea? You must be thirsty after the drive."

"Mom, take a breath." Micah sat down on the barstool at the island and tossed back her long dark hair. "You don't need to wait on me hand and foot, but I wouldn't mind a Diet Coke."

"You got it." Allison retrieved a can from the fridge. "So, another year finished. My God. You only have one left, and you'll graduate." She handed her the can.

"I know. It's gone so fast. Guess I'll have to think about where I want to live and work and all that."

"Not just yet you don't. Get yourself through the internship and the rest will fall into place," Allison replied. "So, how are you holding up with all this?"

"You mean, Dad's wedding?"

"Yeah."

Micah shrugged. "I don't know. It's weird. Like really weird, but I guess as long as he's happy."

Allison tucked a rogue hair behind her ear. Her brassy blonde locks were piled on top of her head in the usual fashion. Her style hadn't changed for several years, but since turning 49 last month, she thought wearing her hair this way made her look younger by drawing the eye up. Maybe, but she hardly needed help looking better than she already did. A slender, toned woman, no one would believe she was nearly 50. "I wouldn't want anything other than happiness for your father."

Micah tossed back her can of soda before returning her attention. "You deserve happiness too, Mom. I know I've been lukewarm to the whole Shane situation, but you look happy."

"Well, it's too early to know how all that's going to pan out, but I appreciate your support." Allison reached for Micah's hand. "It's going to be a tough few days with all the wedding stuff going on, but come Saturday, I'll be there to support your dad. And you should know that Shane will be coming with me. I hope that's okay."

"Of course it is, Mom. I mean, don't get me wrong, I wish it wasn't like this. I wish you and Dad were still together, but I've come to accept it now after putting you through the wringer for so long. I am sorry for that."

"Me too, honey. I could've handled things better, but all that's in the past now. We're only looking forward."

Micah smiled. "Good. I'm so proud of you. Your business and all that. I should've told you sooner."

"Thank you, baby." Allison took in a breath and pulled back her shoulders. "So, your brother will be here in a few hours. How about you and I do a little shopping first? Do you have something to wear to the wedding?"

"Well, I do, but..."

Allison raised her hand. "Say no more. Let's hit the mall."

———

Lucy Boyce was the youngest member of Allison's investigative team at just 21 years old. The dark-haired, slim, quiet young woman, whose knowledge of all things computers was astonishing, had started with the partners after her father passed away only months ago when she was still 20. In fact, Allison owed a lot to Lucy. It had been her father, a hard-boiled P.I., who'd introduced Allison to the business. After his passing, Lucy had been instrumental in helping Allison get new clients because Lucy recommended the team to her dad's former contacts. So, she became the "L" in ACL Investigative Services. Now, she was dating Allison's son. Nolan Hart was a fledgling Triple-A ballplayer on his first season with the Tampa Bay Tarpons. The almost 20-year-old fell hard for Lucy and Allison had been thrilled the two were dating.

Lucy heard Nolan's car pull onto the driveway of the home she used to share with her father and hurried to step outside. Her heart raced and butterflies lined her stomach. It had been almost a month since he'd been able to come home, and she missed him terribly.

He walked along the flagstone path with a duffle bag over his shoulder. His brown wavy hair had grown almost to his shoulders now. Tall and athletic, he was perfect in her eyes and a smile spread from ear to ear as she rushed to embrace him. "Holy crap, I've missed you."

"I've missed you too." Nolan returned the hug with just as much enthusiasm.

"Come in. You must be exhausted. How was the drive?" Lucy led him inside and closed the door.

"I was on a bus for two days with 20 dudes, so not great." He set down his bag. "But after looking at you, I don't even remember who they are."

"What are we going to tell your mom?" Lucy asked.

"Nothing. I'll go see her at 7 o'clock like I told her. Can't a guy see his girlfriend before running home to his mommy first?"

She laughed. "I just don't want her feelings to be hurt. You know none of this has been easy for her."

Nolan continued inside. "It hasn't exactly been a cake walk for me either. Don't worry about my mom. Micah's already there, I'm sure, so it's probably a good thing for those two to have some alone time."

"You hungry? Want something to drink?" Lucy started toward the kitchen.

"I wouldn't mind a beer," Nolan replied.

"What, are you trying to get me into trouble? You plan on showing up at your mom's house with beer on your breath?"

"Seriously?" He followed her to the kitchen. "I am an adult

living my own life. I drink beer with the team—sometimes, when the coach isn't looking."

Lucy opened the fridge. "I did pick up some." She handed him a bottle. "Don't you dare tell your mom. She's still my boss. I don't need her mad at me."

Nolan tossed back half the bottle. "Forget about Mom. I didn't travel across two states to talk about my mom or my dad or his ridiculous wedding. I came here to see you."

Lucy met his gaze. "I'm glad you did."

———

INSIDE THE DEPARTMENT STORE, Allison waited while Micah tried on one of several dresses she'd found. It felt nice doing this kind of stuff with her again. It had been so long. She was glad their relationship was on the mend after so many years. Maybe it had been because Leo started seeing Jenny and was now about to marry her. Maybe that was what it took for Micah to realize her father wasn't pining for Allison and that he'd moved on. They had all moved on.

"Hey."

Allison spun around. "Hey."

Leo stood before her, hands in his pockets and wearing an oversized polo shirt to cover his expanding waistline. "Where's Micah?"

"In the dressing room. She'll be there for a while," Allison replied.

"You have it?" he asked.

"I do. Are you sure you still want it?"

He nodded. "I know you said you didn't find any evidence, but I just—I have to see for myself, you know?"

Allison glanced away. "Yeah, I know." It seemed Leo always

forgot about the sins of his own past, even when focusing on the possible sins of his fiancée. Allison hadn't found any evidence Jenny had actually cheated but did spot her with an old boyfriend a few times. She pulled out the manilla envelope from her large purse. "You're getting married in three days."

He took the folder. "I'm well aware of that, Alli. I should've asked you to look into this when I first suspected, but I tried to ignore it. I tried to pretend I wasn't afraid Jenny was cheating. I imagine you must've felt that way."

"Yeah, it was something like that." Allison took in a breath and glanced at the dressing rooms. "What are you going to do, Leo?"

"With this?" He held up the envelope. "I'm going to look at it. I'm going to look at Jenny's face and I'm going to try to figure out if she still loves him."

"And if you think she does?" Allison pressed on.

Leo smiled at her. His receding hairline and plump midsection didn't change the fact that he had a handsome face. "Then maybe I won't be getting married in three days." He leaned in and kissed Allison's cheek. "I better get out of here before Micah sees me." Leo turned away.

"Hey, Leo?"

He stopped and turned back. "Yeah?"

"Just remember that people deserve second chances. I didn't give you one. So, whatever you decide, try to remember that."

"I will, Alli."

2

A large cross was fixed to the roof of the church. The wooden doors lay behind an arched opening. Guests had begun to arrive on this steamy Sunday morning that saw the sun shining in a bright blue sky.

Charlie sat behind the wheel of her white Chevy crossover, parked with the engine still running. "How are you holding up, Alli?"

From the passenger seat, Allison peered at the church. "Fine. I'm doing just fine. What about you, Micah?"

In the backseat, Micah was dressed in a lilac cocktail dress with spaghetti straps and a plunging neckline. "I'm getting ready to watch my father marry someone who's not my mother, so, not great if I'm being honest. But I have to be here for Dad. You don't, Mom. No one would blame you for sitting this out."

Allison smiled at her. "I know, but I wouldn't be able to forgive myself. I want your dad to be happy and I hope this will make him happy." She spotted Leo's car approach. "There's your dad now. I see Nolan and Lucy with him. We should get inside." Allison opened the car door and stepped out, wearing a knee-length blue floral dress that hung perfectly on her slender waist and was tied off with a bow on the side. And in a rare event, her hair was worn down and flowed long past her shoulders in soft curls.

"Why isn't Shane here with you, again?" Charlie wore a ruffled-sleeved grey dress and low-heeled black shoes that clicked on the asphalt as she reached Allison. Her black spiky hair hardened the otherwise feminine garb that rested gently against her full figure.

"He was going to come—I invited him—but it would've felt too awkward," Allison replied.

"For you or for Shane?" Charlie pressed on as they continued toward the church.

Allison turned back to Micah and took her hand. "I'm proud of you, baby. And you look absolutely beautiful."

"Thanks, Mom. I'm proud of you too. I should have been telling you that all along and I'm sorry I didn't."

Allison gently squeezed Micah's hand as they reached the doors. "Well, here's to the start of another chapter in all of our lives."

The church was quaint, and the pews were filling up with guests. The altar was decorated with flowers in shades of white and peach. Now that the day had come, Allison would've felt better with Shane at her side. Ultimately, it had been her decision to go alone, figuring it was something she had to face head-on. The man she had been married to for 20 years was getting remarried. However, marriage wasn't something Allison would ever be interested in again. What was the point? Her kids were grown and starting their own lives and careers. She worked hard at getting ACL Investigative Services off the ground and so far, it had just recently gotten into the black. No, marriage wasn't in the cards for Allison. Not again.

Micah tapped Allison's shoulder. "Do you want to sit up front with Nolan and me?"

"Oh, no, honey. You two go on up there. Charlie and I will be fine right here. Isn't that right, Charlie?"

"This'll do me just fine." She slid down the row and took her seat.

"Go on. Go be there for your dad." Allison kissed her on the cheek and moved in next to Charlie.

Charlie took her hand. "You did good with those kids, Alli."

"Yeah, they turned out all right." Her attention was drawn to the hall at the right of the altar where Nolan stood with Leo and a man she was surprised to see. "Oh my God."

"What is it?" Charlie looked on. "Who's that talking to Leo?"

Allison's brow knitted. "His dad. My ex-father-in-law. I can't believe he's here."

"Why not? He's Leo's dad."

"Oh, I know," Allison began. "But Leo hasn't spoken to Terry in I don't know how long. And not much at all since his mother died. He's the last person I would've expected to see here."

Charlie studied the two in conversation. "Leo doesn't look thrilled."

"No. I wonder if I should help," Allison replied. "The last thing Leo needs right now is to get into an argument with his dad."

Charlie grabbed hold of her wrist as Allison started to rise. "Alli, wait. This isn't your battle. Not anymore. Leo's a grown man. He can handle it. He's not your problem. He's Jenny's problem now."

"But what about Nolan? He's..."

"Alli, listen to me," Charlie continued. "If you want to truly move on, this isn't the way. Nolan's there to help his dad. Let him help. You have to cut this string once and for all. And if your ex-husband's wedding isn't the place to do it, then I don't know where is."

"Okay. I hear you." Allison turned to face the front. "Leo can handle his own father. None of my business."

"There you go." Charlie patted Allison's thigh. "You should be happy Jenny will be the one to deal with in-law drama. I couldn't stand my in-laws. Thank God they never want to talk to me."

Allison tried to listen with one ear as Leo spoke to his father, Terry. Despite what Charlie said, she knew Leo and his father had a contentious relationship and it concerned her that he was here today. She didn't think Leo would've invited him, so it must've been Jenny. If that was true, it wouldn't sit well with Leo. "Not my problem."

"What's that?" Charlie asked.

"Nothing. Looks like the ceremony's getting ready to start."

Nolan stood next to Leo while they waited for the bride. He was a taller, more handsome version of Leo, but with Allison's tenacity. Jenny's younger sister, who appeared all of about 18, started down the aisle.

Jenny was almost 15 years younger than Allison. She was a teacher at the high school where Leo taught gym class and coached the varsity baseball team. It was a small saving grace that Jenny wasn't the woman who'd lured Leo away from her. Of course, that sounded absurd. Leo did what he did of his own free will. But that relationship went up in flames shortly before their divorce was final. Allison figured it was because Leo had tried to get back into her good graces and she was too stubborn to let him back into her life.

Mild regret masked her face as she looked at Leo in his dark grey suit and tie, gazing lovingly at Jenny as she stood at the entrance, ready to make that walk.

The music began and the guests stood. Allison fixed her eyes on

Terry, who'd retreated to the back of the church. At least he hadn't made a scene, but there was still the reception. As Allison returned her sights to Leo, he captured her look and smiled. But it wasn't the kind of smile she would've expected. Regret lay behind his eyes. Regret for what, she hadn't known. She wondered if Leo confronted Jenny about the ex-boyfriend. If he had, it was possible Jenny wouldn't be walking down the aisle right now. She would've been offended or hurt, and so it was easy to conclude that Leo decided against it. Maybe that was for the best. The idea of karma appealed to Allison, but not at the expense of her children's father. No matter what he'd done to her.

———

THE RECEPTION WAS HELD at Leo and Jenny's home. They lived in a 3-bed, 1990s Ranch-style home in an older neighborhood in the south part of Tampa. Allison was glad she got the house in the divorce, especially since they'd had it remodeled a year before they split up. Hey, she could relish in the small things.

Allison made her way to Nolan. "You looked great up there today, son."

"Thanks, Mom. How are you doing?" he asked.

"Just fine. Where's Lucy?"

"Getting some food, I think." He cast down his gaze. "Are you mad I went to see her before you the other day?"

"No, of course not. She's your girlfriend and you love her. Nolan, you're an adult now, with a job and everything. This is what you're supposed to do."

"I know, but... You know, I can't stay long. I have to get back to the team tomorrow morning. I wish I could be here for you."

"I appreciate the sentiment, but I'll be just fine. Hey, can I ask you something?" she pressed on.

"Sure."

"What was going on between Grandpa and your dad before the ceremony?"

Nolan covertly surveyed the room. "Dad didn't know he had been invited. I guess Jenny thought it was a good idea. Too bad she didn't know that Dad hates Grandpa."

"Your dad doesn't hate Grandpa Terry. He just doesn't get along well with him," Allison replied.

"Yeah, well, Dad was upset. Told him to go sit in the back and be quiet. He did, so I guess that was good. I don't know if he'll be coming here, though," Nolan said.

"Probably just as well if he doesn't." She glanced at the front door. "Oops. Guess Terry didn't get that memo either." Allison grabbed Nolan's arm. "I'll go talk to him. Just keep your dad occupied, okay?"

"I don't think that's a good idea, Mom."

"It'll be fine. Go on." Allison turned to Charlie who had been talking with Lucy. "I'll be right back."

"Where is she..." Charlie's face turned deadpan. "Oh, no."

Nolan stepped toward her and Lucy. "I told her to leave it alone, but you know what Mom's like."

Charlie pursed her lips. "Yes, I do, Nolan. Yes, I do."

It was as though Allison felt her best friend's eyes burning through the back of her skull. She looked over her shoulder at Charlie and offered a thumbs-up. Terry was just ahead, and she smiled on her approach.

"Well, look at you, Alli," Terry began. "Aren't you a sight for sore eyes?" He leaned in to kiss her cheek. "Surprised to see you here."

"I could say the same thing about you," she replied. "How are you, Terry?"

"Doing all right. Still alive and kicking, much to my son's chagrin."

"Oh, now, Leo loves you. You know that." Allison was pretty sure her eyes betrayed her words.

"Sure he does. Well, at least I was here to see him walk down the aisle—again." He laughed.

"I hear Jenny invited you, huh?" Allison asked.

"She did. Kid's okay in my book. A little young, but that's what a mid-life crisis is all about, right?"

Allison chuckled. "I guess so."

"What about you, huh? You got yourself a new beau?" Terry asked.

"As a matter of fact, I do. He's working, so he couldn't be here."

"Is that so? What kind of work?"

"He's a detective."

"Well now, haven't you stepped up. I did hear something about you being a private investigator. Doesn't surprise me one bit. You always had a nose for figuring out folks' secrets," he replied.

His less-than-subtle remark wasn't lost on her. "Thank you, Terry." She turned at the hand that landed on her shoulder. "Leo."

"What's going on over here?" he asked.

"I was just catching up with Terry. Haven't seen him in a long time," Allison replied.

"I thought I made myself clear at the church, Dad." Leo's eyes fixed on Terry.

"Well, I just thought since your wife invited me and all...."

"She was being kind. I'd appreciate it if you left," Leo replied. "This is a family event."

"Last I checked, I was family, or did that change when your mom died?"

Allison stepped between them. "Okay, there's no need to

rehash the past. Terry, maybe you should go. This isn't the time or place."

"You're on his side after what he did to you?" Terry shook his head. "Didn't take you for a fool, Allison." He peered beyond her shoulder. "Oh, now, here we go. Leo's new bride to the rescue."

"Is everything all right?" Jenny arrived, having changed from her bridal gown to a simple white cocktail dress. "Leo?"

"Everything's fine. Terry was just leaving," Leo replied.

"I guess I was." He eyed Allison. "It was good to see you, Alli. You take care of yourself." He turned to Jenny and reached for her hand. "Good luck with that one, and thanks for the invite."

Allison slipped away unnoticed and returned to Charlie and the others. "That went well."

"I see he's leaving, so I guess it did," Charlie replied. "You okay?"

"Yeah, of course I am." She swatted away the notion. "I am hungry, though. I think I'll grab a plate." As Allison started toward the buffet that lay on Leo's dining table, he stood in front of it, sizing up the entrees when she continued. "All good now?"

"As good as it can be." Leo grabbed a plate. "Jenny thought it would be a good idea for Dad and me to clear the air."

"I see that. Bet she won't make that mistake again." Allison heaped a spoonful of rice pilaf onto her plate. "Nice spread. Jenny did good on this one."

"Thanks. Hey, listen, what you gave me before..."

"It was yours to do with as you saw fit," she replied. "I was just doing my job."

"Yeah, right," he added. "Well, at least Dad's gone without incident. That might be a first."

"Did he ask you for money?" Allison shook her head. "I'm sorry. That's absolutely none of my business."

"No, it's okay. He didn't—this time, if you can believe that.

Still, he wanted something. I'm sure he'll let me know what that is in due time."

––––––––

SHANE STOOD on the other side of Allison's front door when she opened it. Her smile widened at the sight of him. "Hey there."

"Hey there, yourself." Shane was still dressed in the shirt and tie he wore for work. "I just finished for the day. Thought I'd stop by and see how you were doing after Leo's wedding."

"A lot of people have been checking up on me today." She stepped aside. "Come on in. I'm doing better now that you're here, anyway. Thanks for coming over." Allison closed the door. "Can I get you a beer?"

"I'd love one." Shane strolled inside. The 40-year-old was fit and trim at about 6 feet and could've been a G.Q. model with his smooth face and sharp jawline. Instead, he chose to become a cop after fumbling through life for too long, unsure of himself. Before Allison, he was a consummate bachelor and now that he had her, he had no idea what he'd been missing.

Allison grabbed two bottles from the fridge. "So today was interesting." She handed him a beer and tossed back a swig of her own.

His brown eyes burrowed into her. "Your ex-husband remarried. I'm sure it was interesting."

"No, not that. I mean, yes, that was interesting. But my ex-father-in-law was there. He and Leo have had a strained relationship for as long as I can remember and especially since Leo's mom died."

"Who invited him?" Shane asked.

"The new wife." Allison smirked and took another drink.

"You seem pretty happy about that."

"No, not really." She raised the corner of her mouth. "I mean, it's a little funny, but no, I'm not happy about it. I just find it interesting, that's all. The ceremony was nice. Jenny did a good job with the reception. But I will say that I'm glad it's over. All of this stuff with Leo and..." She stopped in her tracks.

"What do you mean? What stuff?" Shane pressed on.

"Nothing." She looked away.

"It doesn't look like nothing. What's going on? What don't you want me to know?"

Allison took in a breath and peered at him. "Leo asked me to do a little snooping on Jenny. He thought she might be cheating."

"Is that so? Wow. Wouldn't that be some kind of karma?" he replied.

"Yes it would, but anyway, all I found was that she'd stopped by to see an old boyfriend a few times. I took some pictures and that was it. Leo had to make the call on what to do and he did. To be honest, it felt sleazy; following her around like I did."

Shane held her gaze. "Why didn't you tell me before?"

Allison shrugged. "I don't know. I guess it felt a little weird. I'm sorry." She grabbed his hand. "I don't want to keep things from you. I've been down that road before. I don't want to travel it again."

"Good. Then it's settled. So, how about we forget about your ex and talk about us. Where's Micah? She's staying here, isn't she?"

"She is, but she met up with a friend after the reception. I don't know when she'll be back. Nolan's with Lucy at her place and he has to leave in the morning."

"So it's just us for a while?" he asked.

"For a while, I suppose. Although Micah could walk through the door at any moment," she replied.

Shane returned a mischievous grin. "I'll take my chances."

———

TERRY SAT in his recliner with an open box at his feet. Inside the box were papers and some trinkets. It was what was left of Sue's life. Her will had long since been settled and it wasn't like they had much to begin with. But as he sifted through the papers, he searched for the insurance documents. Specifically, the documents from when they had homeowner's insurance, assuming those papers still existed somewhere. He'd wanted to see the declared value of some of Sue's old knick-knacks. The will left her collection to Leo, but he hadn't wanted it. He had made that clear to her before she passed. If she couldn't be in his life then he wanted nothing else, so now, he had neither. And here it all sat, in boxes inside this shitty apartment.

He retrieved a folder and inside looked to be papers from his old insurance company. "This could be something here." Terry put on his reading glasses and perused the documents, flipping through to find what he needed. "Household items $100,000. That seems high." Terry considered what it was they owned at the time. Apart from some old furniture, not much. "Why would it be so high?" As he read the documents, the details were scant. Nothing was itemized and so the figure must've included everything in their home at the time. "This doesn't help." He set down the papers on the floor next to the box and continued to rifle through it. "Come on, Sue. Help me out here. What's all this junk worth?"

3

The smile on her face said it all. Allison examined the shiny new blue Toyota Camry while the salesman retrieved the keys. Her old Honda, also blue, sat in the parking lot of the car dealership ready to be auctioned off at wholesale. It wasn't worth enough to keep on the lot. Allison was just grateful to get rid of it. The damn air conditioner was still on the fritz. Probably why they low-balled her on the trade-in offer. It hadn't mattered, though. The time and effort it would've taken for her to fix it and sell it on her own wasn't worth it to her.

ACL Investigative Services had done well these past couple of months after a shaky start. She was proud of the work she and the team put in to make that happen. It was finally time to ditch the clunker and treat herself. Yeah, so it was a Toyota. Not exactly a luxury car, but Allison wasn't high maintenance, nor had she had the budget for anything more upscale.

"Here you go, Ms. Hart." The salesman dangled the key fob in front of her. "She's all yours." He peered at her car in the lot and then at the new vehicle. "You have a thing for blue, huh?"

"Sort of." Allison reached for the key. "Thank you."

He opened the driver's side door and Allison slipped onto the velvety beige cloth seats. After he closed it, she took in the delightful new car smell and pressed the ignition. No key required on this one. "Ah, technology." The air blew ice cold, and she reversed out of the lot toward the highway, headed to the office. The girls were about to be surprised.

As Allison drove on, her phone buzzed in the center console. "Damn it. I haven't set up the Bluetooth yet." She retrieved her phone and answered on speaker. "Leo, what's going on? Are you already back from your honeymoon?"

"We're heading back today, actually. Listen, Alli, I got a call from Terry. He says his place was broken into early this morning when he left to run to the store. We're coming home a day early to check it out for him and make sure he's okay."

"Oh my God, Leo. I'm so sorry to hear this."

"I don't know the whole deal, which is why I'm calling. I hate to bother you with this, but Terry doesn't trust anyone else I know, just you."

Allison knew a favor was about to be asked. So much for cutting the strings. "What do you need me to do? I'm driving to the office now."

"Would you mind making a pit stop by Terry's apartment to see that he's okay? He didn't sound good, and I don't want to call the police until I see the situation for myself, but I'd feel better if you checked in on him until I can."

"Yeah, of course I can do that. Is he home now?" she asked.

"He is. I already told him you'd be stopping by. I know that was presumptuous..."

"Don't worry about it. I'll head there now. Just text me the address. I'll call you back after I've checked everything out."

"Thanks, Alli. I really do appreciate it," Leo said. "Call me later."

"Will do. Bye." She ended the call and pulled off the highway at the next exit. "So much for my surprise." Allison pressed Charlie's contact on her phone. "Hey, it's me."

"Aren't you on your way here?" Charlie asked.

"I was until I got a call from Leo..."

"Good gosh, what does he want now? He's calling you while he's on his honeymoon?"

"Yeah, I know, but it's his dad. Apparently, his apartment was broken into and there's no one else who can check in on him. Leo says they're coming back later today but asked me to stop by and make sure Terry's all right. I don't think I'll be long, but I wanted to let you know."

"No problem, Lucy and I will hold down the fort. Not much going on at the moment anyway.

"Thanks, Charlie. I'll head in as soon as I can." She considered for a moment reaching out to Shane, but he didn't handle this kind of stuff anymore. He was in Major Crimes now. Homicides, organized crimes, kidnapping, things of that nature. He'd come a long way since she met him almost five years ago now. The chance encounter at a courthouse changed her life—eventually.

Allison wondered, though, if Terry had called the cops. He wasn't exactly the type of guy who liked having cops around. She wouldn't go so far as to say he was a criminal, but he had done some shady things in the past.

When Leo's mother died, it had been particularly hard on him because he was the one who had to make all the arrangements. Terry went on a week-long bender and left it all to his son to handle. Of course, Leo was a full-grown man at the time, nevertheless, it had brought him even more pain and Allison couldn't do anything for him at the time. Well, she could have, but their marriage was falling apart, and she hadn't wanted to. She could at least help him out now, for whatever that was worth.

Terry's apartment complex was just ahead. The older building was surrounded by small ponds with fountains in the center that shot water a solid 20 feet into the air. The ground floor unit was tucked behind lush greenery down a concrete path and was next to the staircase.

Allison parked her brand-new car and stepped out. She walked along the cracked sidewalk toward Terry's apartment in the heat of the rising sun. If not for her new car and its excellent air conditioning, she'd already be drenched in sweat. It felt good to savor the finer things in life.

Allison arrived and knocked on the door. "Terry? It's Allison. Leo called me." She waited a moment until she heard shuffling feet from the other side. When the door opened, Terry was dressed in a white tank top and sports shorts. "Terry, I'm so sorry, were you asleep?"

"No." He appeared perplexed and scratched at his plump belly. "Leo called you, huh? So you know about the break in."

"That's why I'm here. He thought, since he wasn't going to be able to get back until later today, that I should pop in and make sure you're doing okay."

"Well, come in then. Not that you can do much, but since you're here." He stepped aside.

"Thanks." Allison noticed the place was a mess but couldn't tell if it was because of Terry or whether it had been due to the robbery. "Did you call the police and tell them you were robbed?"

He closed the door behind her. "What for? They won't do shit about it. Just pretend to write stuff down and then leave. I don't need that kind of hassle."

As Allison surveyed the room, she noticed the television was still there. "What did they take, Terry? You really should call the police. If for nothing else, your insurance company will need to have a report filed."

He glanced at his feet and shoved his hands in his pocket. "Right. I guess I forgot about that. Don't you know some cops you can call?"

"I do, but not ones who handle residential break-ins." She picked up her phone. "But let me see if I can call them and get someone out here. It's best to do it while there could still be prints on your stuff." She returned to the call when the line answered. "Yes, hello, I'd like to report a robbery at 2464 Hillsborough Drive, apartment number 1008." She peered at Terry. "When did it happen? Last night?"

"Uh, this morning."

Allison returned to the call. "This morning. No, it's not my place. It's my father-in-law's, *ex*-father-in-law's. I'm just here helping him out." She nodded. "Thank you. I'll wait here with him. His name is Terry Hart. I appreciate the help." She ended the call.

"Ex-father-in-law." Terry shook his head. "Doesn't exactly roll off the tongue, does it?"

"No, not really." Allison returned her phone to her purse. "The police are on the way. I'll hang around if that's okay with you."

"Sure. The more, the merrier." He shuffled into the kitchen. "You want a cup of coffee or something, Alli?"

"No, thanks. I'm okay." She studied the living room. "You weren't home when this happened, right?"

"No. I ran out of coffee and went out to the store at the crack of dawn. Guess they figured they could slip in then." He poured himself a cup and shuffled back to the living room where Allison stood. "The door had been jimmied. I pushed it open, and the lights were off, so I flipped them on. Place was a wreck. I mean, more than usual."

Allison nodded. "Do you know what they took? It's kind of strange that they'd leave the TV. What about a laptop or computer?"

"I ain't got either one of those, Alli. Come on, you know me."

"Right. So what did they take, Terry?"

"Well, here's the thing." He set down his mug and shuffled to his bedroom. "I keep some old boxes of Sue's things in here."

Allison followed him. "Yeah."

"And, well, they're gone. I kept them right here on this wall. Don't know why I still had them, really. I suppose I couldn't bear to part with them."

"What was in those boxes?" Allison asked.

"Just junk. You remember how Sue collected all sorts of shit. Wasn't nothing important."

"And that was all they took?" Allison glanced around the room. "Nothing else?"

"Not that I can tell. It ain't like I got a lot of valuable stuff lying around here, as you can see. That old TV ain't worth anything to anyone. No computers. I don't even have a cell phone. I figure they broke in and saw I didn't have shit, took what they could carry and left. That's why I didn't bother with the cops. What was the point? I only called Leo to tell him his mom's stuff was taken, but he got all funny on me and hung up. Then you showed."

"Well, I still think it's important to file a report for insurance purposes. Whatever was in those boxes could've been valuable, to some extent. I remember Sue collected a lot of different things. You used to have them displayed around the house. Ducks, if I recall. The old decoys. Some figurines. Owls, too, I think."

"That's right. You got a hell of a memory, Alli. But I had no use for all that stuff after she died. Kept it anyway."

The knock on the door caught Allison's attention. "That must be the cops. They got here fast."

"Sure. When I don't need them, they're here lickety-split," Terry replied.

"Isn't that always the way?" Allison walked to the door and opened it. "Morning."

"Ma'am. Are you Allison Hart?" the officer asked.

"Yes, sir. This is Terry Hart, he lives here." She stepped aside.

"Sir, this is your apartment?" The officer walked in.

"Yep. Appreciate you coming, Officer, but as I was telling my former daughter-in-law over here, they didn't take much."

"It's still a good idea to file a report, Mr. Hart. For insurance purposes, if nothing else."

Terry eyed Allison. "Just like you said."

The officer turned to her. "It was the right call, ma'am."

"Thanks. So, Terry says the thieves just took a few boxes of his wife's things. Collectibles and such."

"Anything valuable, sir?" the officer asked.

Terry turned down his mouth and crossed his arms over his full chest. "No, sir. My wife passed a few years back now. That was all I had left of her."

"I'm sorry for your loss. Do you have any photos of what was in the boxes? These collectibles?"

"You know what?" Allison turned to Terry. "I'll bet I can scrounge up some old pictures of the house when Sue still had all that stuff sitting around."

The officer nodded. "That would be helpful—from an insurance standpoint as well." He walked around. "If that's all they took, I'll write up the report and wait for those pictures from you, Ms. Hart."

"I'll work on it this afternoon. I have a good idea of where those photos are at. I'll scan them in and send them over if that works."

"Yes, ma'am." The officer ripped off a sheet of paper from his book. "Mr. Hart, if you'll just sign here. This is the report I'll be filing pending the photos. You can submit that to your insurance company to get reimbursed. Although, I'm sure those things were irreplaceable."

"You can bet on that, Officer." Terry signed the paper. "Appreciate your help."

"That's what I'm here for." He tipped his hat. "You two try to enjoy the rest of your day. Ms. Hart, here's my card. Just shoot me an email and we'll go from there."

Allison took the card. "Sure thing. Thank you." She showed out the officer and turned back to Terry. "Well, that wasn't so bad, huh?"

"I'm telling you, Alli, you're wasting your time going through old photos," Terry replied.

"I don't mind, really. If it'll help with the insurance, what's the harm?" She checked the time. "I'd better get into work. Will you be okay here on your own?"

"Of course I will. No one's coming back here to steal nothing now that they know there's nothing to steal. Besides, my son will eventually come by. Him and his new wife." He eyed her. "Leo was a fool to let you go, Alli. I hope you know that."

She grinned. "Everything worked out for the best. He's happy and I'm happy." Allison leaned in to kiss his cheek. "Goodbye, Terry. Just do me a favor, and make sure you check your door's locked after I leave?"

"Yes, ma'am." He shoved his hands in his pockets and waited for her to leave. His face fell flat as he peered into the living room. "Goddammit."

ACL's OFFICE was on the second floor of a stand-alone commercial building near the east end of the city. The location wasn't the most desirable, but the lease was cheap and the space was plentiful.

Allison finally arrived after signing off on her new car and dealing with the robbery at Terry's apartment. Something in that scenario seemed ridiculously out of place, but in her life, she couldn't tell which one. "Sorry I'm so late."

Her entrance garnered Charlie's attention as she sat at her desk. "Don't be. We've managed to keep an eye on things. How's Leo's dad doing? Did you get all that worked out?"

"I did." Allison walked to her desk that lay against the back wall with a large window behind it. "He sure hasn't changed much. It's no surprise Leo doesn't see him often."

Lucy peered up from her laptop screen. "Why is that? Nolan says his grandpa is kind of cool."

"Sure, because he used to bring Nolan and Micah candy all the time, handed them chocolate bars every time we'd visit. Used to drive me nuts and Leo never did do anything about it. But I'm glad Nolan has fond memories of Terry. I was close to Sue. She was an amazing woman and especially for putting up with Terry. Oh, I've been meaning to show you guys something. Come over here for a minute." She turned to her window.

Charlie eyed Lucy as they both approached Allison's desk. "Did we get that new black van I've been asking for? You know how much I want to park it on the street corner so we can look like undercover feds."

"Maybe we can fit it in the budget next year. Take a look in the parking lot." Allison wore an impish grin.

Charlie peered through the window. "Where's your car?"

Lucy looked out. Her long black hair fell in her face, and she pulled it to one side over her shoulder. "Did Shane drop you off?"

"Nope. I drove here."

Charlie raised a brow. "In what?"

"The blue Toyota down there," Allison replied.

Charlie thrust her palms against the window and stared out. "Are you serious? You finally dumped that old piece of crap Honda?"

"I did. Just this morning. I was so excited to show you guys, then Leo called."

"Leave it to him to ruin your big surprise."

"I don't think he planned on his dad's place getting robbed, Charlie. And I'm here now." Allison folded her arms and smiled. "So, what do you think?"

"It's gorgeous!" Lucy said. "Can we go down and have a look?"

"I thought you'd never ask." She started toward the door and while Charlie and Lucy walked out, her phone rang. Allison answered as she joined them. "Leo, hey, sorry. I meant to call you. I did go and see..." She stopped in her tracks.

Charlie noticed Allison was no longer following just as they reached the elevators.

"What? I was just with him. He seemed fine." Allison shot a glance at Charlie. "I'm at the office, but of course, I'll go now. When are you due back?" She nodded. "Okay. I'll find out what's going on and call you soon. Don't worry. I'm sure everything will be fine. Okay, bye."

"What the hell was that all about?" Charlie asked.

Allison ended the call and sighed. "It's Terry. He's in the hospital. They think he had a heart attack."

4

Dark clouds rolled in across the bay, heavy with rain and flashing like a strobe light. The deep-throated sound of thunder meant the time had arrived. It was 4 o'clock in the afternoon on a summer day in Tampa. Rain came down hard but would finish before the last of the beachgoers could make it to the parking lot.

The drive back from Leo and Jenny's honeymoon destination of South Beach in Miami—not his choice—had taken most of the day. Now, he had arrived at the hospital where Terry was admitted, and Allison waited. Leo hurried inside and headed straight for the information desk. "I'm here about Terry Hart. Is he okay?" Leo's breath was short and quick, as though he'd run all the way from South Beach.

Allison appeared behind him and tapped him on the shoulder.

He spun around with wide eyes. "Alli, is he okay? Is my dad okay?"

She put her hand on his shoulder. "He's fine. Doctor's in with him now and last I heard was that they'll be releasing him soon."

"Oh, thank God." He turned to the nurse who had just approached. "Terry Hart. I'm his son."

"Yes, sir." She sat down and plugged in the name. "Looks like Dr. Patel is with him now. He's in room B-112 if you'd like to go see him."

"Thank you." Leo turned to Allison. "Come back with me?"

"Sure." She had rushed to the hospital this morning after Leo's call and had spent the day with Terry while they ran test after test. "Where's Jenny?"

"I dropped her off at the house. It was a long drive and I told her she didn't need to come down." Leo opened the door and walked inside the semi-private room. "Dad." He eyed the doctor. "How's he doing?"

"He's doing well. The tests all came back normal. It appears as though Mr. Hart's physical symptoms were stress-induced," Dr. Patel replied.

"His apartment was broken into early this morning," Leo added.

"That could well explain the heightened anxiety levels. I see no reason to keep Mr. Hart overnight, so I'll sign his release papers now and you'll be free to take him home." The doctor turned back to Terry. "I would suggest you take it easy for the next few days. Let your son handle your affairs."

"I will, Doc." Terry's voice was gruff as he lay in the hospital bed with an IV drip and oxygen tubes in his nose.

A final nod and Dr. Patel took his leave.

Leo moved in toward the bed. "You're feeling okay to go home?"

"Course I am. Alli's helped me through everything, and I would've been worse off if not for her," he replied.

Leo wore a gentle grin. "I agree. Thank you, Alli. I can't tell you how much I appreciate you coming through for Terry."

She reached for Terry's hand and smiled. "I've known you since I was 22 years old. You aren't getting rid of me now just because Leo's got himself another wife."

Terry squeezed her hand. "I appreciate you, kid, but you should go home. My son's here and he can see to me now. In fact, you should let him take over the whole break-in situation too. You don't need to get wrapped up in all that."

"What's going on with it, anyway?" Leo asked.

"Terry mentioned a few boxes of your mom's collectibles were taken in the robbery," Allison replied. "I said I had some old photos stashed away of when your parents lived at the house in Thonotosassa. A lot of the trinkets showed up in those pictures. I mentioned that to the police to help them locate the stolen items."

"Mom's things were stolen?" Leo asked. "What else was taken?"

"That was it," Terry replied. "Guess they figured something in those boxes might be worth a nickel, so they took them. Left the TV, not that it was worth a dime."

"I can't believe they stole Mom's collectibles. Where did you have them? Why weren't they in storage someplace safe under lock and key?"

"What do you want me to do, son? I got nothing to keep in storage and I had room in the apartment."

Leo's gaze softened. "I'm sorry. I know it's not your fault. I'm just surprised anyone would take random boxes and nothing else. Listen, we should get you ready to go, Dad. Do you need help getting dressed?"

"I'll manage." He pulled up. "Just some privacy if you wouldn't mind."

"Yeah, sure." Leo ushered Allison away and they both stepped out of the room.

After being married to the man for 20 years, she could read him pretty well and noticed his expression. "What's wrong?"

Leo stopped in the hall and peered at her. "What do you mean?"

"I mean, back there, with your dad. Is it because it was your mom's things that were stolen? Is that what's upsetting you?"

"Yes, but it's more than that." He glanced at Terry's room with a narrow gaze. "I don't know. Terry's the same as always and I feel like there's more to this story."

"How so?" Allison pressed on.

"My mom. You know how she loved to collect trinkets."

"I remember," Allison replied.

"A part of me feels like with those things gone, she's gone too. All of her. Nothing left."

Allison took his hand. "Leo, I know how close you were to your mom, and I know Terry was an asshole after she died. I'll admit that something doesn't feel quite right with me about this situation either. I can't figure out why, but you know, he shows up at your wedding..."

"Jenny invited him," Leo cut in.

"Right. So he hangs around knowing you didn't want him there, then he calls you with the break-in story."

"So you agree?" he asked.

"Maybe it's because I've been dealing with too many liars lately with my job, but I feel like he wanted you to show up today instead of me so he could get you to feel sorry for him and then lend him money. It's pretty convenient that nothing else was taken from his place. I get that he doesn't have a lot, but for the thief to choose to steal a few boxes marked 'Sue's things.' That doesn't make a lot of sense to me."

"And then he goes and has a supposed heart attack an hour later," Leo added.

"Which turned out to be nothing more than anxiety," Allison replied. "I remember all the crap Terry used to pull back in the day. All the stuff your mom put up with."

Leo regarded her. "Do you think he's up to his old tricks again because Jenny gave him an opening?"

Allison shrugged. "It's the only thing that makes sense. Was there anything of value in those boxes?"

"I don't know. Mom did have an extensive collection of some really old stuff, but I have no idea if any of it was worth anything. Honestly, if anything was valuable, Terry would've sold it long ago in my opinion," Leo replied.

"And your mom didn't leave her collection to you? I find that hard to believe considering she knew what Terry was like."

"This was back when you and I were going through—everything. I wasn't myself then. But days before she died, Mom asked me if I wanted any of it before..." he looked away. "I didn't want it because it would've meant that I had to acknowledge she was going to die. I wasn't ready to do that. I wasn't ready to lose you and her at the same time."

Allison remembered all too well those painful days. She also remembered during that time that she'd only gone to see Sue a couple of times before the end. And she wasn't there for Leo at all. She'd wanted nothing to do with him. It was something that still haunted her. "Then if all of it belonged to Terry, there isn't much we can do. I can send whatever photos I find and hope that helps them locate the boxes."

"Are you going to hold your breath? Because I'm not," Leo replied.

"It's the best I can do. Now that you're here, you can see to Terry." Allison turned on her heel.

"Hey, Alli," Leo called out.

She turned back. "Yes?"

"Thank you for being there for him today. It was more than you should've been asked to do, but I'm glad it was you."

"Of course. Take care, Leo, and welcome home."

———

THIS WASN'T her problem anymore and yet Allison couldn't shake the idea that Terry was looking to work over Leo as he had always done. It was nothing new, but to feign a heart attack seemed extreme. Maybe she wasn't giving Terry the benefit of the doubt. The man was in his 70s. It was possible with the break-in that it brought on some sort of anxiety attack. But what troubled her even more were the missing boxes. Terry said he hadn't known what they contained except to say that it was Sue's collectibles. Had he cared so little about her, or wished to forget her so much that he hadn't bothered taking stock of what she left behind?

If Terry had needed the money, why not sell the items outright? "Maybe he tried," she whispered to herself on her drive home. "Collect on the insurance?"

The hustle and bustle of the city diminished as Allison made her way home to the suburbs.

The early evening sun was just above the horizon as Allison pulled onto the driveway in her brand-new Toyota Camry. She'd almost forgotten that Micah hadn't known about the car purchase. Charlie and Lucy hadn't even gotten the chance to look at it closely. The one day Allison did something major for herself ended up being about someone else. And that someone else was tied to her ex-husband. The strings were still firmly attached to the Hart family, it seemed.

She stepped out of the car and stood back beneath the muted sky to examine it. The first car she'd purchased all on her own. It was hard to believe a woman of nearly 50 had never bought a car, but that was what happened when one married young.

The front door opened and Micah stepped out in shorts, a tank top, and bare feet. Her dark brown hair was wrapped in a loose bun on top of her head. "What are you doing just standing outside?"

Allison turned back. "Admiring my latest purchase."

"What?" Micah walked out to the driveway. "You bought a car?" She threw her arms around Allison. "Finally! No more sweating my butt off in that old piece of..."

"Hey now, watch it." Allison grinned. "I got it this morning before all the goings on with Grandpa. You like it?"

"Do I like it?" Micah opened the driver's side door. "It's gorgeous. You deserve this, Mom. I mean, you deserve a Mercedes, but you know..."

"I know and thank you."

Micah closed the car door. "How is Grandpa? Did Dad finally arrive at the hospital?"

"He did. He dropped off Jenny and came over. Grandpa's going to be fine. They're discharging him tonight."

"That's good," Micah replied.

"Come on. Let's go inside." Allison started ahead. "Have you eaten yet?"

"No. You?"

"Nope. How about I order some pizza? I'm starving." Allison walked in and closed the door behind Micah. "I'll put in the order on my phone while I'm upstairs getting changed."

"Okay." Micah returned to the living room where a comfy deep-seated beige sofa awaited her.

As Allison walked upstairs to her bedroom, she placed the order and held the phone for a moment, while she sat down on her king-sized bed. She hadn't spoken to Shane at all today and the thought of him brought a smile to her face, so she made the call. "Hi."

"Hey, are you at home?" Shane asked.

"I am. Today's been a little bit crazy and I just realized we hadn't spoken yet, so I

thought I'd give you a call. You want to come by and join Micah and me for some pizza?" His unexpected silence concerned her. "I take that as a no?"

"I know how Micah feels about me, Allison. I also know she's only here for another week or so before her internship starts. I think it's best for you two to spend time alone together. After everything—Leo's wedding—she should be with her mom right now."

Allison peered through her bedroom window into the back-yard. The tall palms that lined her back fence swayed in a light breeze but weren't dense enough to obscure the rooftops behind them. "I see. I'll tell you what, after today, I'd really love to see you."

"What happened today?"

"Too much to hash out over the phone. You sure you don't want to stop by? Micah wouldn't mind."

"Please don't read anything into this, okay? I'm trying to be the good guy here," Shane replied.

"No, I get it. So, I guess we'll catch up later then?" Allison continued.

"Let's grab lunch tomorrow. I'll clear some time, okay?"

"Sure, yeah, that sounds good. Have a good night, Shane." Allison ended the call and fell back onto her bed. She was all about reading into things. It was her job. Maybe Shane really was trying to give her and Micah some space. Honestly, Allison was too old and too tired to put that much thought into it. She cared for Shane a great deal, but this was exactly the reason for her hesita-

tion to date a friend and colleague. The energy romantic relation-
ships took was draining.

She changed into shorts and a t-shirt and returned downstairs.
Micah was curled up on the sofa with her eyes fixed on her phone.
The only part of her that moved was her thumb on the screen. "I
put in the order. Should be here soon."

"Great." Micah's eyes still hadn't left her phone.

Allison regarded her with mild consternation before giving up
and retreating to the kitchen. A bottle of chardonnay waited for
her in the refrigerator. She began to consider the events of the day
—the break-in, Terry's anxiety attack—while she poured a
generous glass. Her gaze drifted into the downstairs hall. A coat
closet lay at the end of that hall just before the utility room. That
was where she kept all the old photo albums.

Allison padded in bare feet down the hall on the light wood
floor, holding her glass of wine. She opened the closet door and
there they were in boxes marked, *photo albums*. "Well, let's see
what's inside."

———

LEO STOOD with Terry at his apartment door under the concrete
catwalk above. "Where are your keys?"

Terry dug deep into his shorts' pocket. "Right here. I already
told you, I'll be fine."

"I'm staying here with you tonight and you'll just have to deal
with it." Leo trailed Terry inside and closed the door. "Are you
hungry? Doctor said you should eat." He started into the small
kitchen and opened the refrigerator door. "Geez, Dad, you don't
have any food in here."

"What can I say? I forgot to go shopping." Terry retreated to
his bedroom. "I'm going to get changed."

Leo opened the kitchen cabinets. "My God, there is literally no food in this house. Dad, I'm going to run out to the grocery store. I'll be back soon." He waited for Terry's reply from behind his bedroom door.

"Fine," Terry shouted.

Leo rolled his eyes and walked outside on his way to the parking lot. "Hell of a way to end a honeymoon." He stepped into his car and pulled out onto the main road. The nearest store was only about half a mile away. As he drove on, he considered what Allison had said about his mother's collectibles. Was it possible Terry's plan was to claim they were worth a lot and get the insurance money? It was something he would do, if he had insurance. There was one thing certain about Terry, he was the type of guy to do anything for a quick buck. Legal or not, if it meant skirting the system or padding his wallet, Terry was all in. Always had been, always would be. But to wait this long, holding onto Mom's things until now, could've meant Terry was in a bind. Maybe Leo needed to dig a little deeper and figure out what the hell was going on.

5

When Allison arrived at the parking lot of the office right on time this morning, she noticed her partners emerge from the building and knew exactly why they'd come down. The excitement she felt after leaving the car dealership yesterday returned and Allison stepped out of her new Toyota Camry when the girls approached.

"We thought we'd come down first thing in case you were called out again by your ex-husband." Charlie examined the car. "Nice ride, Hart. You're doing all right for yourself."

"Thanks." Allison threw her arm around Charlie's shoulders. "Someday, this could be you, too—with a little hard work."

Lucy walked around the car and nodded. "Not too bad at all. You must really like blue."

"My favorite color," Allison replied. "So, what's on this morning's agenda? I need to pay for this thing."

"You remember the pharmacy owners?" Charlie began.

"Sure. Don't tell me they're having problems again," Allison replied.

"No, but they sent someone our way. Let's go back inside and Lucy and I will get you up to speed." Charlie started ahead toward the elevators wearing a loose-fitted short-sleeved dress. It was rare she wore a dress. Said it caused chafing—she couldn't stand it. "Anything else exciting happen last night? Did Jenny file for divorce from Leo, yet?"

"Not yet, but I'm putting together a pool." Allison held open the elevator doors for Lucy. "As a matter of fact, Micah and I had a nice night alone together. Ate pizza, looked at some old photos, and watched a movie."

"Oh, Shane didn't come over?" Charlie asked.

"Nope, just me and the girl. I think he feels out of place with Micah there. She's better than she was now that Leo's married, but I know it's still hard for her to see me with someone else."

"Well, no offense, Alli, but that kid is gonna have to get over herself. You'd better set her straight." Charlie stepped out as they reached the floor. "Nolan doesn't feel that way, does he, Lucy?"

"I don't think so, but then we don't really talk about Allison's love life."

"Thank God." Allison opened the door to the office. "I'm just glad she wanted to come and stay with me for a while before her job starts."

Charlie returned to her desk. "So, about the new prospective client. This is the woman who called late yesterday." She walked to Allison's desk and set down the file. "I don't have much yet because I thought we'd get a chance to discuss it this morning to see if it's worth our time. Considering we're all just sitting on our thumbs right now, I'd say it is."

Allison opened the file and raised her brow as she read. "Well, this is interesting."

"I thought the same thing," Charlie added. "Her divorce is set to be finalized in 4 weeks and she's sure the husband is hiding assets so he doesn't have to give her half. Great guy, huh?"

"We need to uncover said assets," Lucy added.

"This is good." Allison closed the file folder. "Let's get her in here and talk about it."

Lucy returned to her desk and picked up the phone. "I'm on it."

"Okay, so now that's settled." Charlie sat down at her desk when the door opened and drew her attention.

The look on Charlie's face was enough for Allison to quickly step in. "I'll take care of this." She stood to greet him. "Leo, what are you doing here? Is your dad okay?"

"He's fine. Morning, Charlie, Lucy. Nice to see you both again."

Lucy raised her hand in acknowledgment as she continued on her phone call.

"Leo, what a surprise," Charlie quipped.

"Sorry to arrive unannounced." He continued toward Allison, seemingly brushing off Charlie's comment. "Can we talk outside?"

She glanced at the girls. "Hold down the fort?"

"Always," Charlie replied.

Allison followed him out. "What is it?"

"Listen, I know I shouldn't be coming to you. I know how it looks. Charlie just made that pretty clear."

"Don't worry about her. She's overly protective."

"Anyway, it's about Terry. Can you do something for me?" He glanced away a moment. "I feel I've been asking you that a lot lately."

"What do you need?" Allison asked.

"I was wondering if you could look into Terry a little bit."

"What do you mean, 'look into'?"

"Check out his finances for me, if you can do that sort of

thing," Leo replied. "I think he could be in some sort of trouble—money wise. Something's just not right about this break-in. You said he hadn't wanted to call the cops. And then the only things to go missing were my mom's things."

"Speaking of, I pulled out the old photo albums last night that had pictures of your parents' old house. I didn't get through all of them. Terry didn't want me to find the pictures for the cops, which I thought was odd."

"Very. Did you see any of the collectibles?" he asked.

"Like I said, I haven't finished going through them. Micah and I worked on it a little bit last night. But now that you have concerns, I can take a harder look. Do you think Sue's collectibles were worth some money?"

"I'm starting to, which also makes me think Terry must owe people. He's known to dabble in games of chance more than he should," Leo replied.

"I remember." Allison nodded. "I can look into a few things. Check out if Terry's visiting the casinos, the tracks. I don't know how much in the way of financial details I'll be able to get, except whatever I can find on a credit check. That means you'll need to text me his social security number."

"Sure. Thank you, Alli. I can pay you, of course..."

She raised her hands. "Stop right there. I'm not taking your money, not anymore. Seriously, it won't take much effort. I can handle this, and I'll make sure Terry is none the wiser. But what about the photos? I'm happy to send them on to the police to help them find the stolen items and keep looking through them."

"Please send what you have. I can pick up the albums you haven't gone through tonight and we can divide and conquer," he replied.

"That'll work. Why don't you swing by the house about 6 or 6:30?"

"Will do. Hey, thanks again, Alli. I'll let you get back inside before Charlie comes out thinking I've kidnapped you or something." Leo chuckled as he walked on. "See you later."

"See you." Allison returned inside to find Charlie standing in the middle of the room with her arms folded, bearing a death stare. "You don't need to worry. I'm just fine. I can handle a conversation with my ex-husband, Charlie. Just like you can."

"Please." She swatted away the notion. "Like my ex ever talks to me unless he needs something. Oh, wait..."

Allison glanced at Lucy who gave her a similar look. "Don't you start."

"I wasn't going to say a thing. It's none of my business." She laced together her fingers. "But what did he want?"

"He thinks his dad could be in trouble." Allison returned to her desk. "He asked me to look into a few things and see what I can find out."

"And how much are you going to charge him?" Charlie asked.

"Nothing," she replied.

"I didn't know we were doing pro bono work." Charlie turned to Lucy. "What did Cheryl say? You know, the woman who wants to pay us for our work."

"Who's Cheryl?" Allison cut in.

"The file you just looked at," Charlie replied.

"Oh, I didn't catch her first name."

"She said she could come in later this morning," Lucy replied. "I put her down for 11am. I didn't see anything on either of your calendars, but is that going to be a problem for you, Allison?"

"No, I'll work around this. Cheryl's our priority right now."

"As it should be." Charlie appeared to regret her tone and shifted her foot along the floor while she clasped her hands behind her back. "So, like, is there anything you need help with?"

Allison couldn't help but smile. "I get it, Charlie. You think

Leo takes advantage. Maybe you're right. But for now, I'll do what I can for him and no, I think I got this. I appreciate the offer. I'm just going to run a background on Terry and see what pops up."

"Then I'll prep for our meeting," Charlie replied.

Lucy glanced up from her screen. "From what Nolan has said, Terry Hart is an interesting man. And by interesting, I'm pretty sure he meant shady."

"Oh yeah. I wouldn't trust him with my last dollar, that's for sure. He'd try to convince you he could make it two dollars and then disappear." Allison logged into the database and entered Terry's details. Name, birthdate, and the social security number Leo texted.

A moment later, the data returned, and Allison examined it. "Several collectors. Money is clearly an issue." She printed the report and lay it on her desk. Highlighting the worst of the collections report, Allison made note of the account names. Nothing out of the ordinary. A few medical offices, a store credit card, and a..." She put on her readers to be sure. "A horse track."

"What's that, Alli?" Charlie asked.

She peered up at Charlie. "Have you ever heard of a horse racetrack submitting a collections report on someone? Don't they require payment for bets at the time they're placed?"

Charlie appeared to consider the question when Lucy spoke up. "Actually, it's possible. Some of the racetracks offer lines of credit. Small ones, usually, but they have been known to do that, especially the smaller tracks. The big corporate-run places probably wouldn't bother with that. They don't need to, but sure, it's possible."

"Good to know." Allison jotted down the name. "Terry's been known to partake in the odd wager. If he racked up gambling debt, maybe he would do whatever he had to in order to pay it off."

Charlie eyed her. "Like selling his dead wife's belongings?"

"Possibly, but I don't know why he'd go through the hassle of claiming they were stolen."

"Insurance money?" Lucy cut in.

"I'll have to see if he has a renter's policy." Allison returned to her keyboard.

Charlie stood from her desk and walked toward the window. "She's here. Our potential new client."

Allison spun around to see. "She's early. Doesn't matter. I'll put this away for now. Let's set up the conference table with water, pens, paper."

"You got it." Lucy stood from her desk.

Allison grabbed her tablet and notebook and when the door opened, she approached with an outstretched hand. "Good morning. You must be Cheryl Murray. I'm Allison Hart."

"Good morning. I apologize for being early. My last appointment finished sooner than I expected."

"No problem at all." Charlie approached. "I'm Charlie Wells. We spoke on the phone. Why don't you have a seat over here and we can get started."

"Thank you." She eyed Lucy. "That must make you Lucy Boyce. Pleasure."

"Pleasure's all mine." Lucy returned the handshake. "Would you like a coffee or a bottled water?"

"Water, please. Thank you." Cheryl took her seat.

Before Allison stood a wealthy woman. Clothes by Chanel. Bag by Vuitton. "Can I ask you something, Ms. Murray?"

"Please call me Cheryl," she replied.

"Cheryl," Allison added. "It's clear you have the means to hire a firm with far greater resources than we have. May I ask, if you are in the middle of a difficult divorce, why are you not utilizing a firm that can throw their weight around?"

Cheryl revealed a crooked smile and looked down at her hands a moment. "You're very perceptive, Allison. When I spoke to Charlie on the phone, I indicated that my estranged husband was doing everything in his power to hide his assets from me. He has a very good lawyer. I do as well, but I can't ask him to look into the matter in such a way as to keep it from my husband's lawyer. I also can't hire a high-profile private investigator. If I do, my husband will get wind of it. He will adjust and then I will lose. So, after speaking with Charlie, and what you did for my friends, I learned you three could do what I needed to have done without raising the eyebrows of others in the industry, or law enforcement. I need people who can stay off the radar, Allison. I know what you three have done. Will you help me hold my husband accountable so that I don't end up with far less than what I'm entitled to?"

Charlie nodded and glanced at Allison. "As my colleague, here, can attest, I've been in your situation, Cheryl. Not in regard to the money side of it, but I have an ex-husband who did what he could to take me to the cleaners, as they say. So, I understand your point. I think this is something that we can handle for you without raising any red flags."

"Good. I assume you can get started right away?" Cheryl pulled out her checkbook. "I'm happy to provide a retainer. Just tell me how much."

———

TERRY STEPPED out of his old black Chevy Impala and peered at the large building ahead. The noise from the track reached his ears. He shuffled inside and headed straight toward the betting desks. The sound of the race caller on the loudspeaker made him smile. He was back in his element and this time, he was going to square up with the big man. In fact, as he stood at the desk, out of the corner of his eye, he spotted him. "Lou, good to see you."

"You're here. That must mean you have something for me, Terry. Cause if not, then..."

"I got something for you." He pulled a fat envelope from the pocket of his khaki shorts.

Santos eyed him before surveying the floor. "Let's go to my office, shall we?"

Terry followed him back. "It's all there. I'm a man of my word. Now can I place a bet or not?"

Santos took the envelope and examined the contents. He sucked on his teeth a moment and sized up Terry. "Guess we're all good here. I'll see to it the appropriate credit is given. You can do as you like."

"Appreciate that, Lou. Like I said, I keep my word." Terry shuffled out of his office and walked to the betting desk. The bets were placed with what cash he had leftover and Terry walked out into the grandstand. A single white cloud floated in the bright blue sky. Terry aimed his gaze upward. "Couldn't ask for a better day. Sun's shining and I'm in my happy place."

The race was about to begin when Terry felt a hand on his shoulder. He spun around. "Oh, hello. What are you doing here?"

The 40-something man with a narrow build and a few inches on Terry removed his hand. He squinted in the bright light making the wrinkles deepen around his eyes. The light made his red hair look thinner than it was. "Terry. I didn't expect to see you here today."

"That makes two of us. Thought I'd take a few hours to myself. What, are you keeping tabs on me or something?" he replied with a nervous chuckle.

"Just doing what the boss asked of me. I heard you're all squared away."

"That's right. No problems here." Terry turned down his mouth. "You don't need to worry about anything. I got things fully under control." The race started and he spun around. "Come on now 4, you gotta work for me today."

The man folded his arms and watched the race with Terry. "How much you got on this one?"

"Just a 20-spot. I'm being smart." He turned his attention to the track again. "Oh, now, come on! You can do better than that! Let's move!"

The announcer relayed the horses' positions as the race continued. Only 100 more yards. "Almost there. Almost there," Terry said.

The red-haired man gave him the side eye as he looked on.

"Son of a bitch!" Terry slapped the railing in front of him.

The man snorted. "Looks like you picked another loser, Terry. Try not to make a habit of that, yeah?"

6

On a rare balmy night amid the setting sun, Leo rang the doorbell of his former home. Micah appeared on the other side of the front door. "Hey, Dad."

"Hi, sweetheart." Leo walked inside and kissed his daughter's cheek. "Is your mom around?"

"She's in the kitchen. Are you hungry?" Micah closed the door and walked toward the kitchen. "Mom, Dad's here."

"Leo, long time no see." She smiled. "I just got home not too long ago myself. I brought food, so I hope you're in the mood for tacos."

"I could eat." He rubbed his paunch. "Busy day?"

"Yeah, sort of. Looks like we picked up a new client, which is great. I always get a little worried when days go by without the phone ringing," Allison replied.

"That's great. What's the case?" Leo grabbed a paper plate and a couple of tacos. "Don't suppose you have any beer?"

"Of course I do. Help yourself," Allison began. "A wealthy couple is in the middle of a messy divorce. The wife came to see us and asked us to find the husband's assets she suspects he's hiding. And we have to accomplish that without the husband or his lawyer finding out."

"Sounds like a made-for-tv movie." Leo took a bite as he sat down on the stool at the kitchen island. "How do you plan on going about that?"

"I have a few ideas, but the girls and I will brainstorm in the morning. Apparently, the husband has a lot of people looking out for him. People who might be keeping tabs on the wife and her affairs. So, we're going to have to be careful with this one," Allison replied.

"What about all this stuff with Grandpa?" Micah asked as she grabbed some food.

Leo glanced at her. "What do you mean? What stuff?"

"I mean like him getting robbed and stuff. That's kind of serious, right?"

"It is, which is why your dad's here tonight," Allison replied. "We're going to keep sifting through the old photo albums looking for Grandma Sue's collectibles in the pictures. It should help the police, we hope."

"Not to be nosy, or anything, Dad, but how does Jenny feel about all this? You guys just got back from your honeymoon you had to cut short. I mean, she's been pretty cool and all, but it must make her feel—I don't know—left out?"

"Not at all," Leo replied. "She's fine. She understands, now, what Terry's all about. He tried to weasel in through her, but she knows better. Once your mom and I get this situation with Grandpa sorted out, everything will go back to normal."

Allison wasn't so sure. She'd known her former father-in-law long enough to know that he only needed a foot in the door and then he was like a bad rash that wouldn't heal. And with what she already knew about Jenny and how she'd very recently spent time with an ex-boyfriend, she wondered if Leo was just sugar-coating the truth. Of course he was. That was his M.O. It was when they were married, and nothing had changed.

"Speaking of...why don't I grab the albums and we can all sit here and go through them while we eat? That way, Leo can get back home at a decent time, and I can go to bed." Allison walked to the coat closet and retrieved the albums. On her return, she set them on the kitchen table. "Okay, these are the ones Micah and I didn't get a chance to go through yet. We each take one and see what we can find."

Leo wiped his mouth with a napkin and walked to the table to grab an album. As he sat down and flipped through the pages, he smiled. "I haven't seen these pictures in years. Look at how young we were, Alli?"

"Tell me about it. And the kids too," she replied.

"We had a good life, didn't we?" he asked.

Allison held his gaze for a moment. "Yeah, we did."

Micah looked on at her parents' exchange. "It was good for a while."

All three sat at the kitchen table, eating tacos, and looking at old pictures. Allison felt a little like this was the old times, except that Nolan wasn't there.

"Hang on. This was at Grandma's house, wasn't it?" Micah turned the book to Allison. "That one there."

Allison pushed up her reading glasses and peered at the photo. "Yep. And look at that, on the back wall of the living room. You guys remember that old hutch?"

"I do," Leo said. "Are any of Mom's things on there?"

Allison closed in on it. "Yep. That old duck. I remember that thing. Ugly as hell, but your mom loved it."

"She loved all her trinkets," Leo replied.

"I imagine that old wooden duck was in one of those boxes."

Allison pulled off the plastic cover of the album page and carefully peeled up the photo. "Let's set this one aside. We'll create a little pile of photos and then I'll scan them in." Her phone rang and drew her attention. Allison glanced back at the kitchen counter. "Let me see who that is." She stood to retrieve her phone and checked the caller ID. "I'll take this outside. You guys keep looking." She opened the back door and stepped out onto the deck into the light of a half-moon. "Hey, there."

"Hey. What are you up to? You at home?" Shane asked.

"I am. Just sitting at the kitchen table with Leo and Micah going through some old photo albums. We're looking for the pictures of Sue's collectibles for the police."

"Oh, that's right. You mentioned that. Although, I thought it was just you and Micah?"

"Leo stopped by. He's worried Terry's in some kind of trouble and has no idea what might've been taken from his apartment. He wanted to help."

"I see. Well, I guess that makes sense," Shane replied. "I won't keep you…"

"Wait, you just called to say hi?" Her brow knitted. "Is everything okay? I know we didn't get together for lunch like we talked about, but…"

"Yeah, no, everything's fine. I just wanted to hear your voice," Shane replied.

"Listen, tomorrow's looking better for me. How about we meet for drinks after work? The girls and I are working a new case, but it should be fairly open and shut."

"That's great to hear. Sure, I think I can move around a few things. We'll meet up tomorrow. I'll see you then. Bye, Allison." Shane ended the call.

She peered at the phone with some concern. It was hard for her to put herself in his shoes, but it wasn't impossible. Allison sensed he felt like an outsider right now. Maybe she'd been treating him as such. After all this stuff with Terry was over, though, she'd make it up to him. It would all work out. Allison returned inside.

"Everything all right?" Leo asked.

"Fine. It was just Shane." She returned to the kitchen table. "Looks like you guys found a few more pictures. Good. This should help."

———

As morning arrived, Allison threw over her legs to the floor and stood from her bed. It turned out, they'd found quite a few pictures in those old albums last night and she would take them today and scan them into an email to the officer who responded to her call. However, something nagged at her and lent to a somewhat restless night's sleep. Terry's collection report that included the Bayside Downs racetrack. She knew of the place and wondered how often he gambled there. It wasn't outside the realm of possibilities that Terry made up the robbery in an effort to commit insurance fraud and use the money to pay off his debt at the track. She still hadn't found any policy he might've had. That might be something Leo will have to learn on his own since he's a relative.

Allison showered and dressed before heading downstairs for a quick cup of coffee. As she walked by Micah's room, she heard mild snoring. No point in waking her. Allison poured the coffee and made toast. The pictures still lay on the kitchen table. It had been a good night. A night that saw them reliving fond memories of the family they used to be. Apparently, it wasn't meant to last.

Outside, Allison grinned at the sight of her pretty blue Toyota.

She stepped inside, turned the engine, and basked in the air conditioning that blew ice cold. It really was the little things.

Her first thought was to head straight into the office to work on Cheryl Murray's case, but the nagging feeling about Terry wouldn't subside. There had to be something she could do to learn more. Maybe a visit to the racetrack would set her mind at ease. It might be important to know just what kind of relationship Terry had with the people there.

Allison started out onto the highway and drove to Bayside Downs about 25 minutes away. By the time she arrived, the place had just opened. Allison walked inside and headed upstairs toward the betting desks. "Excuse me." She held out her ID. "Is there a manager here that I can speak to?"

"What's it regarding, Ms..." An older woman with short white hair and glasses narrowed her gaze to view the name on her ID. "Hart."

"I have a client, and I need some information about a collections report," she replied.

"Let me see if Mr. Santos can assist. I think he just arrived."

The woman moved out from behind the desk and headed to an office just a few feet away. Allison surveyed the expansive area with concrete floors and steel columns. People approached the desks and appeared to place their wagers before walking out into the stands. She was never a gambler, even when Leo took her to Atlantic City a decade ago to celebrate an anniversary. This was the first time she'd ever stepped foot inside a racetrack. It was nice. She'd spotted a bar downstairs. Ahead were the stands that were sort of indoor/outdoor. And about 100 feet to the left was a neon sign above a set of double doors. "Poker Room." She quickly understood the appeal of a place like this, and especially for a man like Terry Hart. She could practically see the dollar signs flashing in front of her.

"Ms. Hart?"

Allison turned at the sound of her name. "Yes, that's me."

"I'm Lou Santos, the track manager. I also run Customer Service. What can I help you with this morning?"

She eyed his stout frame and receding hairline. He looked to be in his mid-40s. Not exactly handsome, but okay looking. He had a Paul Giamatti air about him. "Can we speak in your office?"

"Of course. Follow me." He led the way to his office and ushered Allison inside. "Please, have a seat."

"Thank you." Allison opened her carrier bag and retrieved the collection report. "I'd like to ask you a few questions about Terry Hart."

He quickly appeared stone-faced. "What sort of questions? And may I ask, are you a relative of Terry's, Ms. Hart? The name and all..."

"Former relative. He was my father-in-law for twenty years."

Santos revealed a crooked smile. "That must've been fun."

"You know Terry well, then," she added.

"You could say that. What do you need to know? I'm not sure I can answer everything, but I'll do my best."

"I was helping him out a few days ago after his place was robbed."

Santos pulled back in surprise. "Robbed? His house?"

Allison nodded. "His apartment. The thing is, only a couple of boxes were taken. Whoever it was left his TV. But to be fair, it was an old TV, so it was probably not worth much. But going back to Terry. I'm helping out his son..."

"Your ex."

"Yes, my ex. He's looking at the possibility of getting Terry some help, as I'm sure you can imagine. I've been asked to learn what I can of his situation here. I see from a background check that the track issued a collections case against Terry."

"Yes, ma'am. However, that will be updated soon to reflect his payoff," Santos replied.

Allison cocked her head. "He paid off his debt?"

"Very recently, as a matter of fact." Santos peered into the hall as though double-checking that no one was within earshot. "Well, I'm not sure how much I'm allowed to say, but since you're family, he paid it off just yesterday. Paid in full with cash." He leaned back against his chair. "I'll tell you something, Ms. Hart. I've known Terry a long time. Man's always looking for a quick buck. Yes, we've extended him credit, but only because we know he's a repeat customer, if you know what I mean. In fact, he was here again yesterday after he repaid the line of credit. The man went right back to placing bets."

"With cash?" she pressed on.

"Yes, with cash."

Allison stood. "Thank you for your time, Mr. Santos."

He escorted her to the door. "What are you going to do about Terry? I hope his son can help him. I'm sorry to say, the man's got a problem."

"I will let his son know what we discussed. Thank you for your time." Allison returned to her car. Turned out, Leo might have been right. Maybe Terry wasn't in trouble because he'd just gotten himself out of it. But if he continued down this path, it would, no doubt, return. The more she considered it, the more she realized the reason Terry had been so hesitant to call the police at his apartment that morning. He hadn't wanted them involved. The supposed heart attack, which turned out to be anxiety, was a distraction meant to throw off her search for the items. But why? Why not come out and say he sold Sue's things? Why risk committing fraud, assuming the items were insured. If Sue's belongings transferred to Terry, why go through all this in the first place? Sell the items, collect the money, and pay off the debt. Something else was at play here and it was time Allison understood what that was.

———

THE DOWNTOWN TAMPA Police Station was just ahead. Allison was about to make an unscheduled stop to see Shane and ask him for some advice. And maybe she could smooth out any misunderstanding he had about last night. The balance between the egos of the ex-husband and the new boyfriend was tenuous, at best.

Detective Shane "Sully" Sullivan worked upstairs in Major Crimes. Their recent romantic relationship aside, Shane was a hell of a detective and Allison leaned on him for advice, much as she had when they were just friends.

She approached his desk. "Hey, stranger."

He peered up at her. "Allison, hey. What are you doing here? I thought we were meeting for drinks tonight."

"Oh, that's still planned, but I thought I'd stop by and ask you a couple questions if you have a few minutes."

"Yeah, sure. Sit down." He waited for her to take her seat. "What's this about? Is it the new case you mentioned?"

"No, actually, it's not. It's about my ex-father-in-law."

"Okay. How can I help?" he asked.

"First of all, can you pull a copy of the police report Terry filed the other morning?"

Shane turned to his computer. "Sure. What do you need it for?"

"I just wanted to double-check something," she replied.

Shane typed in the commands. "Terry Hart. Do you have the address?"

"Yep. The responding officer gave me his card, too." Allison retrieved a sticky note with Terry's address as well as the officer's details.

"Okay, hang on here and let me see what I can find." He glanced at her. "Should be here in the system." His gaze narrowed and he shook his head. "I'm not seeing it yet."

"That's what I was afraid of."

Shane peered at the screen. "Allison, nothing's in the system. Not under his name, or address. There's a note that the responding officer was there... oh, here it is. The note indicates the owner wished to drop the case." He appeared puzzled. "Why would he do that?"

"Looks like Terry hasn't changed in all these years."

"What's going on? I don't understand," Shane replied.

"I can't fully piece it together yet, but there's a reason he didn't want the cops involved. He kept telling me not to bother. That the cops wouldn't do anything anyway. I didn't think much of it at the time, other than it was Terry being Terry. But now? I think he might have committed fraud or something and wanted Leo to be a witness. I don't know exactly, but when I showed up, I might've thrown off his plans."

Shane's dark brown eyes narrowed, and his full lips pressed together. The soft lines in his forehead deepened just a little. "Is this something you want to dig into, Allison? To me, it doesn't seem like it should be your problem. It should be Leo's."

"I won't argue with you, there. This isn't my problem, but I've known that man for most of my adult life, Shane. He's my kids' grandfather. I'm afraid now that he's found a way back into Leo's life, he might drag him into something not exactly kosher. If that happens, the kids could be dragged into it as well. That's where I have to draw the line. I guess I'm looking to preempt all that."

Shane returned a tender smile and wore defeat behind his gaze. "I can't compete with that."

Allison reached for his hand. "I'm not asking you to. That's not what this is about. I need you to understand that. Shane, I had a life before you, the same as you had one before me. Are we going to be able to get past this or is this going to be a problem?"

He shook his head. "Of course it's not a problem. You're absolutely right. I just don't like to see you get pulled into something that could end up blowing back on you, you know?"

"It won't." Her words hardly convinced herself.

"Okay, then. It's your call. Is there anything else I can do to help you out?"

"This is more than enough. Thank you." She stood to leave. "I'm still up for drinks tonight if you are."

"You got it."

"I'll see you tonight." Allison turned on her heel.

"I look forward to it."

She returned to her car and picked up her phone. "Leo, hey, listen, we need to talk about your dad. I'm heading into the office now. Can you break away for a little bit this afternoon?" She nodded. "Great. Come by the office. See you later."

7

Cheryl Murray was a paying client and while Allison endeavored to get to the bottom of Terry Hart's situation, priorities needed to be set. She returned to the office to meet with Charlie and Lucy regarding their newest case.

Charlie was at her desk while Lucy stood at the file cabinet when Allison walked inside. "Morning. I know I'm late again."

Charlie peeked over her reading glasses. "Let me guess. It had something to do with a former family member?"

"Go figure. I needed to look into a few things with Shane." Allison sat down. "How are we coming along on the Murray case?"

"It's been mostly research." Lucy held a file and returned to her desk. "We're looking into the husband's corporate records to see if anything leads us to shell companies. That'd be the first place I'd hide money."

"Maybe an even better place to hide money is in cryptocurrency," Allison added. "Bitcoin, and all the others."

"There would be a digital trail from the bank transferring into a crypto account, wouldn't there?" Charlie asked.

"A lot of different ways exist to move money." Lucy typed on her computer. "From PayPal to Venmo to Zelle. Most would be tied to a traditional bank account, but with crypto, it could be possible for him to skirt around that too, with a wallet."

"A wallet?" Allison asked.

"It's a crypto account. So, like, if someone had $20,000 in bitcoin, it would be in their wallet on a Coinbase-type of site. Which means, if you forget your password, you're kind of screwed. It's a little confusing, but it is something to consider because governments all over the world are trying to come to grips with it themselves in order to prevent money laundering. But as far as shell companies transferring funds to an online bank account, that could be easily hidden from Cheryl as well. It would take a forensic accountant to look into all that."

"Maybe a forensic accountant could look into the crypto thing too?" Charlie asked.

"Yeah, definitely," Lucy replied. "If he or she is good at their job."

Charlie clapped her hands together. "Great. Lucy will investigate that because I honestly have no idea what the hell she's talking about. I'll research whether the husband has a girlfriend. It's possible he might put property or other assets in her name. If we can figure out where he's been spending most of his evenings, we'll find the concubine."

Allison and Lucy traded glances and laughed.

"What?" Charlie asked.

"Concubine? Really?" Allison began. "What is this, the Middle Ages?"

"So I'm working on expanding my vocabulary. So what?" Didn't know I was working with a couple of rubes." Charlie cracked a smile. "I'll head out this morning and see what I can learn from Mr. Murray's schedule. I think Lucy should contact Cheryl and ask about bringing in a forensic accountant." She glanced at Allison. "I guess that frees you up to deal with your family situation."

"Charlie, I can put that aside," Allison replied.

"I know you, Alli. You can't. Don't worry about it. Lucy and I have this under control. If something comes up that we can't handle, you'll be the first one we call. In the meantime, take a couple days to figure out what you need to do. This case isn't going to be solved that quickly. Then, we'll get back together and see where we stand."

———

MAYBE IT WAS BETTER this way, letting Charlie take the lead. After all, they were equals. Both had a financial stake in ACL. Allison was good at rationalizing, and at least the Murray case wasn't life and death, not yet anyway. This would free up Allison to take care of the Terry Hart situation in a matter of days and then move on. But the whole thing needled at her. So, as midday arrived, she left the office to scratch the itch.

She pressed the call button on her steering wheel. "Leo, it's me. Do you happen to have a copy of your mom's will?"

"No, but I'm sure Dad does. Why?"

"You said you told her you hadn't wanted any of her things."

"That's right," Leo replied.

"We were already separated at the time, so I can't recall if there was a reading of the will in front of you and Terry."

"No, there wasn't. I remember saying that it hadn't mattered to me. You know I wasn't exactly myself in those days. I didn't care what her will said."

"Sure." Allison turned down the street toward Terry's apartment. "I don't want to ask Terry for the will. He'll ask questions. What about the lawyer Sue had at the time?"

"If the lawyer still has the will, it's probably in some archived file. It's been a long time, Alli. What's this about, anyway? What are you looking for?"

"I need to know what it says. There could be something in there about her collectibles that Terry's keeping to himself." She pulled to a stop in the parking lot of the apartment complex and looked for Terry's car.

"Okay. I'll dig around some of the old paperwork I have and see if I can find the name of the lawyer," he replied. "Where are you? I thought I was planning on stopping by your office later. You sound like you're driving?"

"I'm working that new case. Just checking out a few things. Let's hold off on you swinging by for now, but give me a call back when you have the lawyer's information."

"Will do. Bye."

Allison hadn't wanted Leo to know she was sitting in front of Terry's apartment building, not until she had proof that he was up to something. Right now, all she had was a hunch. Nevertheless, his car was nowhere to be seen, so there was probably only one other place he might be. "The track."

She pulled out of the parking lot and headed to Bayside Downs when something else occurred to her and she made another call. "Hi. Are you busy?"

"A little, but never too busy to talk to you," Shane replied. "What's going on?"

"How easy would it be for you to get a copy of CCTV footage for me?" she asked.

"Depends. Video from inside a bank vault, not so easy. Video from a street corner, that's something I can do."

"Well, I don't plan on robbing a bank. Here's the deal. Terry claimed his place was broken into," she began.

"Right."

"So, what if we get the security footage from around the apartment building, assuming it exists, and look for a car being loaded with boxes."

"That's actually a good idea. I can probably get my hands on that, but it'll cost you," he said.

With a crooked smile, she continued. "What's the price?"

"Well, you're already having drinks with me later, so how about coming back to my place for the night since you have Micah staying at yours."

"I think I can manage that. Although, tread lightly, Detective. Someone might mistake your fee as accepting a bribe," she laughed.

"If I was going to accept a bribe, it'd be for a hell of a lot more than you spending the night. It'd have to be at least two nights. Seriously though, I can poke around and see what I can find at the building and the surrounding areas. I'll do my best to get to it today, but..."

"Whatever you can do, Shane. Thank you. I mean it. I really appreciate you doing this for me."

"I know you do. I'll talk to you later."

She pressed the end button and arrived at the racetrack. Hunting down any surrounding CCTV would prove whether Terry was telling the truth about a break in. Assuming he was lying made her feel awful, but she'd known this man for many years. He could be slippery, and she couldn't let him slide this time, for his own good and for Leo's.

Allison walked into the building that was a solid 20 degrees cooler than the outside. She had just been in here yesterday talking to the track manager, but now, locating Terry was her goal.

She took the escalator to the second floor where the betting desks were located, along with the top floor of the stands. According to the manager, Terry spent a lot of time here, which meant, even if he'd paid off his most recent debt, it sounded like he'd soon find himself in another tight spot.

She checked the board for the upcoming races and noted the next one was scheduled to start in five minutes. Allison walked out into the grandstand where large blowers above kept the air cooler than on the track below. Whether Terry was here, and her hunch was right remained to be seen.

As Allison surveyed the stands, she spotted Terry standing in the next section over. "Damn it." So her gut was right, but it hadn't made her feel any better. Here was a man who was, only two days ago, laying in a hospital bed having suffered an anxiety attack. This hadn't boded well for Terry's story.

Allison started back into the breezeway to head toward him. She hadn't known what she was going to say except maybe advise him to take it easy after what had happened. But as she made her way, she stopped in her tracks. A man, who appeared to be in his 30s, with an average build and blonde slicked back hair reached Terry before she had. His hands were shoved into the pockets of his black pants, and he wore a serious expression. Allison slipped back into the shadow of a concrete column and observed the meeting. The ambient noise made it impossible to hear the conversation, but based on Terry's demeanor, it hadn't appeared to be a pleasant one. With her phone in her hand, she snapped pictures of the men.

Several moments went by as Allison tried to glean the gist of the conversation without being noticed. Clearly, Terry had been brow-beaten and looked a little stunned as a result. When the serious-looking man walked away, she watched as Terry sat down on the bench in an apparent daze. "This can't be good."

The man walked in her direction and Allison turned toward the track as though watching the race to avoid eye contact. He continued by without noticing her. When he was several feet in front of her, she trailed him. The track was busy, and she could drop back into the crowd easily enough. However, he was stopped by a man who hurried to catch up to him just as he was on his way out the door. Allison recognized him and dropped back but kept her eyes on them. The man was the track manager she'd met yesterday, Lou Santos. Neither looked particularly happy about whatever it was they were discussing. "What the hell is going on?" She kept her sights fixed on the men but had no idea if the conversation involved Terry.

The two eventually parted ways and when the unknown man made it outside, Allison waited for a moment for him to gain distance. Again, she followed.

He stopped outside his car and made a call on his phone while he squinted at the bright sky. Allison looked on, still making her way into the parking lot with no real destination. She needed to take a picture of the man's license plates. It was the only way to learn who he was.

He spotted her. "You lost or something, miss?"

This was a man who knew when he was being tailed. It was her first mistake. "You know, I might be," she replied. "I think I came out the wrong door. I thought I was in this parking lot, but I sure don't see my car." Her nervous laughter was hard to hide.

He grunted and opened the driver's side door of his car. "If I were you, I'd go back inside and get your bearings again. Good luck to you."

"Thanks." Allison smiled while he closed the door and turned the engine. She started back toward the building again as he pulled away. It would be nearly impossible to take a picture now, so she was going to have to memorize the plate. "BZEJ166." In her head, she repeated the numbers as she walked back inside. With her phone in hand, she typed a text message to Shane. "Can you pull a plate for me when you get a chance?"

————

If Allison had been concerned about Terry's financial problems before, now it was who might have been helping him solve said financial problems, and at what cost. The man who had spoken to Terry at the racetrack struck her as someone who was accustomed to getting what he wanted from people. The fact that he'd also spoken to Lou Santos, the track's manager, didn't help to settle her concerns.

It approached late afternoon as Allison returned to the office.

Lucy peered up from her laptop when the door opened. "You're back."

"In the flesh. Hey, where's Charlie?"

"She's still searching for Mr. Murray's concubine, last we spoke."

Allison snickered. "And you?"

"Just narrowing down a list of accountants to talk to and see what they can do for us," she replied. "How did things go for you?"

"Not good. I think Leo's dad could be in trouble, but not the kind Leo thinks he's in."

"What kind then?" Lucy asked.

"The kind that might find him tied to a cinderblock and tossed into the bay." She sat down at her desk.

"Oh my gosh. What happened?"

"I saw Terry at the racetrack. I was about to talk to him when a scary looking guy approached him. I don't know who he is yet, maybe a bookie, but I'm working on finding out. I'll tell you one thing, the way Terry looked after their conversation meant whatever the man said to him, wasn't in jest."

"What can you do about it, though?" Lucy pressed on.

"I got the guy's plates. Shane's running them for me. I need to find out who he is." Her phone rang and she answered the call. "Speak of the devil. You have something for me?"

"Allison, the plates you sent me. The guy's name is Gus Schoeman. His known associates are not the type of people you want to run into while in a dark alley, or anywhere for that matter," Shane replied. "How did you find him?"

Shane struck a tone that worried her. "He was talking to Terry, and it didn't look like a fun conversation. Terry seemed pretty shaken up by it. Then I saw him talking to the racetrack manager."

"You were at the racetrack?"

"Bayside Downs. I'm trying to figure out what Terry's been up to because, like we talked about before, I'm starting to think he could be in debt to some people."

"Some serious people, if this guy is any indication. Allison, did he see you? Gus Schoeman. Did he see you watching him?"

"No, I was careful." So, she'd just lied to him. "Shane, should I be worried about Terry right now?" His sigh was audible on the line. "Tell me the truth. I need to know what he's gotten himself into."

"Well, I don't know what he's into, but Schoeman's part of the Winthrop Group, a suspected arm of the Brunetti family."

Allison smirked. "What? The Tampa mafia? Those guys aren't around anymore."

"Not in the way they used to be. They were big with the casinos here and in Cuba back in the day. The last boss was Vincent Accorsi. He's in his 70s or 80s now and claims to be retired. But the family, they've morphed, combined with other crime families out of New York, New Orleans. Allison, this is no joke. You need to stay away from these people."

"Okay, I get it." Her tone softened. "Maybe Terry's had ties with them since way back. I don't know but Shane, he's clearly in some trouble if this Gus Schoeman is having a heart-to-heart with him. Is it possible they sent someone to break into Terry's house to scare him or try to get money from him? That would explain his hesitation to get the cops involved."

"I'm still working on CCTV from around the area. It's going to take me the day," he replied. "What are you going to do?"

"I need some information from Leo. Once I understand what was written in his mother's will, I'll know what direction to go."

"How do you mean?" he pressed on.

"I have to understand if what Terry claims was stolen had any real value and whether his wife left him the items or put them in a trust for Leo or the kids and he failed to tell anyone," Allison replied. "If I can determine a value, I'll know how much trouble Terry's really in."

"Promise me you won't go tailing this guy," Shane added.

"How can I? Besides, I'm not after Schoeman. I just want to make sure he's not after Terry."

"Fair enough. I'll get back with you as soon as I know more."

"Thanks, Shane." Allison ended the call and looked at Lucy. "I don't know how much you picked up..."

"Enough to know that Nolan's grandpa could be in a lot of danger," Lucy replied.

"That's what I'm working on finding out. I just ask that you don't say anything to him, not until I know more. He doesn't need the distraction."

"I get it. I won't say anything," Lucy replied. "What are you going to do now?"

"Figure out how deep in debt Terry really is. I'm not sure how to go about that just yet, but I'll work on it. In the meantime, keep plugging away at the Murray case. We need to keep our paying client happy."

———

DETECTIVE SULLY HAD ONLY RECENTLY STARTED DATING Allison and that was after months of dancing around the subject. She'd been reluctant, and he'd fallen for her pretty hard. But in times like this, he had to remember that she was also a private investigator whose cases could often place her in jeopardy. Many had already. Now he was concerned this one, which wasn't even a genuine case, might put her in the greatest danger of all. She'd skirted trouble with a corrupt politician, and a dangerous cartel. Could she soon be on the mob's hit list? Not if he had anything to do with it.

"Hey, Sully, what are you working on?" Detective Anton Baylor, who Shane had worked with on the cartel investigation, arrived at Shane's desk. The polished, well-dressed detective was instrumental in that case that ultimately led to the arrest of a corrupt FBI agent, and was a veteran in the department.

"Baylor, good to see you, man." Shane furrowed his brow. "Hey, what do you know about the mob here in Tampa?"

"That's a loaded question," he replied.

"In regard to gambling, bookmaking, things like that. You ever deal with cases like that?" Shane continued.

"Not me. Lopez has though. She went undercover with them about five years ago. Knows the families pretty well. Got out unscathed somehow. You should talk to her."

"Thanks, man. I will. How's things going for you?" Shane asked.

"Same shit, different day, brother." Baylor rapped his knuckles on top of the desk. "We should grab a beer soon, yeah?"

"Anytime."

8

In the nearly six years since Allison's divorce, she'd been to Leo's place about as many times as she could count on one hand, and that was including the recent wedding reception. Now, after some much needed alone time with Shane last night, morning arrived, and it was time to get to work. Leo had relayed to her the information on Sue's attorney. Allison was there to drive with him to meet the attorney.

Allison stood on the concrete covered porch at Leo's home. "Hi, Jenny. Is Leo around?" Allison asked.

"Yeah, of course. Come in." The younger second wife stepped aside and held open the door.

"Thanks. I see you got the place all put back together after the reception."

"It took a while. Can I get you a coffee?" Jenny started into the kitchen. "Leo should be down in a minute."

"No, I'm good. I had two cups already this morning." Small talk was never Allison's thing and especially making small talk with her ex-husband's new wife. She'd spent time around Jenny on various occasions, but never alone. It seemed no matter how much time had gone by since her divorce, talking to the wife of the man she had slept with for 20 years was awkward as hell.

Jenny peered up at the sound of Leo's footsteps. "There he is. Care for a cup of coffee?"

"To go, thanks, hon." Leo turned to Allison. "None for you?"

"I'm good. We should get going."

"Sure." Leo took the cup from Jenny. "I have to head to the school for an athletics club meeting after this, so I won't be back for a while."

"Okay, no problem," Jenny replied. "See you later, Alli."

Only two people called Allison that name. Leo and Charlie. Leo was told, in no uncertain terms, the nickname was off-limits now that they were divorced, though he still fell back on it pretty much always. But to hear it from Jenny made her cringe.

"Come on, Allison. Let's go." Leo ushered her to the door and when he opened it and Allison stepped outside, he continued. "Sorry about her calling you that. She doesn't know."

"Maybe you should say something to her, then." Allison reached for her car keys and unlocked the door.

"What's this? A new car?" Leo smiled.

"Yeah, can you believe it? Finally broke down and got one. What do you think?"

"I think it's great and well-deserved." Leo slipped onto the passenger seat. "Nice. Very nice."

"Thanks." Allison closed her door and pressed the ignition. "A/C works great."

"Good thing. You sure you don't mind dropping me off at the school?"

"Not at all," Allison replied.

"Appreciate it. I'm still not sure how I feel about all this."

As Allison backed out and started along the road, she glanced at him. "About your dad or about going to see the lawyer?"

"Both, I guess," he replied. "I wasn't there for the initial reading. I didn't want to deal with it. But to think Dad might've done something on the sly, well..." he peered through the passenger window. "I should expect it, but not where Mom was concerned. I'm pretty sure she was the only person he truly cared about."

"Your dad loves you, Leo. He just doesn't show it. I know he loves the kids too," Allison said. "We'll go see the lawyer, comb through the will and learn whether the collectibles have any value. And just so you know, given your dad's history, I asked a friend at the Tampa Police Department to pull security video from around the apartment complex."

"You mean, Shane? You asked Detective Sullivan?"

"Yes. Anyway, I thought, if what Terry's been saying is true, and I really want to believe it, then it's likely some security camera around there picked up on the thieves' vehicle and maybe the people inside who broke into his place and took the boxes."

Leo peered at her. "And if you see no one?"

"We'll figure that out if it happens. I prefer to give Terry the benefit of the doubt." She wasn't prepared to tell him about the racetrack yesterday. It was too soon, and it would only worry him. Funny how she still considered his feelings.

"I used to do that a long time ago—give Dad the benefit of the doubt." Leo grabbed onto the handle above the door. "I do like this car, though. You picked a good one."

She grinned. "I've learned how to hold my own, including negotiating. You would've been proud."

"I have no doubt." Leo narrowed his gaze. "That's the building up ahead."

Allison turned into the parking lot. "Are you sure you're okay doing this?" She cut the engine.

"I'm the only one who can besides Terry, so, yeah, I want to know if he's hiding something from me." Leo opened his door and stepped out under the sultry morning sky.

As they approached the entrance, Leo stopped. "What if Terry's lying, Alli? What if he sold Mom's things to pay off some gambling debt?"

"If that's the case, we'll just have to figure out why." Allison followed Leo inside and familiarity crept in. The comfortable feeling that the two were partners again and dealing with situations as a team. But they were far from partners, and both had begun new lives with new partners.

Leo made his way to the reception desk. "Morning. Leo Hart here to see Mr. Brindle."

The receptionist returned a pleasant smile. "Yes, Mr. Hart. I'll let him know you're here. If you'll have a seat..."

Leo nodded and he and Allison sat on the plush linen sofa beneath a painting that looked to be an Aleen Aked, an influential old Florida artist of the 1930s. He bounced his knee until Allison placed her hand on it.

"Relax, Leo. I know this is going to be hard. You never did like talking about what happened with your mother. I get it. But you're going to have to power through this so we can understand the situation."

"I know." He regarded her. "Thanks for doing this, Alli. I mean, I know your job is being a P.I. now and this is kind of what you do, but you didn't have to do this for me."

"Terry is still the kids' grandfather."

A heavy-set man in a blue suit and tie approached with an outstretched hand. "Mr. Hart, Jim Brindle. Nice to see you again. It's been a while." He glanced at Allison. "I'm sorry, and you are?"

"Allison." She returned the handshake.

"Pleasure. Why don't you both come on back and we'll get

started." Brindle pulled the sides of his suit coat taught and turned toward the hall. "My office is just down here. I had to pull the files from Archive. It's been a few years. To be honest, I'm not surprised to see you."

Leo and Allison followed him when Leo continued. "Why not?"

Brindle held open the door and gestured for them to enter. "Well, Terry Hart was an interesting fella, and he had a way about him." After Allison entered, Brindle closed his door and returned to his desk.

"How so?" Leo took a seat next to Allison.

"I can still remember him sitting in the chair you're in right now as I was reading his wife's will. His gaze wandered. His knee bounced. Just sort of seemed nonchalant about the whole thing. That was, until I got to the part about your mother's belongings. Perked up his ears right about then." He shuffled through the papers and slipped on his reading glasses. "How about we get started and you'll probably catch my meaning in a minute." Brindle licked his index finger and thumb before flipping the piece of paper. "Last Will and Testament of Suzanne Lillian Hart."

Allison listened as Brindle read the final wishes of her former mother-in-law. She had loved Sue like a mother and was certainly treated better by her than her own mother. At that time in their lives, when Sue was near the end, their marriage was beyond repair. Leo never handled things like that well. Of course, who had?

"And for my multiple collections, I bequeath to my only son, Leonard Hart, to do with as he sees fit."

Leo sat up. "Hold on. I told her I didn't want her collection."

Brindle pulled off his glasses. "Well, she gave them to you anyway. Mr. Hart, this is where your father, Terry, seemed to have a sudden keen interest." He raised his index finger. "Let me continue and you'll understand why." He read again from the will. "I know my son has refused my collection and I have left specific instructions such that my spouse, Terrance William Hart, shall not sell or otherwise dispose of said collection at any time while Leonard or his children remain on this earth."

Allison's eyes widened. "That's not what Terry said. He said you didn't want them. Nothing about your mom giving explicit instructions to you regarding them." She turned to Brindle. "Were these items ever appraised?"

Brindle shuffled through the papers. "As a matter of fact, they were." He handed the paper to her. "This was done a few weeks prior to Sue's passing. Instructions were given that Terry not be made aware of the value. And since I represented her, he has not been made aware."

Allison held the paper between her and Leo so they could both read it. "Oh my God." She looked at him. "Leo, this one here, the duck decoy, it's worth almost $10,000."

"Why wasn't I made aware of this appraisal?" Leo asked Brindle.

"According to your father, and what your mother wrote, you had no interest. I have a feeling she assumed you'd eventually come around. And you have."

Leo shook his head. "She always could read me like a book. So what happens, then, if the collectibles were stolen?"

"Sorry?" Brindle asked.

"Terry's apartment was broken into," Leo continued. "The only things they took were my mother's collectibles."

"That's curious," Brindle replied. "I assume Terry had insurance?"

"We haven't gotten that far," Allison cut in. "A police report was written at the time but has since been dismissed at Terry's request."

Brindle leaned back in his chair; his round belly protruded. "Even more curious."

"And since they were given to me, what then?" Leo asked.

"Nothing, I'm afraid. Since you rejected the possessions, the items would've defaulted to your father. Even with the explicit instructions not to sell them, which it seems, he hadn't, but rather they were stolen. Of course, at the time, you could've signed over possession to your children in the form of a trust, but... if they were, in fact, stolen from your father's home, the first thing I would do would be to contact the insurance company if he had one. Because I'll tell you one thing, Mr. Hart, any insurance money would be predicated on this appraisal and that money would belong to you."

———

THE DETECTIVE who went undercover to build a case against associates with ties to the Brunetti family had since been moved to another division inside the police department. She was involved in a joint task force with the feds to combat money laundering, and Detective Shane Sullivan was on his way to meet with her.

Shane rapped his knuckles on the doorframe of her office. "Excuse me, Detective Lopez?"

Her jet-black hair was pulled tight in a ponytail. The sharp white collar of her blouse stood tall. And as she turned up her gaze, her cheekbones featured prominently beneath her deep brown eyes. "You must be Detective Sullivan. Come on in."

"Everyone calls me Sully." Shane entered her office and offered his hand. "Nice to meet you."

"Likewise. You can call me Detective Lopez." A playful grin arose on her lips for only a moment before she turned serious again. "You're here about the Brunetti family, so what do you want to know?"

Shane sat down across from her. "A P.I. friend of mine thinks she might have run into some associates of the family. Asked me to look into the associate and since you're familiar, I thought I'd see what you know."

Lopez drew back her shoulders and pursed her full lips. "I know most people think the family is nothing more than legend now. I can assure you, they're not. While they may not have the power they once had, their influence is everywhere in Tampa organized crime. Who does this P.I. friend of yours think is a part of the family?"

"Have you ever heard the name, Gus Schoeman?" Shane asked.

"Sure I have. He's a legit businessman here in the city," Lopez replied. "At least, that's what he wants everyone to think."

"My friend spotted Schoeman talking to someone she knows and while she wasn't privy to the conversation, the person she knows seemed nervous. She got the plates on the car he was standing next to and that was how I confirmed it was Schoeman. I also understand he's part of the Winthrop Group. I imagine you know who they are."

Lopez laced together her fingers. "Oh yeah. You must as well, or you wouldn't be here. So tell me, Sully, how can I help? Sounds like you've done some legwork on your own already."

"I have, but I need to understand if Schoeman is someone to steer well clear of. If so, I need to warn a few folks."

"Steering clear of Schoeman is a no-brainer. However, if he's been talking to someone your friend knows, it's because that someone owes him. Schoeman's usually a 30,000 feet kind of guy. If he's in your face, it might already be too late."

Shane nodded. "I see. Given what you know of these guys,

how much would you say someone would have to be in for to get Schoeman involved?"

Lopez scoffed. "A lot. 10, 15 grand or more, easily. I would advise your P.I. friend to walk away before they're on Schoeman's radar. And if whoever they know is on Schoeman's shit list, it might be time to cut that person loose."

———

ALLISON RETURNED to the office after the troubling meeting with Leo's lawyer regarding his mother's will. It turned out that Terry had been up to his old tricks and likely never stopped, even after his wife died. Now, she waited on Shane to find security video from around Terry's apartment in hopes of spotting the thieves' car, assuming there were thieves. A question that hung in the air after the meeting.

Charlie pulled off her reading glasses as Allison walked inside. "You're back just in time. How did the meeting go?"

"Not great." Allison returned to her desk. "I'm still trying to give Terry the benefit of the doubt, but he is not making it easy. Turns out that Leo's mother had her collectibles appraised and insisted Terry not know the value. She also insisted the items be given to Leo."

"I thought he hadn't wanted them," Charlie replied.

"He hadn't, but Sue knew her husband and knew there would come a time when Leo would come asking about her things."

"Sounds like she knew her husband well," Charlie replied. "Listen, I'm glad you're back because Lucy and I found an accountant I think will get to the bottom of the Murray investigation. We wanted to run the name by you first." She walked to Allison's desk and eyed Lucy. "This was the kid's work, so any credit should go to her." Charlie set down a slip of paper with the name on it. "We should get this guy on board as quickly as possible."

Allison examined the paper. "And he knows to keep this quiet? Cheryl can't afford for her husband to learn what she's doing."

"He knows," Charlie replied.

"Then let's bring him in and get some costs together for Cheryl. The sooner the better," Allison replied.

"Glad you agree because he just pulled into the parking lot."

Allison whipped around to peer through the window. "Oh, okay."

"We figured you were going to be busy with Leo," Lucy cut in.

"No, it's fine. We can't delay the Murray case because of Terry Hart."

"That's what I told her," Charlie replied. "And I like being in charge when you're not here. Maybe when you are here too. We both know this place runs like a well-oiled machine when I'm running the show."

Allison laughed. "It's a damn good thing you're here, Charlie. Now, let's see what this guy can do for Cheryl."

The door opened slowly and a man, who appeared to be in his early 50s, peeked his head inside. "Excuse me, is this ACL Investigative Services?"

"Yes, sir. That's what it says on the door." Charlie approached him. "You must be Ed Lucero. I'm Charlie Wells. We spoke on the phone."

He continued inside and wore a friendly smile that reached all the way up to his light blue eyes. His hair was mostly grey and a little thin on the top. Otherwise, he appeared to keep himself in reasonably good shape. "Ms. Wells, yes, nice to meet you."

"Come in." Charlie closed the door behind him. "This is

Allison Hart, Private Investigator extraordinaire. And this is Lucy Boyce, resident computer expert."

"Ms. Hart, Ms. Boyce, pleasure," he replied.

"Can I get you anything to drink?" Lucy asked.

"No, thank you. I'm just fine."

"We should get started, then." Charlie led him to the conference table. "Have you had a chance to review the files I sent over?"

"Yes, ma'am." He sat down and waited for the others. "I think that if you three want to help Cheryl Murray, the best thing I can do is start by pulling SEC filings on her husband's businesses. From there, I can review corporate tax files as well." He peered at them. "If Mr. Murray is attempting to hide assets from his wife before their divorce, I'll find them."

Charlie smiled with relief. "That's great news, Mr. Lucero."

He regarded her. "Please, call me Ed."

"Only if you call me Charlie," she replied.

"You got it, Charlie."

Allison cleared her throat. "Well, I think Charlie should be your point of contact from here on out. Welcome aboard, Ed."

9

Any detective who had been undercover inside a mafia family for five years and made it out alive was someone whose warnings should be heeded. And after Shane's conversation with the sagacious Detective Lopez, he intended to do just that. Terry Hart was already a blimp on Gus Schoeman's radar. The last thing Shane wanted was for Allison to be one too.

He arrived at the apartment building where Terry Hart lived and gauged the surrounding area in search of cameras. Mainly a residential area, a convenience store lay less than a block away. Anyone coming onto this street would pass by that store. On the opposite corner was a McDonald's. Security cameras would be all over that place. It would help, but Shane needed to learn whether the apartment building, itself, had surveillance. He pulled up to the manager's office near the front of the building.

Inside, a woman sat behind a small desk and Shane approached her. "Afternoon. Is the manager available?"

She scrutinized him for a moment. "Is he expecting you?"

"No, ma'am." Shane retrieved his badge. "I'm here regarding a recent break-in involving one of your tenants. Detective Sullivan, Tampa PD."

"I'll call him up for you." She picked up the phone. "Dave, could you come up here for a minute? There's a police detective here to see you. Thanks." She ended the call. "He'll be right up."

"Thank you." Shane wandered inside the small office that oozed all the charm of the 1990s, complete with brass fixtures and shiny black faux leather chairs.

The manager appeared from the corridor. "Hello, there. Can I help you, Detective?"

Shane spun around. "Sullivan. I'm here about a recent break-in involving one of your residents, an elderly man named Terry Hart."

"Right, yeah. That was just a few days ago. The cops already came out," he replied. "What can I help you with?" The older man with dark thinning hair stood at attention.

"I'd like to see your security camera footage, if possible," Shane said. "We're looking to identify the persons and/or vehicles involved."

"Well, sure. I can pull that up for you, although it might be tough. The cameras in the parking lot are sketchy, at best. Any wind or heavy rain tends to knock them out."

"Anything you can show me would be appreciated," Shane replied.

"Then follow me." The lanky man started back into his office. "Shouldn't take but a minute." He sat down at his computer and typed in commands. "I gotta say, though, I didn't figure this was something a detective would need to do. The cops came and left, and I didn't even know about it until the next day."

"You didn't see the culprits on your security cameras?" Shane asked.

"We don't have any inside the grounds or between the buildings. Just along the back alleyway and the parking lot." He turned to Shane. "Is that going to be a problem?"

"We'll have to see."

Dave pulled up the files. "Here we go. This is from the day it happened." He pushed away from the computer. "Take a look all you want."

"Thanks." Shane eyed the man still in his chair. "You don't mind if I take a seat?"

"No, sir. Do I need to be here for this? I gotta run out to the pool for a minute."

"Go right ahead. I won't be long and if you're not back, I'll let your employee up front know I'm finished," Shane said. "I appreciate the help, sir."

"I'm always willing to help out the local authorities." Dave took his leave.

Shane sat down and viewed the footage. The system was dated. The video was grainy and in black and white. He pressed play and fast-forwarded to the early hours before the break-in, hoping to find a suspicious looking car hanging around, or people scoping out the complex.

Instead, only a few cars came and went. Four cameras were dotted around the lot and captured most of the area. Chances were good that where Camera 3 was stationed was the best spot for a thief to park. The nearby alley would've made for an easy getaway, but carrying boxes through the complex without people noticing was another story. As Shane viewed the footage, he saw nothing out of the ordinary.

According to Allision, the break-in occurred somewhere between 5 and 6 am, during the time Terry had run out to the store for some coffee. It was time to home in on the specifics. "Come on, show me something here. Don't waste my time."

Several more minutes went by as he kept his focus on the

camera nearest to the alley. "Not even a garbage truck. Son of a bitch. No one?"

And just as he was set to throw in the towel, something captured his attention. "What do we have here?" He checked the timestamp. "5:15 am, right on target."

A newer model Chrysler 300 had rolled up to the building at the end of the complex and stopped. No headlights, even while the sun had only just appeared over the horizon. No one had stepped out as minutes passed. "What the hell are you waiting for?" And as he continued to watch, his question was answered. His mouth agape and eyes narrowed, Shane paused the video. "What in the hell?"

———

CHARLIE SHOWED Ed Lucero to the door. "Thanks for coming down. I look forward to working with you."

"And you, Charlie. Thank you." He turned to Allison and Lucy. "You ladies have a wonderful afternoon." As he walked out, he kept his eyes on Charlie and wore a grin on his face.

She returned to her desk, beaming, when Allison chimed in. "Are we going to talk about what just happened with that man?"

Charlie peered up at her with raised brows. "I'm sorry, did I miss something?"

Allison glanced at Lucy and both returned crooked smiles. "Um, it looked like you two hit it off is all I was thinking."

"Did you see the way he looked at her?" Lucy asked.

"Like she was a tall, cool drink of water and he just came in from the desert," Allison replied.

"First of all, I'm more of a pint-sized water bottle, and secondly..." she scoffed and turned haughty, "I have no idea what you're talking about."

But the smile as she returned to her task was what caught Allison's attention. "You like him. He likes you and you like him. There's no denying it, Charlie."

She dismissed the notion with a shrug of her shoulders. "Yeah, well, we'll see."

"Yeah, we will," Lucy replied wryly.

The door flew open, and Shane walked in. "Allison, I need to show you something—now."

She jumped from her desk. "What is it? What's wrong?"

"Charlie, Lucy. Sorry for the interruption." He hurried to Allison's desk. "I copied video files and you need to see them."

Allison took the thumb drive from him and inserted it into her laptop. Charlie and Lucy hurried toward her. "Okay. Now what?" She asked him.

"Open the file. You're going to want to sit down."

"Shane, you're worrying me now," Allison replied.

"Alli, just do as he says," Charlie added.

"Okay, I've opened the first one. What am I supposed to be seeing here, Shane?"

"It's Terry Hart's apartment building. I was there this morning to get the security video files we discussed." He walked around and stood behind her chair. "Fast forward. I couldn't shorten the saved files so there's a lot to go through, but I jotted down the minutes on the timestamp to make it easier. On this video, forward through to minute 05:12."

Allison pressed the button and watched as the video sped through to the exact moment in question.

"Stop. Right there." Shane pointed to the screen. "Watch this." He noticed Charlie standing on the other side and peering over Allison's shoulder. Lucy stood next to her with folded arms, both eager to see what brought him running into their office.

Allison looked on until she spotted it. "What time was this?"

"Just keep watching," Shane replied.

Allison quickly put on her reading glasses and leaned in for a closer look. "Video's grainy."

"That won't matter in a minute," Shane replied.

Allison pulled back as her face turned deadpan. "Wait. Is that? Is that Terry?"

"You're damn right it is and it's about 5:15 in the morning, just around the time he said he had been robbed." Shane pointed to the screen again. "On my way here, I called in the plates on this car. I just got the call back. Allison, this car is registered to the Winthrop Group."

"Gus Schoeman?" Allison asked.

"I doubt it was the man, himself, but it was definitely someone who works for him."

Charlie placed her hand on Allison's shoulder. "And Terry's carrying boxes to him. Holy crap, Alli. Is he doing what I think he's doing?"

"Looks like it," Allison began. "Terry's place wasn't robbed. He handed over the boxes to the man in that car." She turned to Shane. "I don't know the value of everything in those boxes, but the most expensive item inside, or I assume is inside, is some decoy duck. Leo and I saw the appraisal. It's worth $10,000."

"For a duck?" Charlie shot back.

"Oh my gosh," Lucy cut in. "Nolan's grandpa handed over his wife's collectibles to some mob guy. But why?"

"To pay off a debt, I assume," Allison replied.

"Then the guy goes and drops the case," Shane added.

Allison turned back to the monitor. "I think now I know why."

———

THE MEETING at the school ended and Leo couldn't recall a single word his colleagues had said. He'd been preoccupied with the idea that Terry must've figured out the collectibles mentioned in his mother's will had been valuable, at least, some of them, and the story that they'd been stolen was starting to fall apart. Believing Terry had been Leo's first mistake.

His mind still reeled at learning the value of his mother's things. And he was sure Terry would've had them appraised on his own when he got desperate to payoff whatever gambling debt he must've amassed. The worst part was that those items should've been in Leo's hands. If they had been, he wouldn't be sitting here now in the parking lot of the racetrack in search of his father. It was time to confront Terry and get him to tell the truth about what really happened to his mom's treasured belongings.

Leo stepped out of his car and slammed the door. He couldn't see Terry's car in the parking lot. The place was huge. But he had no doubt this was where he would be. If only Jenny hadn't invited Terry to the wedding. Sure, his mom's collectibles would still be gone, but Leo wouldn't have been any the wiser. He would've been completely and blissfully ignorant where Terry was concerned. Yeah, it would've been the easier way out, but sometimes when things got tough, that was what Leo often elected to do.

He walked inside the building and headed directly upstairs to the betting desks in search of Terry. "Where the hell are you?"

"Can I help you, sir?"

Leo whipped around and spotted a plump man wearing dress pants and a button-down shirt. "I was looking for my father. I'm pretty sure he's here."

"Oh? Is he a regular? Maybe I know him. I'm the manager around here," Santos replied.

"Terry Hart. Short guy. Old. Thick hair. Shuffles his feet when he walks."

Santos drew up the corner of his mouth into a smile.

"So you do know him," Leo replied.

"Terry Hart's your pop?" Santos asked.

"Yes, he is. Don't suppose you've seen him today?" Leo asked.

"As a matter of fact, I have. He's out there." Santos pointed toward the grandstand. "You can usually find him third row up on the outside edge of the seats. He likes to make a quick escape and usually from me." He turned on his heel. "Good luck."

"Good luck? Better wish him good luck, not me." Leo marched out into the stands while a race was prepared to begin. He peered left, then right and spotted his father standing at the edge of the third row. He started toward him and when he arrived, he waited for Terry to notice. "Terry?"

His dad turned to him. "Leo? What the hell are you doing here?"

"Looking for you."

"Why?" He returned his gaze to the track. "Hang on, son. The race is about to start. I've got money on this one."

"I'll bet you do." Leo turned his sights to the track when the gates raised, and the horses charged ahead. "I found out something interesting today."

"Come on, Number 5, don't let me down!" Terry shouted.

Leo turned to him. "Don't you want to know what I learned?"

"In a minute, boy." Terry shooed him away.

Leo's jaw clenched and he folded his arms over his chest. "I cannot believe you."

The race only took minutes to finish and when Terry's horse came in dead last, he appeared irked. "Okay, what do you want, huh? You tracked me down for whatever reason. Interrupted my race. So get on with it. Spit it out, kid."

It was all Leo could do to keep from socking Terry right in the jaw. But it wouldn't look good hitting an old man, and, well, Terry was still kind of a badass. "I know what Mom's collectibles were worth, Dad. And I also know they were meant for me."

Terry raised his hands in surrender. "Hey, you turned your back on me after your mom died. You didn't want nothing to do with anything relating to her or her things. What the hell was I supposed to do, huh?"

"Did you sell it all?" Leo asked.

"What? No, of course not. I told you, it was stolen. The damn stress of all that gave me a heart attack."

"It was an anxiety attack, Dad, and I'm starting to question even that."

"Wait now, just hold on, son. What the hell are you saying?"

Leo noticed eyes turning toward them as their voices raised. "I'm asking, did you sell Mom's things to pay off some gambling debt?"

Terry swatted away the notion and shuffled back inside. "I don't need to listen to this cockamamie bullshit." He stopped and turned back to Leo. "You got some nerve, son. Your wife had to invite me to your wedding. You never so much as called me. Now you're accusing me of making up a story about my place getting robbed? Well, screw you."

Leo caught up to him. "You didn't answer my question."

Terry continued. "You know what, son? I don't know what I ever did to you."

Leo scoffed. "Are you being serious right now?"

Terry stopped. "Yeah, I am. When your mom died, I was gutted. You hear me? Gutted. Where were you? Wasn't that around the time you started cheating on Alli?" He shook his head and started on again. "What an idiot. You know she was always out of your league, right?"

Leo had known that since the day they married. "Dad, stop."

Terry had reached the glass doors of the exit. "What? What more you gotta say to me?"

"I need to know if you're in trouble."

"What the hell are you talking about?" Terry pressed on.

"You know what I'm talking about. Look, I'll never forgive you for how you treated Mom and me. And then to learn that her collectibles should've stayed with me."

Terry leaned in. "You didn't want them." His exaggerated annunciation was to prove his point. "And if you're so concerned— that's a crock—then I'll tell you. No, I'm not in any trouble, okay? So you can go on about your happy little life with your happy second wife and stay the hell out of mine." He peered at Leo. "Alli was the only good thing you ever did, and she gave you two beautiful kids. Look how you screwed that up. Why don't you take a look in the mirror, kid, then come talk to me."

———

While Allison could believe Terry would actually do something like this, the reality of it proved difficult to swallow. "What am I supposed to tell Leo?" She paced the office and finally turned to Shane. "Are we talking criminal charges here? He reported a crime that didn't happen."

"Didn't you say you were the one who called the police because Terry hadn't wanted to?" he asked.

Allison nodded. "Yeah, I guess I did, but he didn't stop me."

"What was he going to say?" Charlie interjected. "Oh, no need to call the police. I'm making all this up."

Shane pushed off the corner of Allison's desk. "I think we're all missing the bigger problem here."

Allison stopped in her tracks. "Which is?"

"Terry Hart is involved with some very dangerous people. The kind you don't want to get on the wrong side of."

"So if he got in the red with them again," Allison continued. "And he has nothing left to sell to pay his debt…"

"Then I imagine Terry Hart won't be a problem to anyone after that," Shane replied.

Allison returned to her desk. "I have to call Leo. He has to know what's going on." She picked up her phone and pressed his contact number. "He's not answering. Damn. Voicemail." When the message finished, she continued. "Leo, it's me. I have some information you need to know about your dad. Call me as soon as you can. Bye." She returned her attention to Shane. "Is there anything I can do in the meantime?"

He peered at all of them. "The best advice I can give you is to stay the hell away from Terry Hart."

10

Beneath the porch light, Allison and Shane stood at her front door. She reached for her keys and unlocked it. "Micah's out with a few of her friends right now."

Shane followed her inside. "Does she know about any of this with her grandpa?"

"Some." Allison closed the door behind him. "I'm not sure what to tell these kids about all this. Terry was always kind to them, brought them gifts. But he was never really there for them, same as he wasn't for his own kid." She started into the kitchen. "Beer?"

"Please." Shane pulled out a stool at the kitchen island. "I think it's best you bow out of this entire situation. I know you want to help Leo..."

She returned with two bottles and opened the tops. "I need to convince Leo to back off and let Terry handle his own problems. None of this would've come out had Jenny not pulled Terry back into their lives. A fact I'm sure Leo hasn't missed." She sipped on her beer.

"Not to sound callous, but I don't care what Leo does so long as you steer clear of it," Shane replied.

"It's a little callous, but I understand." A knock on her door drew her attention. "Is that Micah? Why isn't she using her key?" Allison started toward the door while Shane looked on.

She turned the handle and opened it. "Did you forget your keys?" But on the other side wasn't who she'd expected. "Leo?"

With glassy eyes and a slight sway, he replied, "I don't have keys to this house anymore."

Allison glanced at Shane, who was still in the kitchen, before turning back to Leo. "Are you okay, Leo? Have you been drinking?"

"Just one—maybe two drinks," he replied.

She peered outside and spotted his car. "Geez, you drove here? You clearly had more than two drinks. Get inside."

Leo staggered a little as he walked in and glanced into the kitchen. "Oh, you have company."

Shane raised his bottle of beer. "Hey, Leo."

"Detective Sullivan." Leo turned back to Allison. "Sorry to interrupt. I didn't know where else to go."

"How about home to your wife?" Allison walked into the kitchen. "I'd offer you a beer, but I think you should have a cup of coffee." She turned on the pot. "I tried calling you earlier this afternoon, but I got your voicemail."

"I haven't been taking calls." Leo dropped onto the kitchen stool next to Shane. "How's it going, man?"

"Fine." Shane's expression suggested otherwise.

"Where's Micah?" Leo asked Allison.

She returned with a cup of coffee and set it in front of Leo. "With her friends. I thought you were her at the door."

"Yeah, I'm sorry to come over unannounced." He sipped on

the brew. "I found Terry at the racetrack. Big surprise, huh? I wanted to tell him I knew about Mom's appraisal."

"What did he say?" Allison asked.

"Told me to butt out, and reminded me that I hadn't wanted anything to do with Mom's things after she died. I hate it when he's right."

Allison turned down her gaze a moment. "There's something you need to know, Leo, something Shane found earlier today, which was why I called."

"Okay." He turned to Shane. "What is it?"

"I'm sorry to be the one to tell you this, man, but your dad." Shane peered at Allison with uncertainty until she nodded for him to continue. "Your dad, he dropped the investigation into the robbery; requested that it be dropped, actually. Allison asked that I look into a few things, and I found CCTV footage from the complex parking lot." He tossed back a swig of beer, appearing hesitant to continue.

"And?" Leo pressed on.

"On the video, we saw your dad carrying boxes. He gave them to a man whose car is registered to the Winthrop Group."

"What the hell is the Winthrop Group?" Leo asked.

"A company with dubious connections run by a man with known ties to a crime family in the city. Allison was pretty sure the boxes Terry handed over contained your mom's collectibles."

"The ones he claimed were stolen," Leo added.

"Yeah, man. I'm sorry, but it looks that way," Shane replied.

Leo chuckled and rubbed his eyes. He chuckled again, a little louder this time until he went into a full-on belly laugh.

"Leo?" Allison pressed her hand on top of his.

"No, no, I'm fine." He calmed his laughter. "Doesn't that just figure? I mean, I knew my dad was a piece of shit. Why should this surprise me?" He creased his brow and looked at Shane again. "And you're sure about this?"

Shane nodded.

"Son of a bitch." Leo stood up and staggered toward the door. "Thanks for the coffee, Alli."

She brushed off the familiar term and caught up with him. "Leo, wait, you're in no condition to drive. I can't let you leave."

"Why not? You did six years ago," he replied. "Why is now any different?"

She wanted to be angry with him but tried to remember he wasn't himself right now. Leo was a lot of things, but spiteful wasn't one of them. "I'm trying to help you out. You can sleep it off on the couch." She led him to the sofa. "You might want to call your wife. Either she can come and get you or you can stay here, but you aren't getting behind the wheel of a car right now."

Leo peered at her with his phone in hand, ready to call Jenny. "You're a good woman, Alli. I always knew that."

Allison returned to the kitchen. "I'm so sorry about all this."

Shane reached for her hand. "Don't be. It's fine. I'm sure his wife will come and get him."

The front door opened and drew Allison's attention. "What now?"

"Mom?" Micah walked inside. "Is that Dad's car..." her gaze was pulled to the living room. "Dad? What are you doing here?"

Allison caught up to her. "He's had a little too much to drink. He's calling Jenny to come pick him up."

"Why is he here? Why didn't he just go home?" Micah asked.

"Good question," Shane mumbled under his breath before he threw back another swig of beer.

"It's just stuff going on with Grandpa. Dad's upset and that's all it is," Allison replied.

Shane walked into the foyer. "I should go. This is clearly a family situation."

Allison thrust her arm against his chest to stop him. "No, wait."

"He's right, Mom." Micah turned to Shane. "No offense."

"None taken." He grabbed his keys from his pants pocket. "I can give Leo a lift home, too, if you want."

Allison peered into the living room and spotted Leo slumped back on the sofa, asleep. "Thanks, but I'll see to it Jenny knows to get him. I'll talk to you tomorrow?"

"Sure thing." He nodded and kissed her cheek. "Good night."

Allison secured the door behind him while Micah had gone to her dad's side and picked up his phone.

"Mom, I don't know his password. I can't see if he called Jenny or not."

Allison bowed her head a moment to collect herself before heading into the living room. "I'll just call her myself." With her phone in hand, she made the call. "Hi, Jenny, it's Allison. Did Leo..." She grinned. "Right, okay good. He's crashed out on the sofa, and I couldn't see on his phone if he called you. Great. No, I appreciate you coming. See you in a little while." She ended the call. "Jenny's on her way now."

"What's going on, Mom?" Micah asked. "Dad doesn't get drunk."

"Not generally, no. It's between Grandpa and him. They'll have to work it out." Micah was a grown woman now, but Allison felt the need to protect her from whatever it was Terry managed to get himself into. She'd felt terrible about Shane, though. He'd never been married and had no children. This must've seemed so foreign to him. He'd only come over at her request and now he was gone.

"Leo? Leo, come on now." Allison shook him awake. "Jenny's coming to get you. Let's get you up and out of here, huh?" She turned to Micah. "Hon, can you give me a hand?"

"Sure." Micah helped him up.

"I'm sorry, girls. I let you both down," Leo mumbled. "I let my girls down."

"No you didn't, Dad. It's okay to get drunk once in a while. I've done..." she trailed off and shot a glance at Allison. "I mean, it's okay."

Allison pursed her lips. "Uh-huh. We'll get into that another day." When the knock sounded, she knew this time it was Jenny. "Your ride's here, Leo. Get up. Let's go." She pulled his arm around her shoulder. "Micah, grab his other arm and help him up."

"Got it."

They shuffled him to the door and when Allison opened it, Jenny stood on the other side.

She glared at him with her hands on her slim hips. "Can you walk on your own?"

"I'm fine. I'm fine," Leo replied.

"We'll help you get him into the car," Allison added.

"Thanks." Jenny turned around and started toward the car, opening the passenger door. "I'll drop him off back here in the morning to get his car. Thanks for this, Allison."

"Don't be too hard on him. This whole thing with his dad has thrown him for a loop," she replied. "And we both know this isn't normally what Leo does."

"I know." Jenny buckled him in and closed his door. "Still, it was good of you to make sure he didn't get behind the wheel again."

"Of course." Allison peered out into the street while Jenny slipped into the driver's side. Her gaze narrowed when she noticed a car across the street in front of the neighbor's house. On returning her attention, she waved to Jenny. "Bye."

Jenny backed out of the driveway and started on.

Allison turned around and pulled Micah close. "Let's get back inside. It's muggy as hell out here." She led Micah to the door but stopped and looked again at the car.

It started up and drove on without its headlights. "What in the world?" Allison had learned to trust her gut and right now, her gut was telling her to make note of the car and the plate, if she could get a look at it. But as it drove on, she pulled back to avoid being seen.

"Mom? You okay?" Micah asked as she stood in the hall.

"Yeah, fine. Sorry."

———

TERRY STEPPED out of his car and shuffled along the walkway toward his downstairs unit. After the confrontation with Leo, he'd waited in his car until Leo left before going back inside. He wasn't going to prove the kid was right about his gambling troubles. But now, as it hit 10pm, he'd gone home, dead broke once again. And not without a word of warning from the manager, Lou Santos. No more lines of credit, he'd burned that bridge. Nevertheless, Schoeman could still be counted on, he thought. Keeping in good with those guys was key to Terry's success.

He dug into the pocket of his khaki shorts and retrieved his house key, but on trying the handle, he noticed the door was unlocked. "What the hell?" Terry pushed it open and stepped inside. His hand ran along the wall and found the light switch. "Jesus." As the light filled the room, he took in the scene. The sofa was overturned. Cans of beer and soda lay scattered on the floor as though someone had dumped the recycling trash can into his living room. The place had been ransacked. "Just calm down." He placed his hand over his chest. "Relax. Breathe." Going back to the hospital only for them to tell him he was having an anxiety attack wasn't going to happen. And worse yet, he knew no one would come to his aid, not after the way he talked to Leo. Calling the cops? Forget it. Terry was on his own. He shuffled inside, kicking away the cans in his path. "At least they didn't take the TV."

Anyone else would've thought they'd ransacked the kitchen too, but the dirty dishes had been there for days, so had the pizza boxes. He continued through the small one-bedroom apartment until reaching his room. Terry flipped the switch and thrust his hand over his mouth. On the wooden headboard he'd had since he'd gotten married, were the words, *"payback's a bitch"* carved into it. "But I paid off you sons of bitches."

It was clearly a warning, but why? Had Gus learned that Allison called the cops? But he fixed it. He made sure the case was dropped. "I don't get it. What the hell did I do?"

———

Jenny pulled into the garage of their 3-bedroom home. She peered at Leo, who had just been roused by the opening of the garage door. "Let's get inside and put you to bed."

As she walked around to help Leo out, she spotted a car driving slowly by. Her eyes fixed on it for a moment until it sped up and disappeared down the street. She opened Leo's door. "You're going to have to help me, Leo."

He groaned. "I'm sorry, baby. I messed up."

"Yeah, you did. I had to go to your ex-wife's house to pick you up, but we can talk about that tomorrow when you're sober. Let's just go inside."

He pushed off the seat and nearly tumbled into her. "Terry's an asshole."

Jenny tucked her shoulder under his arm and steadied him. "So you've said."

"I mean, he's a real asshole. I wish you hadn't invited him to the wedding."

"I'm sorry, Leo. I didn't know. You never said why you weren't close to him." She closed the door and ushered him inside. "I didn't mean for any of this to happen and certainly not for you to be hanging around Allison because of it."

He scrunched up his face as he walked into the kitchen. "Are you jealous of her or something? Cause you know..."

"Yeah, yeah. I know. And no, I'm not jealous. I just don't like the idea of you running to her every time you have a problem."

Leo stood on his own feet and aimed his index finger at her. "Now you listen here, I can handle my own problems. I don't need you or Alli to help me." He stumbled and reached for Jenny's arm.

"Yeah, I see that. Why don't we just talk about this in the morning before you say something you'll regret?" Jenny helped him through the hall and into their bedroom. "Sit down." She slipped off his shoes and socks and got him into the bed. "Sleep it off. I'm going to read for a little bit."

"You're not coming to bed now?" he pleaded.

"Nope. Night." She switched off the light. Jenny returned to the living room and reached for the blinds on the picture window behind the sofa. She peered out and noticed the car again. "Okay, what's going on?"

––––––––

Before Charlie Wells became the "C" in ACL Investigative Services, she worked for the State of Florida in Fraud

Investigations. It was how she came to know Allison, and the two were as close as sisters ever since. It helped that they had a lot in common. Both divorced. Both had kids. The difference was that Charlie's boys were younger than Allison's children. She shared custody of them with her deadbeat ex-husband, who was a son of a bitch most of the time.

Her job had been a supplement to Allison's, who was a field investigator at the time. Charlie did the paperwork while Allison gathered physical evidence.

Charlie had become well-versed in fraud research over the course of her career. And when something niggled at the back of her neck, something that didn't seem right, she followed up, and her instincts were usually spot on. That was how she felt now in light of the Terry Hart situation. While her focus had been on the Cheryl Murray case, she felt comfortable now with Ed Lucero working on it. Her cheeks flushed a little at the thought of him.

The high-value decoy duck stared back at her from her laptop screen. Allison had forwarded the photo to her that she'd found in an old album. Charlie questioned why Terry Hart would've claimed it had been stolen. Terry had handed over the collectibles to a man he was no doubt indebted to. And after learning what had been in his wife's will, it became clear why he hadn't sold the items himself. They weren't his to sell.

She pulled up eBay and searched for similar items wondering just how much something like that might go for. The appraisal stated $10,000, but resale was always a little different. And what about the rest of Sue's things?

The screen populated with ads for a lot of these wooden ducks. Some in pretty bad shape, some looked like they'd never been touched. Apparently, this was a popular collector's item. She noticed several decoys were for sale anywhere from a few hundred dollars to several thousand. "Oh my gosh." Charlie slipped on her readers and peered closer at the screen. She double-clicked on the image to enlarge it. "No, it can't be." Her eyes darted to the photo Allison sent and then darted back to her screen. "Sure as hell looks like the same one."

11

Terry's apartment had been put back together. No more cans, no more trash. The furniture, such as it was, had been returned to its original state. Even the dishes in the sink had been washed. He was shaken by the event and worried that this time, he might not be able to talk his way out of trouble. After tossing and turning in bed last night, desperate to figure out what exactly had gone wrong, he knew one thing; Gus Schoeman wasn't happy.

This time, however, he was going to keep what happened last night to himself. It was supposed to have been Leo who turned up the day of the bogus robbery. Terry had it all planned out to a T. Yeah, he knew his son was on his honeymoon, but it all added depth to the story. Leo would rush back and be a witness for Terry that his place had been broken into and things got stolen. He'd already known Sue's collectibles were untouchable to him, per her will. But hey, if he was robbed, not his fault, right? It hadn't worked out that way and the cops got involved.

It must have been the reason Schoeman sent his cronies to overturn his place. Well, message received—loud and clear. It hadn't seemed to matter that Terry dropped the investigation. Screwing around with Gus Schoeman might have been a mistake. Hindsight being what it was.

Terry buttoned one of his many loud Hawaiian shirts and snatched his keys from the breakfast counter in the kitchen.

He shuffled outside and stepped into his old black Chevy Impala before keying the ignition and heading onto the highway.

Terry arrived at the Winthrop Group's office in a high rise near Downtown Tampa. He stepped out of his car and headed toward the entrance. The glass doors parted as he arrived, and he walked inside the cold lobby. The front desk was just ahead. "Good morning. I'm Terry Hart here to see Mr. Schoeman."

"Is he expecting you?" asked the young man wearing a shirt and tie.

"No, sir, but he'll know why I'm here," Terry replied.

After looking the old man up and down, he picked up the phone. "Let me try his office." A moment later he called out. "Sir?"

Terry approached the desk again. "Yes."

"Mr. Schoeman said you can go up. Third floor. Second door on the left."

"Thank you, young man." Terry patted down his thick salt and pepper hair and tugged on his shirt as he made his way to the elevator. The doors parted on the third floor, and he arrived at the office. With a knock, Terry was granted entry.

Gus Schoeman leaned back in his executive chair and regarded Terry with indifference. His thin blonde hair and hollow cheeks made him look much older than he was under the harsh office lighting. "Terry. I'm surprised to see you here. How are things?"

"I think you know how they are." He shuffled inside. "Spent the night cleaning up my place trying for the life of me to figure out what happened."

"Sorry, I don't catch your meaning," Schoeman replied.

"Sure you do." Terry lowered himself onto the guest chair with a grunt. "I just can't figure out what I did. I thought we were square."

"Oh, you thought that, did you?" Schoeman leaned over his desk, resting on his pointed elbows. "So did I, until my associate mentioned that a few of the items you handed off as collectibles were worth diddly squat."

"Now, hold on. That can't be right. I took that stuff to an antiques store. Fella there said that duck alone was worth thousands. Not to mention the rest of it. I wasn't pulling your leg, Gus. I promise you that."

"Appraised value, maybe, but not on the streets. And the rest of that ticky-tack shit wasn't worth enough to buy me a steak dinner. Terry, you're into this for 16k. I paid off your 10k line of credit, then you go and pull a stunt like this."

"No, you're mistaken," Terry began. "You should've easily been able to sell those things for the rest of what I owed you."

"I'm mistaken?" Schoeman nodded with a downturned mouth. "How about you do that, then? I'll give you back what's left. You sell it, then come back to me with the rest of the cash. I'll deduct what we got for what was sold already. Something like five grand was all we got." He eyed Terry. "I was doing you a favor by taking that shit off your hands. I'm done helping. So I suggest you do what you gotta do and come back here by the end of the week with the rest of the money you owe me."

"I don't know that I can unload the stuff that fast," Terry replied.

"Then I suggest you figure out another way. One way or another Terry, you'll be giving me the remainder of the cash, all 11 grand you owe me, by the end of the week or we're going to have ourselves another sit-down. Trust me, you don't want that."

———

IT WAS a bright blue morning and yet as Allison made her way to the office, she felt like she was being sucked down into a rip current, a dark tide that was pulling everyone under and threatened to drown her entire family.

She was the first to open the office as light spilled in between the slats of the window blinds. A slight musty smell lingered in the old building and worsened on the more humid days like today.

The first thing on her to-do list this morning was to call Shane and apologize for last night. Leo showing up drunk at her door wasn't her fault, but she could imagine how it made Shane feel. Allison made the coffee, opened the blinds, and sat down at her desk to make the call. "Hey, it's me. Are you busy?"

"Yeah, I'm at a crime scene right now. Can I call you later?" he asked.

"Oh, of course. I'm sorry to bother you. Talk to you later."

The office door opened and Charlie walked inside as Allison ended the call. "What's wrong? Why are you here before me?"

"Nothing's wrong. I wanted to get a jump on the day, so I came in early," she replied.

"Uh-huh. Something happened last night. You told Leo what we learned about his dad and the robbery, didn't you?" Charlie headed straight for the coffee on the back credenza.

"I did, but it didn't happen like you think. Leo drove to my house—drunk—and it all went downhill after that."

"Holy crap. Okay, I wasn't expecting that. That must've gone over well with Shane. He followed you back to your place last night, didn't he?"

"Oh yeah, it went great having my drunk ex-husband show up while I was with my cop-boyfriend. I'm surprised Shane didn't arrest him."

Charlie poured a cup of coffee and was heavy-handed with the creamer. "I would've paid to see that, though. Sounds like you had an interesting night. But so did I." Charlie walked to Allison's desk and handed her a sheet of paper. "Take a look at that. Tell me it isn't the same one from the picture you sent me."

Allison slipped on her readers and examined the paper. "This is an eBay listing."

"Yep," Charlie replied. "Take a look at where the seller is located."

"Here in town." Allison flipped over the paper and returned it again. "I don't understand. How could we possibly know for sure this is the same decoy Sue owned?"

"We don't, but it sure as hell looks the same. I think we should find out a little more about the seller." Charlie peered at her. "Alli, this could be linked to the crime family Shane mentioned. Terry gives these collectibles that didn't belong to him to Schoeman's people to pay down his debt. The most valuable item then turns up for sale online, meaning they used a fence. That's a crime."

"Yeah. And the trail will lead straight back to Terry, exposing Schoeman and maybe his ties to the family too." Allison set down the paper. "First thing we need to do, then, is to verify that it's the same decoy."

Charlie started back to her desk. "I'm working on that this morning. I put a call into the appraiser listed on Sue's paperwork. The one who initially appraised the decoy. He's working on confirming my suspicions now. I sent him the eBay listing this morning before I left the house, and he already had his own photos from the appraisal."

"Then that should answer the question," Allison replied.

"What would that mean for us? For you?" Charlie asked.

Allison shrugged. "I'm not sure. It could put Terry in hot water, more than he already is."

"Then we do our best to make sure the finger points to Gus Schoeman and his people," Charlie added. "Get an arrest, get these guys off the streets and out of Terry's life. Leo can then get Terry out of his life if that's what he wants."

"This family and their associates have run organized crime in Tampa and the state for something like 70 years. I don't think our little P.I. firm is going to bring them down. Best we can do is protect ourselves and the ones we care about," Allison replied.

"How about we just see if the decoys are the same, huh? Then we can figure out what to do with the information. We can find a way to do this without Leo getting involved." Charlie's attention turned to the door. "Morning, Lucy. Hey, did your dad ever have any run-ins with organized crime families?"

Lucy looked around as if the question had been directed at someone else. "It's 8 o'clock in the morning and I haven't even sat down yet."

"Sorry," Charlie smiled. "But did he?"

Lucy walked to her desk. "Well, I can't recall anything in particular, but I'm sure he must've in his time. He dealt with a lot of shady people. Is this about Terry Hart?"

"Yes," Allison cut in. "Could you check your dad's files for a man named Gus Schoeman? Also, anything referring to the Winthrop Group."

"Sure. I'll work on it now," Lucy replied. "Oh, should we follow up with Mr. Lucero on any progress he's made on the Murray investigation?"

"I'll do it," Charlie jumped in.

"Go right ahead," Allison replied. "I'm sure he'd love to hear from you."

Charlie's cheeks revealed a hint of pink as she picked up the phone.

"Are you blushing?" Allison asked. "Wow, you must really like this guy."

Charlie shrugged. "Eh, he's all right."

"Sure." Allison snickered as her attention was drawn to her phone. "Hang on. It's Shane. I'd better get this." She answered the call. "Hi, sorry about interrupting you earlier."

"Don't be. You didn't know. I had a minute, so I thought I'd call you back. What's up?" he asked.

"Now's probably not the right time, but I wanted to apologize for last night..."

"You don't need to, Allison. You can't control other people's actions."

She sighed. "Still, I feel awful about it."

"It's fine, really. Is that what you were calling about? I'm still on scene, so I should probably get back..."

"Actually, there was something else. Last night when Jenny picked up Leo, I stood at the door and waited for her to pull away. When she did, I noticed another car start up from out of nowhere. I wasn't paying attention, so it could've turned the corner onto my street, or it could've been there already. Point being, it looked out of place."

"You got plates you want me to run?" he asked.

"I do, if you wouldn't mind. Knowing who Terry's been consorting with and all that...If you have a minute sometime today. I'd just feel better knowing whether I should be worried. I know it wasn't the car I saw in the parking lot next to Gus Schoeman."

"Hang on. You saw him at his car?" Shane asked.

"Uh, yeah. I was looking for my car and he was right there..."

"Allison, did he talk to you? Did you tell him who you were?"

"Did I talk to him?" Her brows raised. "No, well... he might've said something like, 'are you lost,' because I was looking around for my car. I kept looking for my old Honda and not the new one." She laughed nervously. "No big deal. He has no idea who I am."

"Did he see you get into your car?" Shane pressed on in a serious tone.

"No, I went back inside. Shane, it was really nothing..."

"Give me the plate from the car last night. Make and model, too, if you can remember it," he cut in.

She dug through her laptop bag for the slip of paper. "I'll text it to you now. I was going to call Leo and give this to him too just to be sure they keep an eye out for it."

"Good idea," Shane said. "Okay, I got the text. I'll see what I can find out. Sorry, I don't mean to be a jerk. I just worry."

"I know and you're not a jerk. If anyone is, it's Leo." She laughed.

"At least we agree on that. I'll call you when I have something. Bye, Allison."

"Bye." She ended the call and looked at her partners. "So, let's talk about Cheryl Murray."

———

TERRY RETURNED to the racetrack to try his hand once again. It was the only possible way he could hope to begin to pay back the people he'd have given anything not to owe at this moment. No doubt, another friendly chat with Lou Santos would transpire. He and Schoeman were tight and that didn't bode well for Terry.

He'd repaid his debt to the track. Sure, it was with money from Schoeman, but for now, he was square with Santos. Maybe Santos would even consider extending another small loan to increase his odds of bringing home some extra cash. Winning thousands of dollars to get out from under Schoeman was another story altogether, but this was a good place to start.

"Lou, good to see you today." Terry waltzed into the man's office like he owned the place.

"Terry, why am I not surprised to see you in here?" Santos replied. "To what do I owe the pleasure?"

Terry sat down in the guest chair. "Well, seeing how I've been diligent about repaying my debts, I wondered if the delightful management at Bayside Downs would kindly extend me a small sum of money with which to play today."

Santos raised a brow. "You're kidding me, right? Come on, Ter, you gotta be pulling my leg right now."

"I'm not and I don't understand why you would think so," he replied.

Santos pulled up in his chair. "Because you got nothing left to offer, man. What can you provide as collateral, huh? Come on, what do you have that will ensure I don't lose my job by giving you another line of credit."

Terry dug in his shorts pocket and retrieved his keys. "Here. She's free and clear and worth at least seven grand."

The man eyed the keys. "Your car? You want to put your busted up old Impala as collateral? Geez, Ter, I don't know how the hell you'll get home then. And seven grand? You're shitting me, right? I've seen your ride. No way that POS is worth more than 3-grand."

"All right. Five. I'll put up my car for a $5000 line. That's more than fair and you know it," Terry replied.

Santos eyed him. "Brother, you got balls, I'll give you that. You think I don't know who's been fronting you cash lately? Now you come to me wanting me to do the same?" He pulled out a pad with forms on it and began writing. "It's your funeral. I'll give you a 4k LOC." He tore off the form and handed it to Terry. "Standard repayment agreement. Nothing more. You can't pay it back,

Bayside Downs will own your car. Do you hear what I'm saying to you?"

"I hear you and you won't have to worry about that." Terry took the slip of paper. "Pleasure doing business with you, Lou. Today's going to be a good day. I can feel it."

When Terry left the office, Santos waited for him to fall from view before he picked up the phone. "It's me, listen, Terry Hart was just in here. Yeah, I know. He put up his car this time. I gave him 4 grand. He'll blow through that in a few days." He nodded. "I know the drill. You'll get the same percentage we agreed upon. I'll leave that up to you because it's you he'll have to answer to. Got it. Later."

———

GUS SCHOEMAN WAS BORN and raised in the Sunshine State. Tampa had been his home since he was plucked from his street hustle at the age of 19 by a man who went by the name of Sal. That was all he knew, and he had been smart enough not to ask questions. Sal introduced him to people. People he still knew today. Sal was gone now. Passed on some years ago. And Gus had moved up in the organization. He was a busy man and screwing around with the likes of Terry Hart gave him indigestion.

A middle-aged man with a crew cut and dressed like he was about to hit the links popped his head into the office. "Excuse me, Mr. Schoeman? Am I interrupting?"

Schoeman waved him in. "No, come in. You got something for me?"

"I do, sir." He handed over a file folder. "This is the information you asked for on Mr. Hart's associates, or family, as it were."

"Specifically, the blonde," Schoeman replied.

"Yes, sir. It's all in there. According to our guy at the precinct, she's a private investigator here in the city."

Schoeman opened the folder. "Yep. Same woman I saw at the track pretending like she was lost, or something. And our boy, Terry, is related to her."

"Was. Ms. Allison Hart was Terry's daughter-in-law up until about six years ago. It doesn't appear as though Terry Hart had much to do with any of his family..."

Schoeman closed the folder. "Until now."

12

The idea that Terry arranged for his wife's valuable collection to be used to pay off his gambling debt pissed off Allison. Sue had been the only person who could've managed to put up with that man for as long as she had. Nevertheless, Allison hadn't wanted anything bad to happen to Terry, and certainly not to Leo. However, Charlie had a point and maybe there was a way to get a fencing charge slapped against the man who supposedly sold the collectible along with the people who bought it. It was possible to keep Terry and Leo out of the picture if they played it right. Learning whether the decoy was one and the same was the first step in that process.

Allison opened her door and slipped behind the driver's seat of her new car. After Charlie closed her door, she pressed the ignition. "You have the address?"

"I do. They close at 6. We'll be fine if we avoid the highway and miss the rush hour traffic," Charlie said.

Allison rolled out of the parking lot. "I'm hesitant to find out who was in that car last night. The more we learn about Terry's problem, the more exposed we are."

"If it was one of the people Terry owed money to, then these guys aren't messing around, Alli. You don't start following family members of the guy who owes you if you're not serious about getting the money back," Charlie replied.

"That's what concerns me." Allison turned onto the parkway toward Riverview. "Let's stop by the station and hit Shane up for an answer after this, assuming he's around. He was at a crime scene this morning. With him being in Major Crimes now, I don't know how much help he'll have time to offer anymore."

Charlie peered through the windshield. "We need to be able to lean on more than just Shane, that's for sure. But I'll tell you, I am starting to feel like we're not giving Cheryl Murray the attention she deserves."

"And we're dumping everything on Lucy." Allison turned onto the street where the seller of the decoy duck had a storefront. "We ask to see the duck. Ask if he has an appraisal and if there's any chain of possession."

Charlie opened her door to step out. "You know, you're starting to sound like a private investigator or something."

Allison stepped out. "Gee, I try so hard not to."

Charlie reached the entrance and opened the door. The store was crammed with antiques and smelled of all things old and musty. "Should've brought my can of air freshener."

"I'm not sure that would help." Allison started ahead toward the register. "Hi, good afternoon."

A silver-haired slender woman dressed in a white silky blouse stood behind the counter. "Good afternoon, ladies. How can I help you?"

Allison retrieved the printed listing. "We would like to take a look at this."

The woman slipped on her reading glasses that hung around her neck. "Let's take a look here." She examined the listing. "Oh, yes. I remember this. It's rare we ever see something of this value. Are you two interested in purchasing it?"

"Possibly. We'd like to take a look if it's here," Allison replied.

"Certainly. It's in the back, getting ready to be transferred to our other location. We didn't think it would sell here. I'll go get it for you." She spun around and disappeared behind an arched opening.

"The first step in our master plan is complete," Charlie said.

"Our master plan? Are we evil villains now?" Allison asked.

Charlie raised her hand and twisted her invisible mustache. "I could be." She eyed the woman as she emerged from the back and nudged Allison. "Here we go."

"This is the decoy here." She carefully lifted the lid to the box. "As you can see, we're keeping it well protected." The duck was wrapped in brown paper and surrounded by bubble wrap. "Give me a minute to unpack it."

Allison and Charlie waited a painstakingly long time for the woman to unveil the prized duck. When she set it down on the glass counter, Allison was transported to a time when she was a young mother and recalled sitting in the living room with Sue while the kids were outside in the swimming pool with Leo. The gold sofa was covered in plastic and matched the shag carpeting. The Harts didn't have much in the way of money and redecorating was a mere dream to Sue. But Allison recalled the conversation. Heartfelt and wonderful, she also remembered seeing this duck. Yes, this was the same one. It was hard to believe Allison could still remember it, but it somehow felt like it was only yesterday.

The elderly woman with kind eyes studied her. "Ma'am, are you all right?"

Allison was drawn back into the present. "Yes, sorry."

"I asked if you wanted to see the appraisal," the woman added.

"Please, yes, that would be great."

When she retreated once again behind the arched opening, Charlie leaned into Allison. "Hey, you okay? You went away on me there for a minute."

"Just brought me back, is all." Allison lay her fingertips on the wooden duck's back. "You were right, Charlie. This is the one. I can't believe I'm looking at it again after all this time."

"So you remember it?" Charlie asked.

"I sure do." She sighed. "I wish I could buy it back for Leo. His mother loved this thing." Allison spotted the woman again and returned a smile.

"Here you are. This appraisal was done just the other day when we received the item," she replied.

"Can you tell me who sold this to you?"

"I can't give you the name of the gentleman, but I can tell you it had been in his family for some time."

As Allison examined the document, she looked again at the photos of the duck. This was indeed the very same as Sue and Terry had in their home so long ago. What was important, here, was who performed the appraisal and whether that person was tied to the Winthrop Group. "I see here the name of the company who appraised it. Could I jot that down?"

"I don't see why not." The woman handed Allison a pen. "Are you looking to ensure its authenticity because I can promise you, we only deal with licensed appraisers."

"I have no doubt," Allison began. "I'd just like to learn if there might be more of an ownership trail. Maybe there was another appraisal done on this item. That would be of record, if I'm not mistaken."

"It should, but it's impossible to know for sure. May I ask why that's important to you?" the woman pressed on.

"Just as a confirmation. It's a large purchase and I need to be sure this is not a replica," Allison replied. "Even the best eyes can be fooled sometimes."

"I suppose, and I'll try not to be offended." She chuckled.

"Please don't be," Charlie cut in. "This is how she is with everything."

"I appreciate your time and I'm sure I'll be back ready to make the purchase." Allison started to turn but stopped to look at Charlie. "I'll bet the appraiser at the Winthrop Group will be happy to know this appears genuine."

"I'm sorry? Did you say the Winthrop Group?" the woman asked.

Allison turned back around. "I did. I'm here on their behalf."

"Well, there must be some mistake then because, you see, someone from their organization sold this to us."

"Oh, wow. I see." Allison creased her brow. "That is strange. But then again, you did say it was only a couple of days ago that you acquired it?"

"Yes, that's right."

Allison returned a knowing smile. "You know what? I'll bet word hadn't reached the acquisitions department yet. With such a quick turnaround, I'll bet that's exactly what happened."

"So you don't think you'll be purchasing the duck after all?" asked the silver-haired woman.

"I'll confirm one way or another. I'm so sorry for the confusion but thank you for your time." Allison started ahead and Charlie followed.

When they returned to her car, Charlie stepped inside and waited for Allison to close her door. "That was pretty damn smooth, Alli."

"I thought, what could I lose, huh?" Allison pressed the ignition and pulled away. "Now, let's see if Shane's gotten anywhere on that car."

They drove on toward the Downtown Tampa Police Station when Charlie broke the silence. "So, how's he been handling all this stuff with Leo's family? Must be hard on a guy who's been a bachelor his whole life."

Allison glanced at her. "I can see he feels out of place. When Leo showed up at my house drunk, Shane did his best, but I know he felt awkward. We all did, frankly, but then when he left, there was definite weirdness between us."

"I'm sorry to hear that, Alli, I really am. I'm sure Shane will get over it. He's going to have to, or you guys aren't going to last long. I suppose it's one thing I don't have to worry about too much. The boys' dad never steps foot in our house. He shows up at the curb, never gets out of his car and messages the boys to come outside," she scoffed. "But the relationship you and Leo have would be hard for any man to accept."

Allison glanced at her. "Is it that bad?"

"Bad?" Charlie asked. "No, not bad. Close, I'd say is the right word. There's nothing wrong with being friends with your kids' father, but there is a line, Alli. You have a tendency to step over it."

"I'll work on that." She parked near the front of the station-house and turned to Charlie. "Do you think I'm taking advantage of my relationship with Shane?"

"How do you mean?"

Allison shrugged. "He pulls a lot of strings for us. He jumps on anything I ask him to. I'm starting to think maybe I am. Do you think outsiders see it that way?"

"First of all, it doesn't matter what outsiders think. Do you care for him?"

A grin drew up on her lips. "Yeah, I do."

Charlie opened her car door. "Then that's all that matters.

Screw what other people think. And if you feel that the relation-ship might be getting lopsided, you're the only one who can do something about it."

"You never did pull any punches, Charlie, that's why I love you." Allison stepped out of the car and started ahead.

As they walked inside, Officer Carol Moyer was at the desk. "Evening Allison, Charlie. What brings you two by? Like I couldn't guess."

"You know us well, Carol," Allison began. "Looking for Sully, if he's around."

Carol was a beat cop who wore her hair in a tight low bun. Her plump cheeks revealed a softer side to an otherwise authoritative mien. "Believe he's at his desk upstairs."

With a nod and a smile, Allison started upstairs while Charlie trailed. Detectives and officers appeared hurried and hadn't taken notice of the investigative partners as they made their way to the Major Crimes Unit.

When the bullpen came into view, Allison spotted Shane at his desk. "Hey, there."

He drew up his gaze and appeared pleasantly surprised. "Alli-son, Charlie. I didn't know you two were stopping by. I'm sorry, but I was actually on my way out. I'm working a case right now."

Allison held up her hands. "No need to be sorry. I should've called first. We were in the area and thought we'd stop in to see if you found anything on the car from last night."

He surveyed his desk as though searching for something. "You know what? I have a couple minutes to spare. I put in the request earlier. Let me follow up." Shane picked up his phone. "Ritten-house, it's Sully. Anything come back yet on that plate?" He nodded. "Yeah, send it over now. I'm here. Great. Appreciate it." He ended the call. "It's on its way over now." Shane refreshed his screen. "And here it is."

Allison walked behind his chair and peered over his shoulder. She leaned into him and whispered in his ear. "Thanks for doing this. I owe you- again."

A grin played on his lips. "I'll take payment later. Okay, so this is what we have." He pointed to the screen. "Looks like the car is owned by the Winthrop Group. Not a good sign. But you said it wasn't the same car you saw at the racetrack, right?"

"No, this one was different," Allison replied.

"It appears to belong to the same people, and I don't like that at all. It means they know who you are and where you live."

"Alli said it did appear to follow Jenny and Leo," Charlie cut in. "I agree with Shane. I don't like this. Who told them about any of you? Was it Terry, and why would he do that?"

Allison pulled upright. "We're talking about an organization, bookie, loan shark, or whatever, that Terry probably owes. And it looks like he offered his wife's collection as payment."

"Where they promptly sold it off to another party, who was the apparent fence for them," Charlie added.

"And now these people are keeping us in their sights. Why? If Terry paid them, why get his family involved?" Allison pulled in a deep breath as she considered the idea. "Leo knows what Terry did, but this adds a new element to it. It adds a new element for all of us. It's time to warn Leo that he needs to stay as far away from his father as possible."

Charlie peered at her. "That's good advice for all of us right now."

13

Concern grew over the family's safety after Allison learned who had been parked outside her house last night. This was no longer an effort to understand whether Terry had gotten himself in deep with a bookie, or a racetrack—he clearly had. The concern was now, had Gus Schoeman, head of the Winthrop Group with ties to the Brunetti family, determined Allison's family could be seen as collateral to keep Terry Hart in line.

It was a small saving grace that Nolan wasn't around. He had already gone back to his team. However, Micah was staying with Allison until her internship was set to start in another week. While she'd wanted her daughter there, the risk was too great now. Maybe Allison was overreacting, but when it came to her children, no measure to ensure their safety was too great.

As evening arrived, Allison had sent Charlie home and she was on her way to sort this out with Leo. Shane's words of caution were about all he could offer at this point. Bringing charges against Terry of falsifying a police report or slapping Schoeman with a charge of selling stolen goods wasn't going to solve this problem. If anything, it would only bring more.

Leo's house was just ahead, and his car was parked in the driveway. While he already knew about the will and how his dad had paid off his gambling debt by handing over his family heirlooms, telling him that he and his new wife would need to look over their shoulders was a whole other issue. Jenny would be scared. She and Allison were hardly friends, but this wasn't something she would've wished on anyone.

Allison knocked on the door and Leo opened it. "Hi. Can you spare a few minutes?"

"Sure. I got your text. Jenny's working late tonight. I told her you were coming. Come in." Leo stepped aside. "Have you eaten dinner? I was just about to warm up some leftover pizza."

"That sounds delicious. Thanks." She followed Leo into the kitchen that was slightly dated with light maple cabinets and Corian countertops. She suspected Jenny would've preferred to update it to look more like Allison's. It had taken her years for her to convince Leo to put the money into the house. As far as Allison was concerned, Jenny hadn't put in her time yet. When it came to money, Leo wasn't one to part with it willingly.

She sat down at the kitchen table. "The girls and I have been looking into a few things regarding your dad."

"So you mentioned." Leo handed her a bottle of beer. "I assume this is bad or you wouldn't be here."

"It's not great, Leo." Allison took a drink.

He placed two slices of warmed pizza on a plate for her. "I want to apologize for last night. First of all, I should never have gotten behind the wheel..."

"No, you shouldn't," she replied.

"Secondly, I shouldn't have come running to you. It's not your job anymore and I'm sure Shane didn't appreciate my being there either."

"He was okay. He understands we share kids. You got lucky nothing happened to you."

Leo took a bite of pizza and joined her at the table. "You're here because of the car you saw last night, right?"

"Among other things, yes. I didn't think too much of it at first, but I made note and figured I'd look into it."

"Well, Jenny saw it last night too. She didn't write down a plate number or anything, but she did tell me about it after you sent me the message earlier."

"So whoever was driving it decided to stick around here, huh?" Allison asked.

"Looks like it. I have to tell you, Alli, both Jenny and I are a little on edge over this. What should we do?"

"Look, Leo, your dad is up to his eyeballs in gambling debt. I've been keeping my eye on him, and I saw him at the racetrack talking to who I later learned was Gus Schoeman. It wasn't a friendly chat, I can tell you, and this guy has ties to a known crime family. And when I spoke to the racetrack manager, he told me Terry had just recently paid off a $10,000 line of credit. And that was after the supposed robbery, which we now know was a lie."

"Geez, 10 grand? A crime family?" Leo shook his head.

"Then earlier today, Charlie and I tracked down your mom's decoy duck. The most valuable of the items she owned."

"How did you do that? Where is it? Can I get it back?"

"You have $7000? That's how much it was, and I didn't have that kind of cash laying around," she replied.

Leo appeared deflated. "Right, yeah."

"We found out who sold it to the antique shop where Charlie tracked it down. Leo, it was the same group Terry appears to owe money to. The Winthrop Group—Gus Schoeman. They sold it to write down some of Terry's debt, is our best guess. Charlie thought we could bring charges against the antique store and the Winthrop group for fencing, money laundering. But I don't know if they'd stick, and it would expose us all to the crime family."

"My God, Alli, what are we going to do?" Leo asked.

Allison tossed back a long drink of her beer. "I'm here because I think you and Jenny need to be on alert. And it's best if you stay away from Terry."

"They know where we live," Leo said. "I can't believe this."

"I'm so sorry, Leo. I wish I had better news for you."

———

SOFT LIGHT SPILLED into Terry's apartment from the streetlamps outside his building. It was 2 o'clock in the morning as he slept soundly in his double bed. And when they came inside, he hadn't heard a single noise.

The two men, dressed in black, used hand signals as they made their way through the apartment. They were already familiar with it since they were the ones who'd ransacked it two nights ago. The smaller guy walked to the fridge and pulled out a half-full bucket of chicken. He examined a leg and shoved it into his mouth.

"Let's go." The larger man headed into the short hallway and opened Terry's bedroom door, gesturing for his partner to follow. "Go around," he whispered.

That was all it took. Terry's eyes clicked open and his gaze darted between the shadowed men. He raised his hands for protection. "No, wait."

The big guy thrust his ham hand over Terry's mouth and held down Terry's shoulder with the other.

His partner grabbed Terry from the other side. "Now what?"

"You gonna stay quiet?" The man asked him.

Terry nodded.

"You'd better, or it's your funeral." The big guy pulled up Terry while his partner helped. "You're gonna walk on out of here, you got it? I ain't dragging your fat ass, you understand?"

His hand was still over Terry's mouth and so he could only nod.

"Good." He peered at his partner. "Grab his shoes. We'll give him that much." He looked at Terry again. "Boy, you must've really screwed up for us to have to come here again. Don't know what you did, man, but I doubt you'll do it again, huh?"

Terry shook his head and mumbled something but with a hand over his mouth, it was indiscernible.

"Yeah, didn't think so." The man glanced to his partner. "Move fast and keep quiet."

"You got it, boss."

Terry stayed on his feet, though he struggled to keep his balance. He didn't move like a young man anymore, but the men holding onto him didn't seem to understand that as they dragged him along. When the big guy finally removed his hand, he tried to get in a word. "This is a mistake. I worked all this out with Gus. Just ask him."

"Be quiet, old man." He opened the front door into the night and beneath a cloudy sky. The heavy air was still, and the crickets chirped. Light came from the few streetlamps that hung over the parking lot as they approached. "Just get in nice and quiet and you'll be just fine."

Terry nodded as they shoved him into the back seat of an old Ford Taurus. At least it was roomy. His kidnappers slipped inside and closed their doors.

"I'm telling you, this is a mistake. I've got everything all worked out," he pleaded.

"Is that so, old man?" The big guy turned the engine and

pulled out of the parking lot. "Then maybe you should've told your private detective to keep her nose out of our business dealings."

Terry's brow knitted. "What the hell are you talking about?"

"Allison Hart. You two related or something?"

Terry didn't answer but appeared to catch on to what must've transpired. "She doesn't know anything. I don't know what she's done, but I haven't said squat to her, I swear I haven't."

"Might as well save it for Mr. Schoeman. It's him you'll have to convince."

Terry lowered his gaze. "Holy shit, Alli. What the hell have you done?"

———

WHEN LEO ARRIVED at Terry's apartment first thing this morning, he expected his dad had still been asleep when he hadn't answered. He rang the bell this time and waited. "Come on, Dad. Wake up." Despite Allison's warning to stay away from Terry, Leo was there to make sure his dad wasn't going to bring any more trouble to the family.

Still, there was no answer. "Damn it." He knew Terry kept a spare key around back where he had a small fenced-in concrete patio. He'd said as much when the call came in about the supposed robbery. His unit was on the first floor, and they all had patios. The upper units had balconies. Leo reached under the potted plant just outside it.

He walked around to the front again and unlocked the door. "Dad, you up?" Leo stepped inside. "This place is a mess." Continuing inside, he spied the kitchen where he noticed a half-full bucket of fried chicken sitting on the counter. "Dad?" Terry might have been a slob, but he never wasted food.

Leo continued through the small hallway and into Terry's bedroom. "Where the hell are you? Dad?" He turned around and peered toward the bathroom. "That's it." Leo returned to the living room and pulled his cell phone from his pocket. "Alli, it's me. I'm at Terry's apartment right now. I know you said to stay away. I just wanted to tell him not to drag us into his problems and lose my number, but he's not here." He nodded. "No, I checked. His car is in the parking lot. Alli, he's gone, and by the look of things, I don't think he left voluntarily. Okay, thanks. I'll see you there in a few minutes."

———

ALLISON SET down her phone and peered through the window behind her desk. "Leo's coming."

Charlie looked up from her laptop. "Why? What's he need you to do now? I thought you talked to him last night."

Allison turned around and looked at her partners. Dread masked her face. "Terry's missing."

"Oh my God." Charlie closed her eyes a moment. "Is he sure? Did he try to call him?"

"He was inside Terry's apartment. No sign of him even though his car was there." Allison sighed heavily. "So much for us walking away from this."

"I'm sure there's an explanation," Lucy cut in. "Should we call Shane?"

"No, not yet. I need to get my head around it and make sure Terry's not just hiding out first. We can handle this for now unless we see otherwise."

Charlie poured a cup of coffee at the back credenza. "Did we bring this to a head, Alli? We were the ones looking into the collectibles and asking questions."

Allison pursed her lips. "I don't know. Maybe. Maybe I've been blaming Terry for pulling us in and I didn't help the situation. I thought I was being smart bringing up the Winthrop Group to the antiques dealer."

"It was my idea," Charlie added.

Lucy picked up her cell phone. "I feel like I should tell Nolan."

"No, please don't," Allison replied. "All it'll do is worry Nolan and he has a game today. I don't want to do that to him. I'm not going to tell Micah yet either. She's still staying with me for now, and it'll only upset her."

Lucy set down her phone again. "Just makes me feel helpless to do anything."

Allison slipped on her reading glasses and peered at her computer. "Let's think about how we can tackle this."

Charlie walked toward her desk. "We know the apartment building has cameras. That'd be our best shot at seeing if anyone came for Terry."

Allison nodded. "Exactly. Let's work on that and I think I'll go back to the racetrack and talk to the manager again."

"How will that help?" Lucy asked.

"He has a relationship with Schoeman. I don't know what that entails yet, but there's something going on between them. It's time I explore that a little more." Allison's attention was drawn to the door.

Leo walked inside and nodded to the partners before he turned to Allison. "Alli, what the hell am I going to do? I know I said I was done with him, but..."

"I'm sorry about this, Leo," Charlie cut in. "But don't jump the gun just yet."

"Charlie's right," Allison began. "Let's think through this, okay? Then we can decide if it's time to get the police involved."

"Of course we need to get the police involved. There's no choice. He's gone, Alli. I can't just ignore that," Leo said. "Despite everything, he's still my dad."

"I get that. What I don't want to do is to make a bad situation worse. Look, Terry dropped the break-in investigation. That doesn't look good. And now you want to go to the police and tell them Terry's missing without being certain?"

"Okay." Leo shrugged. "How do we get certain?"

———

THE BOATS ROCKED GENTLY in their slips and the sound of the bay reached Terry's ears. They'd arrived in the dark of night, but he knew right away where they were. Now, as daylight arrived, he still sat on a cot inside what looked to be a janitor's closet. They'd left him here and he hadn't known where 'here' was, but he knew he was by the water.

"You messed up this time, Ter," he said to himself. But what concerned him was that he thought he had a deal. Now, with the mention of Allison, well, he figured she stuck her nose where it hadn't belonged. She'd always been smart and intuitive. It made sense she went in the direction she had with her career after Leo split.

When the door opened and daylight spilled in, Terry wasn't surprised by who stood on the other side. "Gus, what the hell's going on, man? I thought we had a deal?"

Schoeman walked inside and shook his head. "Ter, Ter, Ter. We did have a deal until I learned you got some P.I. snooping around my business. P.I.s usually have cop friends. Which means, shit's about to go south real quick if I don't put a stop to it. Hence, your current predicament." He gestured as if presenting Terry to the room.

"She's family, or used to be. I don't know what you think she did. I made sure the robbery investigation was dropped and I figured we be copacetic, you know?"

"No, I don't know," Schoeman replied. "She knows about the collectibles, meaning she knows about the Winthrop Group. How long do you think it'll take her to put two and two together and learn what I got going on with the track? You brought her into my business, Terry. That's a problem. And let's not forget about the rest of the money you owe me. The cards are stacked against you, man."

"No way she knows anything about anything. I never said shit to her. I wouldn't screw you over like that, Gus. I swear I wouldn't. I can talk to her. Get her to back down. What else can I do? Tell me, Gus. I'll do whatever you ask, just like always."

Gus moved in and loomed over Terry, who still sat on the edge of the cot. "Find a way to get her off my back or I will." He turned away but stopped short. "And get me the goddam money, Terry. You got two strikes against you, my man. There are consequences."

14

In the span of a few hours, Allison realized the tables had turned in her relationship with Leo. Terry was nowhere to be found. And the tell-tale sign that something was amiss was his old Chevy Impala that still sat in the parking lot of his apartment complex. She'd insisted they wait. They searched Terry's stomping grounds; the track among them. He was gone.

"Thank you, Alli." Leo steadied his gaze as he sat in the passenger seat of her car. "Look, I know Terry's an asshole, but I can't wait this out. We've checked everywhere. We have to get the police involved."

And there it was. Allison had become the face of calm. She would have been the first to admit that in her marriage, Leo had been unflinching in his resolve when things went awry. Still, a part of her considered that waiting to bring in the cops had been the wrong call. They would find out soon enough.

"I'll do the talking. I know a lot of these guys and they'll help us through this, okay?" She peered at Leo. "I just need you to keep your cool and we'll get through this."

"I don't understand why you can't just get Shane to help," Leo replied.

"He doesn't deal with missing persons' cases. And he's working on a homicide right now. I can't ask him to pull his resources." She placed her hand on his shoulder. "Don't worry, we'll find Terry."

The two stepped out of the car and walked inside the station. Allison approached the front desk. "Hi, Carol. Who can I talk to about filing a missing persons case? I didn't call Sully. I know it's not his area. Can you help us out?" She glanced at Leo. "This is Leo Hart. It's his father."

"Oh my gosh. Yes, of course. Let me get the detective on duty right now."

"Thank you." She turned to Leo. "I'm sorry about all this. You just got back from your honeymoon and now this is happening."

"I know who Terry is," Leo began. "He's a small-time hustler with a penchant for gambling. But this time, I think he might've gotten in over his head. As far as the honeymoon, well, I'll try to make it up to Jenny when this is over. At least she won't make the mistake of calling on Terry again."

Allison noticed the officer returning with a detective in tow.

"Allison Hart," Carol began. "This is Detective Dean Cooper. He'll help you with the paperwork."

"Thank you." She offered her hand. "Detective Cooper. This is Leo Hart. It's his father who we're looking for."

"Hart? Are you two related?" Cooper returned a quizzical gaze.

"Not anymore." A slight grin emerged on her lips and quickly faded. "Detective, Leo's father, Terry Hart, has been in some trouble recently and now we can't seem to track him down anywhere."

"I see. Why don't you both come on back and you can tell me

more?" Cooper started into the bullpen. The detective was a slightly older man, in his early 50s, appearing to have kept himself in fit condition. His graying hair was full; worn short and parted sharply on the side. Though not entirely polished, and with a hint of rebellion in his gait, he carried himself with purpose.

Cooper gestured to the guest chairs as they arrived at his desk. "Please, both of you have a seat. Terry Hart? You say he's been in some trouble recently. Tell me about that."

Allison turned to Leo. "Go ahead."

Leo proceeded to tell him about the supposed break-in and the collectibles, ending on the way he saw Terry's place this morning.

"I can understand why you're concerned." The detective slipped on reading glasses and peered at his computer screen. "I see here that the B&E robbery case was dropped."

"Yes, sir," Leo replied.

"With no explanation from your father?" Cooper pressed on.

"I didn't know about it right away. Alli looked into it when she got one of her hunches."

Cooper set his sights on her. "That's right. You're a private investigator?"

"I am. ACL Investigative Services. We've been up and running for less than a year, but things have gone well."

"Good to hear." He narrowed his gaze. "Come to think of it, maybe I have seen you around here."

"A good friend of mine works in Major Crimes. Detective Sullivan," she added.

He nodded. "Sully, right. Good guy." Cooper laced together his fingers and rested his hands on his desk. "Okay, listen. I can get you going on the paperwork to file a missing persons' report. Your father is elderly, doesn't get around well. We can probably even get a silver alert issued if that's the route you'd like to go..."

"If?" Leo asked.

Cooper held up his hands. "I say 'if' because based on what you've just told me, there's reason to consider whoever he owes money to, as you suspect he does, might be looking to put a scare into him to pay up. If that's the case, and we get the ball rolling on an alert and BOLO and all that, I'm concerned it might put him at an increased danger." He turned to Allison. "You mentioned the apartment building's security footage showed Terry Hart handing over these valuables."

"That's right. And I don't know if this is anything or not, but we've seen a suspicious car at my house when Leo was there. He then seemed to follow Leo when he left. I wasn't sure at the time if it was anything, but I made note of the car and Sully checked it out for me," Allison replied.

Cooper nodded. "Who did it belong to?"

"It was owned by a company called the Winthrop Group."

The detective turned down his lip. "I'm not familiar with them, but I'll look into it. Here's what else I'd like to do. We can go ahead and file the report, but I think it would be in Terry's best interest to hold off issuing any silver alerts. We already know his car is still at his apartment, so a BOLO doesn't do us much good."

"Then what do you plan to do?" Leo asked.

"I know you've checked out his place already, but I'd like to take a look for myself. Get a feel for how the property was left. Examine Terry's vehicle, and any more surveillance video the apartment manager has. Use whatever tool we have at our disposal to find clues as to where Terry might've gone."

"Detective, does this sound like it could be a kidnapping? I asked Leo to hold off on coming here so we could have a look for ourselves. It sounds like I made a bad call," Allison said.

He pressed together his lips until they turned white. "It's hard to say right now. My gut tells me, given Terry Hart's history, you acted in a reasonable manner. That said, gambling rings, organized crime, all that's big business in this town. It often gets drowned out because of drug smuggling, and that's what these guys count on—not a lot of attention from law enforcement. So, how about you just let me take it from here and I'll see what I can find." He stood up and grabbed his keys. "Mr. Hart, I suggest you go home. There's nothing more you can do right now. I'll keep you posted."

"What are you going to do?" Leo asked.

"If you have a key, I'd like to get to your dad's place first, like I said. If you don't have a key, I'll talk to the manager."

Leo looked at Allison. "Will you go with him? You're the one who uncovered all this about Dad. Please, Alli. No offense to you, Detective, but she's very good at her job. If it's possible, I'd like her to be involved in this."

Allison had worked with a few of the detectives in the department already, but she sensed that Detective Dean Cooper preferred to go solo. "I'm not sure that's a..."

"You want to come along, I don't have a problem with that," Cooper jumped in. "So long as you don't contaminate my scene or get in the way."

That was a favorite saying among the detectives that she would contaminate their scene. "I'll stay out of your way and won't touch a thing."

Cooper revealed a tight-lipped grin. "All right then, let's go."

"I'll call Jenny and have her come pick me up." Leo eyed Cooper. "Thank you, Detective."

Allison reached for Leo's hand. "I'll call you if he finds anything." She hurried to catch up with Cooper, who was already a few steps ahead. When they walked outside as afternoon started to slip away, she turned to him. "I'm sorry about back there. Leo insisting that I come. Just know that I defer to your expertise."

He stopped and squared up with her. "No need to kiss up to

me, Allison. Can I call you Allison? Besides, maybe you'll be useful."

"Sure. My car's over here. I'll meet you there." Allison started ahead toward Terry's apartment and made a call to Charlie. "Hey, it's me."

"How'd it go?" Charlie asked.

"Detective Dean Cooper is taking the reins. He seems to be on board with the idea that Terry got himself into some trouble. We're on the way back to Terry's apartment. He wanted to check it out himself first. How are things going on your end?"

"I just got off the phone with Ed Lucero. Sounds like he might have found something."

"What did he find? Tell me it's big. Tell me Cheryl's husband is the lying backstabber she thinks he is," Allison replied.

"I don't know about that, but Ed's tracing back a series of banking transactions that span the better part of a year."

"So, he was hiding money from her?" Allison asked.

"It appears that way, but he needs more information. The kind of information that would mean Cheryl's husband might figure out what she's been up to."

"We can't let that happen." Allison turned off the highway. "There's no other way for him to uncover what those transactions meant?"

"I think Cheryl will have to make that call, Alli, as to whether she wants Ed to dig into it further. If her soon-to-be-ex finds out, he might find a way to hide what he's done and get her for accessing accounts she shouldn't have had access to."

"What do you think we should do?" Allison asked.

"Cheryl Murray's husband is wealthy and powerful. I'm not sure what he would do to her, financially speaking, or us, as a business trying to succeed in this city," Charlie replied. "That said, you know I've never been one for backing down. So, with our client's approval, I'll make sure Ed can keep going until he has the evidence to nail Mr. Murray to the wall."

"Then let's do it," Allison replied. "Listen, I'm at Terry's apartment. I'll let you know if we pick up on anything. In the meantime, thanks."

"What for?" Charlie asked.

"For being my partner. Gotta go. Bye." Allison ended the call and opened her car door, catching up to the detective who'd already arrived. "That's his apartment there, on the corner."

He peered at the building. "You have the key?"

"Yes, Leo gave me the one he had. I'll show you around." Allison walked along the sidewalk toward the breezeway where Terry's unit lay near the end of the building. She unlocked the door and stepped inside. "One bedroom, one bathroom down that hall there. Then you have the kitchen and living room here."

Cooper placed his hands on his hips. "Great. I'll take it."

Allison snickered and quickly realized he had a sense of humor. Good to know. Maybe he wasn't as tough as he appeared. "I'm happy to show you other units." She walked toward the kitchen. "But seriously, aside from spotting Terry's car in the parking lot, when Leo came inside, he saw this sitting on the counter."

"A half-eaten bucket of chicken," Cooper replied.

"Leo said it was cold when he was here, like it had just been taken out of the fridge."

"And not put back. Okay. Got it." He started ahead and surveyed the living room. "I have to tell you, Allison, if Terry Hart is in the hands of people he owes money to, this case is going to get a whole lot bigger."

"How so?" she asked.

"For starters, kidnapping, extortion. Sounds like organized crime to me. Nothing to trifle with."

She drew in her brow. "Detective, should we be worried for Terry's safety? I mean, really worried?"

"I understand this man is, or was part of your family. I don't mean to scare you and I apologize for doing so. My mind tends to run off in a million directions when I start a new investigation. You never know where it will lead. So, while a healthy dose of worry is warranted, it could also be a matter of Terry Hart going into hiding to keep away from the folks who want his money. You said yourself the man staged a break-in at his own house. We should consider the possibility he's staged this too."

"What about looking at the security video from last night and yesterday?" she asked.

"Yep, I'll get on that, but I'll need a warrant," Cooper replied.

"The manager cooperated with Detective Sullivan when the break-in happened. I think he'll accommodate us."

"Then have at it. See if he'll turn it over. Make sure to get a copy. I'll stick around here and see if anything grabs my attention."

"Okay, thanks." Allison left the apartment and made her way to the manager's office. On entering, she noticed an older lanky gentleman behind the desk. "Hi, there. I'm Allison Hart. Terry Hart's daughter-in-law. Are you the manager?"

"I am. Don't tell me Terry's place got busted into again."

"No, it's not that." She lowered her gaze a moment. "Some things have been going on with Terry lately."

"Right, the robbery," he replied.

"Yes, there's that, but it looks like the issue could be a little more urgent than we first thought. You were so helpful to Detective Sullivan the other day. I was hoping I could view additional security footage from yesterday evening?"

"I don't understand. What's happened now?" he pressed on.

"We think Terry might be struggling with Alzheimer's. It looks as though he's wandered off and we can't find him. With your help, I could figure out what direction he might've gone."

"Oh my Lord. Yes, of course. Come on back to the storage room. That's where I keep the video." He peered over his shoulder. "What happened to the detective from before?"

"He's on another case right now and asked me to handle it for him. I'm a private detective."

"Well, all right. Let me show you what I have here." He fiddled around with the keyboard for a moment. "Hang on. What's this?"

Allison drew closer with interest. "Everything okay?"

"Well, no. Seems I don't have the files you're looking for," he replied.

"You don't have them? I don't understand."

"That makes two of us, Ms. Hart." He turned around in his chair. "The video's been erased is what I think has happened. Look." He spun back around. "I try to pull up last night. Nothing shows up until damn near 3am."

"What about earlier in the evening? We'd been in contact with him until later last night," she said.

"I'll give that a try." The manager keyed in more commands. "Would you look at that? Video stops after about midnight and doesn't pick up again until almost 3. What do you make of that, Ms. Hart?"

Allison pulled back. "I wish I knew. Thank you for your time." She started out.

"Wait! Ms. Hart? What about Terry?"

She stopped at the door and turned back to him. "I'm sure everything's fine. But you know what?" Allison walked toward him again and handed him a card. "Do me a favor? If you see anything unusual going on at Terry's place, would you call me?"

"Yes, ma'am."

"Thanks." Allison hurried back to the apartment where she found Detective Cooper inside taking photographs. "Detective, we have a problem."

———

TERRY SAT on his cot and noticed the shadow cross beneath the locked door. They'd kept him here all day and he wondered if anyone cared, if anyone was looking for him. But why would they? He only had Leo and he'd burned that bridge long ago. Even Alli had probably gone sour on him after all the recent hubbub.

If Gus Schoeman was trying to scare him, then mission accomplished. Terry was hungry, thirsty, and sore. They'd smacked him around a little. Nothing too serious, but enough to make their point. He wasn't a young man anymore and his body ached from sitting on the cot. He needed to take a crap too, but so far, they'd left him only a bucket. He wasn't taking a dump in a bucket, that was for damn sure. He still had some pride. Time would tell if it lasted.

The door opened and Schoeman walked inside. "Terry, how you holding up, man?"

"Doing all right. Still wondering why the hell I'm here."

"Really? Well, you look like shit, no offense." He moved in closer. "Listen, old man, I think my point's been made. So what are you going to do to get me my money?"

"I can sell my car. I got family. They'll lend me some cash."

Schoeman roared back with laughter. "You serious? That's your plan? Ask your family for cash?" He shook his head. "I could be wrong, but I don't see that happening. And what, you think I don't talk to Santos? You already put up your car as collateral. Jesus, man, when the hell you gonna learn? Schoeman stood inches in front of Terry and towered over him. "What I see happening is this. I see you finding any way you can to scrounge up the full 16k you owe me. I don't give a shit how you do it, but you got three days."

"But what about what you got from the..."

"How do I know what your shit's really worth? That deal's gone. The buyer backed out cause you had your P.I. daughter-in-law snooping around, talking about other appraisals and shit. Look, I care about getting my money. I'll cut you loose. See to it you get a ride back home or wherever the hell you need to go. But in three days, you don't have my cash, well..." He pulled back again. "Guess I'll have to pay a visit to that pretty private investigator daughter-in-law of yours. I'll be sure and let her know that your problem is now her problem. I don't think she'll give me any push-back when I tell her all about Nolan and Micah."

"No. No, please. I'll get your money. I swear it, Gus. I'll get it. They don't have anything to do with any of this. None of them," Terry replied.

"Well," Gus shrugged. "You got three days to show me the cash, or they're gonna have something to do with this. Now stand up."

Terry pushed up off the hard cot.

Schoeman peered over his shoulder. "Follow him over there. Get yourself cleaned up, Ter. You look like shit." He stepped out after Terry and walked toward his guy. "Give him a lift."

"Sure thing." The man followed Terry as he walked to the bathroom.

Terry pushed inside the restroom door and stood in front of the mirror. He splashed water on his face and pressed an abrasive paper towel against it. The bruise on his cheek looked worse than it felt. His skin was paper thin now, and he bruised like a Georgia peach.

"Let's go in there."

Terry looked at the door from where the voice came and took in a breath. He shuffled out again and took in the surroundings for the first time. It was almost dark outside. *An old office building?* he thought.

"Boss wants you to make a good impression, so he says to take you to see the pretty blonde."

Terry closed his eyes. "I don't know where she's at."

"How about we try her house, yeah?" the man replied.

"No. Just take me home. That's what Gus said."

"He changed his mind." The man grabbed Terry's arm to hurry him along.

Terry was led outside into an empty parking lot. The sun was setting, but it wasn't quite dark just yet. It must've been after 7pm, at least. Maybe Alli would be home. He didn't think he was going to have a choice in the matter now.

"Get in, old man." He pushed Terry into the car. "And put this on until we get clear of this place." He tossed in a handkerchief.

"Ouch! Damn it." Terry's elbow struck the center console as he tumbled onto the seat. He knew where Alli lived because Leo used to live there too. He prayed she wasn't home, and this goon would have to take him back to his apartment. "What about my son? Why can't I just go there?"

"Boss's orders were to take you to the blonde. Sorry, pops. Put on the damn blindfold now." The man turned the ignition and pulled out of the lot. "Where to?"

Terry relayed the address and tied the handkerchief around his eyes. Several minutes had gone by when the man spoke up again.

"You can take off the blindfold now."

Terry removed the handkerchief, and nothing looked familiar to him for about five minutes until the guy turned down Palm Avenue. Alli's house was in this neighborhood.

"She should be just down this street, yeah?"

Terry nodded.

"Good." He continued until he pulled in front of the house. "Here we are. Let's go, man. Time's a-wasting."

"Please don't do this."

"Already done." He slammed the door and walked to the passenger side. "Out you go."

Terry stepped out and didn't see any cars in the driveway. That was his first glimmer of hope.

The man knocked on the door and when it opened, Terry looked on in horror.

"This man belong to you?" the guy asked.

Micah's face twisted in fear as she stared at Terry. "Grandpa? Oh my God. Are you okay?"

"He'll explain everything. Nighty night." He pushed Terry inside and walked away.

Terry stumbled in but soon regained his balance. "I'm fine, kiddo. I'm just fine."

"You're not fine. I'm calling Mom." Micah made the call on her cell. "Mom? Where are you?"

"I'm at the police station working on something. Micah, is everything okay?"

"No. No, it's not. Some guy just dropped off Grandpa. Mom, he's hurt. Someone hurt him."

"Oh no. Micah, lock the door and do not open it for anyone. You hear me?"

"Yeah. Mom, what's going on?" she asked.

"I'm on my way."

15

Allison placed a bandage over Terry's scuffed and bruised cheek while he sat next to her on the sofa. Detective Cooper went back and forth to the front window, peering out in search of the abductor's return when headlights caught his gaze. "Looks like Sully's here."

Allison headed toward the foyer. "I'll get the door. Leo, would you finish taping this for me?"

"Sure." Leo took her place on the couch. "How you doing, Dad?"

"I already told you all that I'm perfectly fine," Terry replied.

Relief masked Allison's face at the sight of Shane on the other side of the door. "I'm glad you're here. Come in. Detective Cooper is in the living room with the rest of us."

Shane stepped inside and gave Allison a peck on the cheek. "Are you doing all right?"

"Me? I'm fine. Terry, on the other hand, not so much." She closed the door behind him. "I didn't want to bother you with this. I know you're busy working another case."

"Bother me? You should've come to me earlier."

"There's nothing more you could've done that Detective Cooper hadn't. I can't pull you off another case and, to be honest, at the time, we had no idea what was going on except that Terry was nowhere to be found. It didn't become an abduction until he showed up at my door, beaten and bruised." She glanced into the living room. "I just can't believe Micah was the one who had to handle it."

"Is she okay?" he asked.

"I think so." Allison led the way into the living room. "Detective Cooper, I think you know Detective Sully."

"Good to see you, brother." Cooper offered his hand. "I hear you've done some of the legwork on this already."

"Just as a side gig to help out a friend. I ran the situation by Lieutenant Duran. We agree that I'm only here as backup. Whatever you need from me, man," Shane replied.

"Appreciate that. I figured we'd set up a sting. Not sure how much you know, but from what Terry, over here, has said, he's got 72 hours to come up with the money. Gus Schoeman issued a not-so-subtle threat against the Hart family if he doesn't pay up." Cooper paced the living room. "We could go and arrest Schoeman now for kidnapping since Terry can ID him, but we both know what that'll mean for him if we do."

"I'll be missing for good," Terry replied.

"That, and we'll get the attention of the Brunetti family," Cooper added. "These guys have no qualms taking out cops or anyone else. Sixty-odd years of their influence in this city shows us that. After talking with Allison, she filled me in on the connection between Schoeman and the family. We have to handle this with kid gloves."

"These are people we don't want to screw around with, I agree. But Schoeman can't get off free and clear for what he's done. Family or not, he committed a serious crime," Shane replied.

"You have noble intentions, my friend, but all is not lost. A workaround could be to arrange for us to get the cash and do the drop however Schoeman wants to do it. Tampa's finest will be there to pick off whoever shows up for the money. We'll do our best to work him and get him to talk about Schoeman and his business partners. If he can finger the family, Schoeman will go down without a fight. Problem solved."

Shane dropped onto one of the side chairs. "I'm not sure it'll be that easy. You know Detective Lopez?"

"Heard the name," Cooper replied.

"She went undercover with the family a few years' back; thought they were growing their influence in the drug trade. Never did get anything solid. The family doesn't have the same power they once had, but they have enough to shake down guys like Terry and get away with it. Getting anyone to talk might be a miracle."

Allison stepped up. "I don't mean to butt in, but I've got my kids to think about. My son is traveling right now. Do I need to call him back here?"

"Mom, he could lose his spot on the team. You can't ask him to do that," Micah replied. "If anything, I think he'll be safer with them than he would be here. I don't feel safe here."

"It's my fault," Terry mumbled.

Allison hadn't wanted to pile on him, even if he was right. "Micah, I know all this sounds scary, but nothing's going to happen to you or any of us."

"Your mom's right," Shane cut in. "I'm sure Detective Cooper will want to set up a patrol around the neighborhood, but it might be best you stay close to your mom until we get through this." He turned to Cooper. "What do you think?"

"Patrols, definitely. And yeah, I'd stick close to home for the next few days. Look, this is all to scare Terry into paying up. We will find a way to bring charges against Schoeman."

"I agree," Shane interjected. "But we'll still take precautions."

"Leo, I think Terry should stay with you and Jenny for the time being," Allison said.

Up until now, Jenny had sat quietly on the loveseat while everyone discussed Terry's problems. Up until now, they had pulled her in. "These people know where we live too, Leo." That car drove right by our house. Same one that Allison mentioned. I'm sorry, but he can't stay with us. No offense, Terry."

"None taken," he replied.

"What about setting up patrols around our house too, then, Detective Cooper?" Leo asked.

"We'll keep eyes out for the cars we know of right now. Patrols around both neighborhoods. And then in a few days, this will all be over," he replied.

Allison regarded him. "I wish I had your confidence, Detective."

A HALO of moonlight formed around Allison's bedroom curtains. The soft glow inside offered just enough light to see Shane's silhouette. She nestled against his bare chest as they lay in bed. "Thanks for staying tonight. I don't like feeling vulnerable, but that's exactly how I feel right now."

"You're entitled to your feelings. It's your family; your kids. It would throw anyone for a loop. I have to say, though, it does feel strange being here with Micah in the next room," he replied.

"She's hardly in the next room. She's down at the end of the hall with plenty of room between us. And she is a grown woman. I think she understands that her mother has a sex life."

"I never once thought about my parents having a sex life." He shuddered.

"No one does, but after what we've all been through over the past several days, Micah sees what you mean to me. She's watched her father move on with his life and I think she's finally getting to that point with me."

"I mean something to you?"

"Stop." Allison gently smacked his chest. "Of course you do."

He kissed her forehead. "Good. I'm glad to hear that because you mean a lot to me, too. I'm just pissed that your family's getting dragged into this situation. This isn't your problem."

"Terry's made it my problem. I don't know if what you and Detective Cooper have planned will work, or whether it'll snag Gus Schoeman. There's still the possibility of bringing charges against him for selling stolen goods."

"Maybe, but it was people who worked for him who did it. And that would mean they would've actually had to steal something. Terry handed over those things willingly, at least that's what the video shows. I don't see how any of that would hold up in court. Not to mention, bringing charges against someone like Schoeman would be a big deal. I don't know how high up he is in the organization, but I have no doubt it would rattle cages," Shane replied.

Allison pulled up onto her elbow and her long brassy blonde hair draped over her chest. "If there was more there to build on, you'd have a better chance." She glanced up at the ceiling. "What if I can prove that the racetrack manager is working with the Winthrop Group?"

"In what way?"

"Lou Santos. I've talked to him a couple of times when Leo

asked me to root around Terry's finances. I learned Terry had been extended a line of credit with the track, which for someone like him seems a huge risk. Then he paid it off in its entirety after he handed over the valuable collection. I've spotted Lou Santos and Gus Schoeman together. They seemed to know each other well. It's just a little too coincidental for me to see them together. I still have to put the pieces together. I think it could be a situation of either kickbacks, or money laundering, maybe skimming off the track. I don't know, but I'd like to find out."

"I'm not going to convince you to stay away from Terry now, am I?" Shane asked.

Allison placed her hand on his cheek. "It was too late for that the moment they showed up at my door."

———————

TERRY HAD 72 hours to come up with $16,000. That part was in the hands of the fine Tampa police detectives. However, Allison wasn't about to sit this out and she'd made that clear to Shane last night after Terry all but ensured Schoeman knew everything about her and her kids. But going it alone wasn't an option and so when she arrived at the office this morning, getting her partners on board would require a small bribe. And that bribe came in the form of warm doughnuts.

When Allison walked inside, she hardly got out the words.

"Doughnuts?" Charlie practically leapt from her chair. "What's the occasion?" She took the box from Allison's hands and set it on her desk.

Lucy's brow raised as she peered curiously at the box. "I just put on a fresh pot of coffee too."

"Help yourself." Allison reached her desk. "I wanted to talk to you guys about something, but maybe we should discuss Ed's findings first?"

"He came through." Charlie took a bite of a Boston Cream. "The money transfers were traced back to Cheryl's husband without setting off alarm bells. I didn't get into how he managed to do that, but he did say a friend owed him. That was good enough for me."

"Will it give Cheryl the proof she needs?" Allison asked.

"More than enough," Charlie replied.

"That's great news. Let's keep Ed Lucero in mind for future work," Allison continued.

"Well, we know Charlie will, anyway."

"He might've asked me out on a date Friday," Charlie added. "I had to think about it. You know, check my schedule and all that, but..."

Lucy's mouth dropped. "Shut up! That's awesome, Charlie. It's about time. I'm happy for you."

"Me too," Allison said. "He seems like a great guy."

"Hey, if he doesn't kidnap me during the date, I'll count it as a win." Charlie snickered. "So, anyway, what's this thing you wanted to talk to us about? As if I can't guess that it must have something to do with Terry Hart."

Allison turned down her gaze and felt her eyes sting a little. "Shit," she whispered.

"Hey." Charlie appeared to notice and walked to her desk. "What's wrong?"

Allison looked up again and regarded her partners. "You know I got that call last night from Micah and I had to drop you off at home."

"Right. You said something about Terry showing up, which I thought was great because, you know, he just disappeared. It's a good thing he was all right," Charlie replied.

"Yeah, no, it's great. But I left out a few details, mostly because I hadn't known them when Micah called, but when I got home, I got the gist of the situation."

Lucy made her way to Allison's desk. "What happened?"

"Well, Terry was taken by the people who he owes a lot of money to. They slapped him around a little. Nothing too serious. Uh, anyway, they gave him 72 hours to come up with the money. But the thing is, these people, Schoeman and who knows who else, they know about the kids. They know where I live."

Charlie closed her eyes a moment. "Okay, what can we do about this? What's Shane say about it?"

"He was there, so was Detective Cooper, who helped Leo file the missing persons' report." Allison drew in a deep breath. "Long story short, the police will be patrolling our neighborhood and Leo's. They're putting together a plan to get the money and hand it over to Schoeman's people."

Lucy's expression hardened. Her jaw clenched and her hands balled into fists. "Okay, so what's *our* plan? I know you won't let this stand."

"You're damn right I won't, not when it involves my kids," Allison replied. "But I don't have a fully formed plan yet, that's what I need you two for. So, Terry has 72 hours to come up with the money he owes. I'm not looking to get in the way of the police's efforts on that front."

"Won't that help anyway?" Lucy asked. "If they catch the guys, that's it, right?"

"It'll put some of Gus Schoeman's people out of commission, but I'm not quite convinced it'll take out Schoeman himself. He has people around protecting him, like the Brunetti family. And then there's Lou Santos. He's the guy who runs the racetrack Terry frequents."

"Tell us what you have in mind, Alli, and more importantly, are you sure you want to do it?" Charlie asked.

"Oh, I'm sure. The goal is to help build a solid case against Schoeman. He's the man we need to get behind bars to keep him far away from my family. Our part in this will require some recon first. Over the next few days, I want Charlie to go to the racetrack and place some bets." She looked at Charlie. "I'll front you the money. It needs to be enough for the manager to take notice, but not so much that it starts to stink of a setup. The goal here is to get in with Lou Santos and figure out if he's connecting people to Schoeman and what part Schoeman plays."

"How much are you willing to lose, Alli? I have no knowledge of horses or betting at all," Charlie replied.

"I can help with that," Lucy jumped in. "Dad had a client a few years ago. I can't recall his name off the top of my head, but he was a gambler. Got into a lot of trouble with debt. I think it was dogs, but it could've been horses. I'll have a look."

"Where's this man today? Have you seen or heard from him since your father passed?" Allison asked.

"He was at Dad's funeral. I know he felt that he owed Dad for helping him out of a tight spot. I can ask for some pointers so it doesn't look like Charlie doesn't know anything about the races. I think it'll be enough to pass the smell test."

"Okay then." Allison nodded. "And as far as the money, let me worry about that. We aren't talking the kind of money Terry owes Schoeman. Like I said, just enough so you catch the manager's eye, and we'll make up a sob story as to why you started placing bets."

Charlie raised her index finger. "Oh, I know. I can say my husband is sick and we're facing bankruptcy because we can't pay for the medical bills..."

"That's great, but then how would you explain why you're using what money you do have for gambling?" Allison asked.

"Good point." Charlie narrowed her brow as she appeared to consider another story. "Okay, how's this..."

———

Now came the balancing act. Shane was already working a homicide and was still a rookie in the Major Crimes division. Pulling his resources from that case was ill-advised, even with Lieutenant Duran's blessing. Something he wasn't sure he'd get considering the shaky start he'd had with his new boss. So, how was he going to keep a foot in the door on Cooper's operation that was supposed to keep Terry Hart safe? More importantly, it was supposed to keep Allison and her family safe. It was time to see how much progress Cooper had made and figure if there was room for him to step in without stepping on toes. "Hey, man." Shane arrived at Cooper's desk. "Just coming to see if you needed a hand with anything and how the money acquisition was coming along."

Detective Dean Cooper leaned back at his desk and pushed his hand through his salt and pepper hair. "I got the buy-off from the lieutenant to get the cash. He's pushing it through the system now and we should have it by tomorrow morning. It'll be marked bills in the event we lose our guy."

Shane sat down. "Sure. Sure. What about the pickup time and location?"

"Terry Hart and his son dropped by earlier this morning. Said Terry got a call to meet on Wednesday night, 11pm, at the site of the new high-rise condo building under construction near the bay."

"Smart. They probably won't have cameras installed on the perimeter yet," Shane replied. "What's the plan? Terry makes the drop, we make the arrest?"

"Look, Sully, I appreciate you stepping in, especially since you were in on this early, but I can handle it on my own. You're already working a homicide. I mean, I get that you're friends with these people. Maybe more than friends with the P.I. Fine, not my business, but I prefer to work alone."

"I'm not trying to horn in on your case. I just want to help. I can be there with the rest of your team. I'll do whatever you need me to do. Like I said before, I'm here for backup."

Cooper regarded him with a raised brow. "All right. I plan on driving out there tonight to scope a stake-out location. You're welcome to come with me and see what will be waiting for us on the night of."

"Okay, sounds good," Shane replied. "I'll meet you here at the end of shift?"

"Sure thing."

———

THE DARK BLUE 2005 Shelby Mustang rolled on toward the construction site with Detective Cooper behind the wheel. The muscle car looked like a shadow against the backdrop of the harbor.

Shane sat in the passenger seat. "Where'd you get this car?"

"Bought it off some widow whose husband picked it up as a project car but died before he got around to fixing it. I rebuilt most of it. Felt bad for the lady, so I gave her a little more than it was worth, given its condition. Still, it's worth a hell of a lot more now that I've restored it."

"I'll bet." Shane stepped out under a clear dark sky charged with heavy air. A strange feeling weighed him down. Was it jealousy? No. No way was he jealous Cooper was working with Allison and drove a badass car. What the hell did he have to be jealous of? Shane could get any woman he wanted. This guy, Cooper, was all right, but...

"Are we just going to stand here all night or are we going to have a look around?" Cooper asked.

"Sorry." *Shake out of it man. You got nothing to worry about with Allison. Just because she's beautiful, and smart, and has her own P.I. firm...*

"Sully?" Cooper was ten steps ahead of him. "Let's move. I don't want to be here all night. Am I keeping you from something?"

"Right behind you." Shane hurried to catch up to him. "Why here?"

"I had a chance to look into who owned this building, figuring it might be the Winthrop Group, but no. It's like they picked a place that would make it easy to lose a body, you know?"

"Maybe so." Shane surveyed the area. "Bay's right there. Dark as hell out here. I don't know, man." He stopped and looked at Cooper. "This is starting to look like a setup."

"Get Terry here, take his money, and give him a nice hard shove." Cooper nodded. "Yeah, it does look that way."

16

By mid-afternoon on the day before the scheduled drop, the plan was set, and Charlie was ready. She tugged on her black tunic shirt and double checked in the decorative wall mirror in the office that her hair wasn't even going to think about moving. "I'm starting to feel like the guinea pig of the team."

Allison examined Charlie's appearance. "This time, I guarantee that no eyeglass-wearing, humble-looking accountant is going to take you." She reached for Charlie's shoulder. "But we would understand if you didn't want to go through with this. We'll figure out another solution. I don't want you to feel like you have to do this, Charlie."

"I don't. And I do know that this is different from before. I mean, really, I can't go too wrong placing a few bets." She turned to Lucy. "Which reminds me, your friend is going to text me, right?"

"It's all set up. You take a picture of the board and he'll review it and return a bet that looks legit, but would be unlikely to win," she replied.

"And the money?" Charlie turned back to Allison. "How much?"

Allison opened her handbag and retrieved an envelope. "There's $1000 in here. That should draw some attention. If all goes to plan and you lose everything, you'll go back tomorrow with another grand."

"Cripes, Alli, where did you get the money? You have a sugar daddy I'm not aware of?"

"Don't worry about it. I do have a budget, but I think this will, at the very least, get you noticed. Especially since you've never been there before."

"And don't forget my je ne sais quoi," Charlie began. "It draws people to me like moths to a flame."

"Or flies to shit, but whatever..." Allison laughed. "All kidding aside, I think we're ready to do this. Lucy and I will follow you and I'll stay in the parking lot. I want to watch for anyone who trails you out or anything unusual. Lucy will go inside and keep eyes on you too." She peered at Charlie. "You won't be alone."

Charlie spun on her heel. "Then let's go."

The thing about Charlie was that rarely did anyone see her as anything but tough, a little snarky, and determined to get her way. Nevertheless, there was a side of her that she kept to herself and maybe only showed one other, who was Allison. A vulnerability existed deep down that only reared its head in times like these. That vulnerability developed during the course of her marriage to the boys' father. An asshole by anyone's definition, and one who provoked that weakness in her.

As the team drove on in separate cars, their ultimate goal of helping to build a case against Gus Schoeman, Charlie arrived at the huge parking lot of the racetrack. Allison and Lucy were in Allison's car and rolled up behind her. Charlie peered through her rearview mirror and returned a thumbs up. "I got this, Alli," she whispered.

When Allison returned a nod, she drove on finding a nearby parking spot with a line of sight to Charlie's SUV.

The warm subtropical breeze threatened to muss Charlie's hair as she stepped out. Her skin chilled the moment she walked into the building. The concrete floor and high rafters let the air conditioners blow hard and cold. Charlie pulled back her shoulders and climbed the stairs to the second-floor betting desks, and grandstands. Screens above showed the day's races and the results of ones that had finished. With her phone in her hand, she discreetly snapped a photo and texted it to Lucy's gambler-friend, who Charlie suspected may still dabble in the game. Lucy was set to follow her inside and so she kept an eye out. "She's here. Just do your job," Charlie whispered under her breath.

When her phone buzzed with an incoming message, there was palpable relief. It was the friend with the wager she was to make and now Charlie could move ahead with the plan. Behind one of the desks was a man who smiled at her, appearing to await her approach. She obliged. "Hi there."

"Hello, ma'am. Here to place a bet?" he asked.

"Yes, sir." She relayed the information to him.

"Okay then. Here's your ticket."

Charlie handed over the cash and grabbed the ticket. "Fingers crossed!" she said to him. The stands were ahead and she made her way out, gazing out onto the track. The place was packed. She had no idea so many people were interested in horse races. It was the middle of the day in the middle of the week, and she wondered what kind of jobs these folks had that allowed them to indulge. Maybe it was the kind of job she should get.

The ticket read that the race was set to begin in 5 minutes. With her eyes trained on the horses inside the stalls, she couldn't help but wonder where Lucy was hiding. And where was this manager Allison talked about? She hadn't seen anyone come within 10 feet of her aside from other patrons. Was this really going to work or was this...

"And they're off..."

The race had begun, and Charlie jumped to attention. For a moment, she hoped to win. This was why the people were here. The adrenaline rush, of course. The payout on such long odds would've been pretty good according to the text she received from Lucy's friend. She could give Allison back the grand and keep the rest to sock away and take the boys on a nice vacation before her eldest goes off to college.

However, within moments, the dream of all that money vanished. The race was lost and so was Allison's grand. Charlie pursed her lips and shook her head. It was time to tuck her tail between her legs and lick her wounds, all the while, hoping the manager was watching somewhere. Getting him to take notice of her so that she might understand if and how the deal between Schoeman and him worked, was fading fast.

With her head hung low, Charlie retreated inside to the cold air, metal columns, and concrete floors. There was one thing she could do before making her final departure. Charlie reached into her bag and retrieved her wallet. Opening it, she peered inside as if looking for money. She pulled out one of her credit cards and glanced between it and the nearby ATM. It was the icing on the cake. The broke and lonely older woman gazing longingly, wondering if she should place another ill-fated wager. *I should've been an actress*, she thought.

Finally, it was time to exit Stage Left; the performance undoubtedly leaving an indelible mark on the powers that be. At least, she hoped.

Charlie slowly walked downstairs and the doors leading out

were just ahead, giving this manager one last shot, but no, nothing. And there was to be no looking back. Lucy would be there somewhere, no point in searching. Charlie must keep up the act. It was her only job. With the keys in her hand, she reached her SUV and unlocked the door. "Job done. I hope to hell it worked."

———

TODAY HAD BEEN a gamble and not just the bet Charlie placed at the track. It was a gamble as to whether Allison had made the right call on the entire plan. No one was paying her and, in fact, she'd just lost a grand, not exactly chump change. So who really stood to lose and why was this so important to her?

It was the end of a long day when Allison walked into the house. The fruits of her labor, Charlie's labor, really, was yet to be determined. For now, she was just glad to be home and wanted to have a nice dinner with her daughter.

"Micah?" Allison closed the door behind her. "Why aren't the lights on?" She walked through to the living room and switched on the lights. "Micah? Are you here?" Her car was out front, but that meant nothing since her friends could've picked her up. The thing was, she'd promised Allison to stick close to home until this was over. "Micah?" She marched to Micah's bedroom and opened the door. "Damn it."

Allison reached for her phone and pressed Micah's number. The line rang once, twice, voicemail. It was in a mother's nature to worry about her kids. Worry about where they were and whether they were safe. And most mothers didn't have people like Terry Hart in their family. So when Allison's pulse quickened and fear balled up in her gut, her daughter's safety was at the top of mind. She double-backed through the halls and opened the front door once again, walking to Micah's car in the driveway. The hood was cold to the touch. Allison spun around in search of the patrol car that was supposed to keep an eye out at the house. It was nowhere to be seen.

She walked inside and called the one person who could help. "Shane, Micah's gone."

"What?" he asked.

"Her car's here, she's not, and I don't see the patrol anywhere. I'm trying not to panic, but it's not working."

"Okay, take a breath. I'm right in the middle of something but let me call Detective Cooper and find out where the hell the unit is. Stay on the line, Allison. I'll put you on hold and call him now."

She waited while there was silence on the other end and the only thing she could hear was her own heartbeat.

"Allison, are you still there?"

She jumped to attention. "Yes. What's going on, Shane? I have to find Micah."

"Cooper is heading your way now. He's putting a call into the unit to get his location. You should see them soon..."

"It's Micah, Shane. I need to find her."

"Call her friends and see if any of them have seen her today. That will give us some idea where she was last seen..."

"Last seen? Jesus." Allison swallowed hard.

"You know what I mean. Do that, and by that time, Cooper will be at your door. We'll find her, Allison. She's probably with a friend."

"I told her to stay close..."

"She's a college kid. She's going to do what she wants. Keep trying her on her phone, too. Text her, whatever. Do you have a locator app on her phone?"

"Not anymore." Allison rubbed her brow and peered through the living room window. "I think that's the patrol car. I'll call her friends now."

"Keep me posted. And Alli?"

"Yeah?"

"She's fine. I need you to remember that," Shane replied.

"I'll try." Allison ended the call and walked outside, waving down the unit. The officer rolled down his window and she leaned in. "Have you seen Micah?"

"That's your daughter, right?" he asked.

"Yes. Did you see her leave at all today?" Allison pressed on.

"No. I've been on shift since about 3pm. I can call the officer who was here earlier and find out what he knows."

"Please do that. Detective Cooper is on his way," Allison replied.

"Yes, ma'am."

She turned around and headed back inside. Her mind raced. Where could Micah have gone? She knew the risks. But Shane was right. At the heart of it, Micah was barely 21. Just a kid who maybe didn't fully understand just how dangerous the situation was. "She's not stupid." Allison argued with herself, and no one was winning.

She made the calls to her friends and either got no answer or no one had seen her. Strike One. Allison picked up the phone again. "Charlie, can you come over?"

"What's wrong? Are you okay?" she asked.

"Micah's gone. I'm freaking out over here." Allison paced the living room with her hand on her forehead.

"Oh my God. Where's Shane?" Charlie asked.

"He's on a case. Detective Cooper is headed over now. I talked to the officer who's patrolling. He didn't see her leave. Her car is here. Her friends haven't seen her."

"Alli, it's okay. Just calm down a second. I know you're scared. Sit tight, I'm on my way."

When the line went dead, Allison's attention was drawn to the window where headlights shone through. "Cooper." She headed outside again in a whirlwind of agitation, confusion, and fear. "Detective, what do we do? No one's seen her today. She's not answering her phone."

"Let's go inside and take this one step at a time." He ushered her into the house. "Have you contacted her friends?"

"Yes. No one's seen her. I asked the officer outside. He said he's only been here since 3 o'clock. Can you talk to the other patrolman who was here?"

"I'll find out what's going on now. Will you at least sit down?" he asked.

"No. I can't." Allison was coming apart at the seams. "I have to call Leo. He has to know what's going on."

"Of course. You should call him. In the meantime, I'll be right outside, okay?"

She nodded with the phone in her hand. As the detective closed the door, Leo answered the line. "Leo, have you seen Micah today?"

"No. I talked to her this morning. Why? What's going on, Alli? Talk to me."

"I can't find her. Micah's gone. Our daughter's gone."

17

If it was unclear as to whether Allison's decision to go after evidence against Gus Schoeman had been the right one, it was crystal clear now. Her mind was all but certain Micah's disappearance was tied to Schoeman. He'd made good on his threat about her kids but hadn't lived up to his end of the bargain. The deal was that Terry had 72 hours to pay up. It had hardly been 48 hours and it was looking more and more like Micah was a casualty of Terry's arrangement.

Allison picked up her phone. "I'll try her again."

Leo, Charlie, and Detective Cooper huddled in the living room with none of them appearing certain as to what would come next. Cooper had made all the calls he could make. No one wanted to put to words what they all believed had happened.

Allison's eyes darted at Leo as a glimmer of hope sparked in them when the call was answered. "Micah? Oh my God, where are you?"

"Your daughter is fine, Mrs. Hart."

Allison hadn't recognized the man's voice on the other end of the line but could venture a guess. "Mr. Schoeman, let her go. She's done nothing to you. Our family has done nothing."

"No, none of you have done anything to bring this on. Terry Hart has."

"You said 72 hours...." Allison peered at the detective who moved closer to listen in on the conversation.

"Assurances, Mrs. Hart. This is how we get assurances."

"By taking one of my children? I don't know how that assures you Terry will come up with money he doesn't have," Allison replied.

"The schedule stands. Tomorrow night at 11pm, Mrs. Hart. Terry knows where, and I trust you'll relay to him the message. He'd better have the money by then. Your daughter will be just fine so long as that's the case. And I'd keep the cops out of this if I were you. If I get a whiff of pig, it'll be your daughter who pays the price."

The call ended and she looked at the detective. "He has her. Oh my God. What are we going to do? Can't you go after him?"

Charlie moved in and squeezed Allison's shoulders. "They're not going to hurt her, Alli, not if they want their money."

"You didn't hear his tone. He doesn't care about Micah. He didn't bother to keep to the original agreement. How can you say they won't hurt her?" Allison turned to the detective. "You should've arrested Gus Schoeman when he took Terry. Now look at where we're at?" Her eyes reddened.

Cooper turned away a moment. "Allison, I'm so sorry about this. I do think your friend is right. They won't harm your daughter. Frankly, with these types of people, they would've already done it to send a message. And unfortunately, whoever was on the other end of that call didn't give us a name."

"It was Schoeman. It had to be," Allison replied.

"We can't prove that," Cooper continued. "Look, the drop's

still on for tomorrow. Nothing's going to change hands until we see your daughter. They won't get a dime until we have her back."

———————

THE DETECTIVE STEPPED up patrols around the neighborhood, though as far as Allison was concerned, it hadn't mattered. Micah was gone. The patrols didn't do any good for her then, they wouldn't do any good for her now.

Allison ran her index finger around the top of her water glass as she hunched over on the sofa. "You don't have to stick around, Charlie. I appreciate it, but…"

"No buts. The boys can handle themselves for a while. They won't be doing anything more than playing video games anyway. That's all they've been doing the entire summer."

Allison's phone buzzed on the coffee table. She shot a look at Charlie and quickly noted the caller ID. "It's just Shane." She answered. "Hey."

"Allison, I'm coming over now."

She closed her eyes. "No. No, you don't need to. Detective Cooper did everything he could. There's nothing more we can do but wait."

"I should've been there for you…"

"You're on a case, Shane. It's okay." Allison's emotions caught up to her. "I just want her back. I can't believe this is happening. You were right to tell me to stay away from those people, but I didn't listen. I was naïve to think I could stand up against them."

"Stop. This isn't your fault. It's Terry's fault," Shane pressed on. "I don't think you should be alone right now. I should really come over."

"Charlie's here. I told Leo to go home thinking Terry might reach out to him, or something. I don't know, I just didn't want to see the look on his face anymore." Allison sighed. "There has to be something I can do, Shane." Before he could say anything else, she continued. "Listen, I can't talk right now. I just need to think things through."

"Yeah, okay. I understand. Please know that Cooper is doing everything in his power to find Micah. We all are."

"I know. Unfortunately, I don't think those powers are enough. Good night, Shane." Allison set down her phone again and looked at Charlie. "That came off harsher than I meant it to."

"I'm sure he understands." Charlie placed her hand on Allison's thigh.

Allison revealed a tender grin. "Maybe." After a moment, she sat up tall and turned to Charlie with a knitted brow.

"What is it?" Charlie asked.

"Shane mentioned to me earlier today, before all this happened, that he and Detective Cooper surveyed the drop site last night."

"Okay." Charlie revealed a curious gaze. And?"

"He didn't get into too much detail with me other than to say that he was going to look into who owned the building to see if it has anything to do with Winthrop Group." Allison reached for her laptop on the side table. "What if they have Micah at one of the properties they own? Where else would they have her if not someplace easily accessible for them?"

Charlie nodded. "All right. Hey, it's worth a look as far as I'm concerned."

Allison punched in the keys. "I'll run a property records search for them and see what turns up. My God, Charlie, what if they have her at one of their properties?"

"We wouldn't know which one and would have to search them all," Charlie replied. "Is that what you want to do? Don't get me wrong, I'm game if you are, but I'm just asking."

"I don't know. It's a shot in the dark, but sitting here and doing nothing where Micah's concerned…"

"Yeah. Not going to happen," Charlie cut in. "I'll follow you. You just tell me where and when."

"Thanks, Charlie." Allison studied the screen as the search continued. "It should be easy to narrow down. The building would most likely be empty."

"Some place out of the way, maybe?" Charlie asked.

"Probably." She pointed to the screen. "They own quite a few but look here."

Charlie leaned closer. "A cluster of office suites near the Port Tampa docks. Let's put a star next to that one."

"And this here, the industrial complex near East Bay Raceway Park," Allison added. "We can scratch off the couple of residential buildings. I'll plug in these other two locations and look to see if they're currently being leased." She peered at Charlie. "This one has two empty suites."

"The one at the industrial park near the bay. So, what do you think? Should we call Detective Cooper and ask him to check these out?"

Allison considered the idea. "I want to go check it out myself first. I'm not sure he'd be willing to run on my gut feeling. You heard what he said."

"He wants to keep the status quo until the drop. Yeah, I heard," Charlie replied. "But you could be right about this."

"If I am—if I get there and see signs of life. Anything that might suggest Micah is being held there, then I'll make the call. You don't have to go with me, Charlie. This is something I should do on my own. You have the boys to think about. You should go home."

"Nice try, but I don't think so. My concern, though, is that if there are cameras on the perimeter of the building, and someone is inside, they'll see us coming. We could make a bad situation worse if they have her there, Alli."

"I want my daughter back. I might be wrong about all of this, but I have to try. I'll take precautions to avoid surveillance."

Charlie stood from the sofa. "Okay then. We should go."

―――――

IN THE LATE hours of the night, the building appeared in the distance, illuminated only by streetlamps and pathway lights at the front. The adjacent bay glimmered under the half-moon.

"This is it." Allison slowed the car and turned off the headlights. "We'll stop here and walk the rest of the way to be sure the car isn't picked up on cameras."

"There's not much cover for us if we're on foot either," Charlie replied.

"If the suites are empty, there might not be active cameras in the first place."

Charlie opened her car door. "We won't know until we try. Let's find Micah. It's past my bedtime."

Allison joined her as they headed toward the back of the buildings across from the docks. "This is a sketchy part of town."

"Yeah, well, you didn't think they'd keep Micah at the Ritz, did you?" Charlie quipped.

"Right, assuming she's here and I'm not wasting our time," Allison said.

"It's not a waste of time to look for your daughter, even if we are a couple of middle-aged women walking around an industrial park after midnight." She smiled. "Kidding. We'll be fine. Place is empty by the look of it."

"Third building on the left," Allison cut in. "That's the first of the two vacant suites."

"Then that's where we'll go, but we need to find some kind of cover. Let's get close to the back wall of the building. It would most likely be a blind spot if there are cameras." Charlie's short legs carried her quickly to the back of the building. "Alli, this way."

Allison hurried to join her. "You're faster than you look." She pressed her back against the wall. "We should be good here."

"So we stick to this wall like glue and start shuffling along." Charlie continued ahead. "If we get a hint of a feeling that Micah is here, she won't be alone."

"I understand. I'll make the call to Cooper. This is it, here." Allison grabbed Charlie's shoulder. "Hang on. Let's figure out the best way to look inside."

"I see the back entrance just ahead."

Allison nodded. "There's a window a few feet before the door. I'll go there and take a peek inside. You stay here until I give you the go-ahead." Dew clung to the window as the stifling heat and humidity lingered. She looked back to see Charlie exactly where she left her. But as she took another step, the back door opened and Allison gasped. She flattened her back against the wall. *Oh shit, oh shit, oh shit.* She wanted to look back at Charlie, but any movement could catch the eye of whoever now stood at the door.

The man held it open with his foot while he lit up a cigarette. The flame illuminated his face for only a moment, revealing his fire-red hair. He pushed open the door, and now Allison couldn't see him at all. But if he stepped out another few inches, they would get an eyeful of one another.

Allison's breath caught in her throat. Her phone was in her back pocket, doing her absolutely no good at the moment. *Just go back inside.* And as if she possessed the mind-bending powers of a Jedi, the man pulled back and the door started to close. Her foot shuffled atop the loose gravel of the asphalt pavement as she prepared to turn around and go back.

The door stopped. The toe of his shoe was visible beyond it. He wasn't going back inside, not anymore. Allison squeezed her eyes shut, damning herself for making the noise. She glanced at Charlie and they both knew this was it. Time to run.

Allison sprinted and reached Charlie. Within seconds, the two were headed toward the road.

"Hey!" The man tossed away the cigarette and hustled after them. Lissome, his long legs carried him at nearly twice the pace of the girls.

Allison was steps ahead of Charlie and slowed a little.

"Move, damn it!" Charlie demanded. "Go!"

They were in the middle of the empty street, hurrying to make it to the other side and back to the car. But Allison knew this man was faster. "Oh, God. He's catching up."

"Don't look back. Run!" Charlie was nearly out of breath.

"We won't make it to the car," Allison began. "Follow me." She darted to the left and the hard turn nearly caused her to stumble, but she pressed on with Charlie behind and the man closing the gap.

The light of a nearby liquor store captured Allison's attention. *Thank God.* She turned back and waved Charlie on. There it was, the entrance to the store. Allison opened the glass door and held it. "Hurry, Charlie!"

Charlie hustled inside while Allison ran to the checkout counter. "A man is after us."

The cashier's face masked in confusion.

"He's coming," Allison said.

The woman at the counter didn't say a word and only nodded to the cold storage. Allison returned a nod and both she and Charlie rushed toward it and stepped inside.

The room was dark, and Allison didn't dare turn on the light.

The air was painfully cold as the sweat on her skin chilled. He must've caught up by now and was inside.

Charlie pressed her shoulder against Alli's. "What now?" she whispered.

"Wait," Allison mouthed in return. She wondered how long they would have to stay in here. The woman at the counter had saved their lives, for now.

"Cripes, it's freezing in here," Charlie whispered.

Allison pulled her close and the two huddled together for warmth. When the door opened minutes later, Allison lost her breath, not knowing who stood on the other side.

"You guys can come out now. He's gone," the young woman said. She held the door and Allison and Charlie stepped out.

"He's really gone?" Charlie asked.

"Yes. I told him no one came in. He didn't believe me and looked around himself. Then he finally left." She secured the door and started back toward the checkout. "You guys steal something from him or was he just a creeper?"

"A definite creeper," Charlie replied. "Thank you."

"I'd stick around for a few minutes if I were you. I can go out back and walk like I'm taking out the trash or something and see if he's hanging around."

"You have no idea how much you helped us," Allison replied.

"I been there. I have some idea." She walked to the door and peered through the glass. "I don't see him, but I'll go have a walk. Maybe go sit behind the counter, yeah? Just in case he comes back in."

Allison started toward it. "Yeah, thanks."

The two squatted low behind the counter while the woman stepped outside. Charlie peered at the expensive liquor on the shelves. "Makes me really want a drink right about now, huh?"

"Yeah. I could use one." Allison rubbed her forehead. "I don't know how we got out of that, Charlie. I really don't."

"Luck," she replied. "And I was the 100m dash champion at my high school, so you know..."

Allison chuckled. "I'll bet you were. I've never seen you move so fast. Come to think of it, I've never moved that fast."

"Seriously, though, Alli, did you see anything? Did you see Micah?"

"No. He opened the door before I could look, but she must be there. Why would that man have been there unless he was sent to keep an eye on Micah?"

"What do you want to do?" Charlie asked.

Allison's phone buzzed in her back pocket. "It says unknown." She answered the call. "Hello?"

"You have a collect call from...

"Mom?"

Allison's eyes welled as she heard her daughter's fractured voice. "Micah. Accept the charges! Accept the charges!" The line clicked. "Micah, where are you? Where are you, baby?"

"They took me. Mom, someone grabbed me and took me to some building. I've been there for hours. I don't know where." Her sobs grew louder. "Then, I ran. I just ran. The guy who was watching me went out for a smoke. That's what he said. But he was gone for a long time and I thought, I don't know, but I thought I could get away. So I did. I just ran. I don't know where I'm at now. Some payphone maybe a mile away. I'm not sure. Mom, I'm scared."

"Is she okay?" Charlie demanded.

Allison struggled to contain her emotions. "I know you are, baby. It's okay. Are you hidden right now?"

"There's like a little park in the distance. I see a swing set. It's so dark, though. I can hide in the trees or something over there. Can you come get me? Please, Mom."

"Yes. Yes. I'll come get you. I think I know where you are and we're not far away."

"What?" Micah asked.

"It doesn't matter right now. I'll look at my phone's map for the park. I'll find you. Don't move from there, okay? Stay there and we'll be there in just a few minutes."

"I won't go anywhere. Please hurry."

"We will." Allison ended the call and the front door opened again.

"He's gone," the woman said. "You two can come out."

Allison stood up as relief washed over her. "Thank you so..." Her face turned deadpan.

The man held a gun to the young woman's head. "I figured you two were here."

18

The earthy scent of the damp soil beneath Micah's feet lingered as she crouched low behind a tree. The only noises were that of the crickets. No cars traveled the road in front of her at the late hour. She'd walked the few feet to the small park from the only payphone she'd seen while running away from the man who held her captive. It may have been the first payphone she'd seen in person and not on some old television show. Her cell phone had been taken away when the man shoved her into the backseat of his car.

"Where are you, Mom?" Her dark, straight hair clung to her cheeks as sweat trickled down. It had been twenty minutes and still no sign of her mother. Should she risk coming out into the open again to call her dad, or wait a little while longer? "You have to get out of here." Micah returned to the nearby payphone, exposed and afraid. The collect call was made.

"Dad? Dad, it's me."

"Micah?" Relief sounded in his tone. "Where are you? Are you safe?"

Her eyes welled. "I got away. It all happened so fast. I called Mom and she said she was coming but it's been too long. I don't know where she is. Maybe the man who took me found her. Dad, please help. Please come get me."

"Tell me where you are. I will find you."

"I'm at a payphone near a little park. There's not a lot out here."

"Give me the number on the payphone. I'll track down its location."

"Um, okay." She relayed the number.

"Are they still after you?" Leo asked.

"I—I don't know. I haven't seen anyone at all since I escaped."

"Okay. You said there's a park nearby. Go back there, take cover. I'm on my way. If I can't find you, I'll call back to the payphone. Will you be able to hear it from the park?"

"Yes, I think so. It's really quiet out here. Dad, I'm scared. Why didn't Mom come? She made it sound like she was close by."

"I don't know. I need to go now. I'll locate the payphone and head your way just as fast as I can. Micah, I'm coming to get you. Don't be afraid."

"I love you, Dad."

"I love you too, sweetheart."

Micah hung up and returned to her spot behind the tree. She had no idea of the time without her phone. And so what felt like an hour, might have been only minutes before she finally spotted headlights slowly approaching. She peeked around the tree. "Dad." Micah stood up and hurried toward the street. "Dad, I'm here. Over here."

Leo stopped the car and jumped out. "Oh my God." He pulled Micah into an embrace as she sobbed. "It's okay. You're safe now. I got you."

"I don't know where Mom is. Can you call her?"

Leo pulled back. "What happened? Did they hurt you?"

"No. I'm okay. Dad, we have to find Mom."

"Okay, okay. Get in the car. I'll try her phone, but don't worry, we'll find her."

————

THE LANKY MAN holding the gun to the young woman's head eyed Allison. "You're the mom, aren't you? How the hell did you know where she was?"

"I don't know what you're talking about. My friend and I were interested in some office space and saw the building. Decided to drop by," she continued.

"Really? At this time of night in this part of town, you two cougars decided to wander around in search of office space?"

"Don't know what to tell you," Charlie added. "We were having drinks earlier and passed by here on our way home."

"Then why'd you run?" he pressed on.

"Like you said, it's a sketchy part of town," Allison began. "We weren't expecting to see anyone. You scared us, so we ran." She glanced at the gun. "I guess we were right to be scared, huh?"

He pushed the woman away and she stumbled back to the checkout counter. "You know, I can make a call and find out real quick who you are. If I find out you're lying, that's when you'll really need to be scared."

Allison had already met Schoeman. It would only take a call to him to confirm her identity. If they made the wrong move now, it could cost them their lives and the life of the young woman who had tried to help them.

"Wait," Allison cut in. "I'll tell you who we are and why we're here."

He lowered his gun and eyed her. "I'm listening."

"I was hired by Lou Santos, who works at Bayside Downs. Terry Hart told him he'd been kidnapped by Gus Schoeman's people, which I assume includes you. And then that he was set free but on the condition of payment within 72 hours..."

"I know all this already, lady. You'd better come up with a better story. I'm losing my patience."

"Lou was trying to set you up. He asked me to look into the Winthrop Group and its properties. My colleague and I were checking out the property when you showed up and scared the shit out of us. I don't get paid to know all the details of Lou's plan, but he asked us to check things out." She glanced at Charlie, who was slightly slack-jawed in apparent marvel at Allison's ability to spin a tale from thin air.

The gunman's face screwed up as though a foul odor reached his nose. Allison studied him, wondering if he believed her. His current expression suggested he hadn't. It was a stretch, a grasp at a final straw to save their lives. She just needed him to bite and hoped for a chance that he might set them free. But at least Micah was safe. Still, she had Charlie to worry about. She would rather die than let anything happen to her.

The loud blast rang in Allison's ears. Her head hummed and her eyes widened as she turned to Charlie. Both examined one another to confirm if either had been hit. It wasn't until Allison looked at the woman that the pieces fell together.

The long-legged man with fiery hair crumpled to the floor. Blood pooled around him.

Charlie reached out. "Alli? Alli, can you hear me? Are you okay?"

Her voice was muffled while the ringing continued. Allison turned to her. "I'm okay. I can't hear you very well." She glanced at the young woman who held a rifle in her hands. "You shot him."

With her pinky finger in her ear, she rattled it around. "It was either him or us. He wasn't watching me. Just you two. Figured that was our best shot at making it out of this alive."

Allison wrapped her arm around Charlie. "You're okay?"

She nodded before turning to the woman. "Thank you."

"He seemed like a piece of shit, so the world's probably better off, am I right?" She set down her rifle. "Better get the cops down here. You two should go. It'll be less messy if no one knows you were here, yeah?"

Allison shook her head. "But..."

"Nope. Just go. No cameras in here. No one's gonna know nothing. Besides, I think you two need to lay low for a while. I'm going to venture a guess that guy doesn't work alone."

"She's right, Alli. We have to go and find Micah." Charlie ushered her toward the door but stopped and turned back to the woman. "I'm not sure how we can repay you."

"We're open 24/7. Tell your friends about us." A wry smile drew up on her lips.

Allison and Charlie walked out of the store.

"We have to get to that park." Allison held her phone and looked up the location on the app. It has to be this one here. It's only a mile or so away." Her phone rang and she glanced at the caller ID. "Leo?"

"I have her, Alli. She's safe. Here, talk to your daughter."

Allison's lips trembled. "Micah?"

Charlie looked on in relief.

"Mom? Oh, thank God. I waited. You didn't come, so I called Dad. Are you okay?"

"Charlie and I are fine. I'm sorry I told you to wait. I thought... it doesn't matter. What matters is that you're okay. And so are we."

"Dad drove me home. Do you need to talk to him?" Micah asked.

"No. Just tell him we're fine and we'll be there soon. I love you so much, honey."

"I love you too, Mom."

Allison ended the call. "Let's get the hell out of here so I can see my daughter."

Charlie smiled. "You sure? I was thinking we should stick around for a while and see what else happens."

———

ALLISON PARKED the car in the driveway and cut the engine. Micah must've seen her arrive because the front door swung open and she rushed to the car. Allison stepped out and pulled Micah into an embrace. "Oh, baby. Thank God you're okay."

"I'm so sorry, Mom. I was stupid. I saw a package on the porch, and I opened the door to get it. There he was."

"None of this is your fault, sweetheart," Allison cut in. "None of it. He lured you outside. I'm just so happy you're home."

Leo trailed Micah outside and peered at Allison. "Jesus, Alli, what the hell happened tonight? Did you get her free?"

"Let's just go inside. I need to sit and take a breath."

"I thought Charlie was with you?" Leo continued as he started inside again.

"I dropped her off at home. The boys were there alone and I told her I'd bring her back here in the morning to get her car." Allison kept her arm around Micah as the two walked in. She kissed her cheek and finally let her go. "We were there."

Micah smiled. "It had to be you. I just knew it."

"Come on. Let's sit down." Leo ushered them to the sofa. "I'll get you some water. Micah, do you need anything?"

"I'm okay, Dad," she replied.

When Leo returned, Allison took the glass and swallowed it down in a single gulp. She took in a breath. "He's dead."

"What?" Leo lowered himself onto the side chair.

"The man who had Micah. He's dead. I don't know if anyone else was there with him..."

"Did you kill him?" Micah asked.

"No. I honestly don't know how we made it out of there alive. He came after us. He saw me and Charlie and we darted like bats out of hell. We found ourselves hiding inside an all-night liquor store. The cashier, a young woman, probably not much older than you. She killed him. He would've killed all of us if she hadn't."

Leo jumped from the chair. "Did you call the cops?"

"She did. She also insisted we leave. Look, Leo, I know this is a lot to take in. It's a lot for me to take in, but the goal was achieved. Our daughter's home."

He pressed his hand against his forehead. "My God, Alli, but at what cost? How did you find her?"

"Does it matter? It's one more thing we can use against Gus Schoeman. They held her at a building his company owns. I wouldn't be surprised if it was the same place where they took Terry. They have to arrest him now." She reached for Micah's hand. "I think you should stay at a friend's house. Until this is over, you shouldn't be here. I thought it would be the safest place for you, but clearly it isn't."

"Mom, I won't leave you."

"You have to, Micah. Nolan is safer away, like you said, and that's what you need to do too." She peered at Leo. "Don't you agree?"

"Your mother's right. In the morning, let's get you out of here. You've got that job starting soon anyway." He turned back to Allison. "Then we can finish this once and for all."

_____

LEO HADN'T WANTED to leave, but Allison insisted they would be fine, and that Detective Cooper had stepped up the patrols. Now, all that was left to do was tell the detective that she'd somehow managed to secure Micah's freedom. She and Charlie. They were a hell of a team, including Lucy, even if she hadn't been with them tonight. More than ever before, Allison realized how much she needed her partners.

She stood at the front window with her phone in hand. It was nearly 3 o'clock in the morning, but a cop would answer. That's just what they did. "Detective Cooper? It's Allison Hart. We got her back—Micah, she's home."

"What? How?" His tone was groggy. "Where are you?"

"Home. My partner and I did some digging and took a shot that Micah was being held at a vacant building owned by the Winthrop Group. We hadn't really expected to find her there, but she managed to escape when her captor came after us."

"Jesus. I'm on my way."

The line went dead before she had a chance to tell him not to bother. Of course, he would've anyway. The hitch in this plan was that while they survived the night, Schoeman would soon learn, if he hadn't already, that Micah escaped, and his man was dead.

Reluctance took hold as she prepared to call Shane. He would be disappointed that she'd taken such a risk, but it hadn't mattered to her. Micah was her daughter. Allison wasn't going to leave it alone until she had her back.

She waited for the line to answer. "Hey, it's me. Micah's home."

_____

Detective Cooper texted his arrival as Allison spotted the incoming message. The hour was beyond late, the sun would be up soon, and he was kind enough not to knock on the door. She'd just checked on Micah and noticed she'd finally fallen asleep. Allison's nerves were still too frayed to think about sleep.

She opened the door. "You didn't need to come over."

Cooper had a commanding presence and when he stepped inside, the room was his. "Yes, I did. I also called down to the station after a shooting was reported in the area that I think you might be familiar with."

"You want my side of the story?" She closed the door. "I can put on some coffee if you're interested."

"No thanks. I think I know how this is going to go. You and your partners decided to take matters into your own hands to find your daughter."

"Detective," Allison followed him into the living room. "If it had been your kid…"

"I would've followed the advice of the very smart detective running the investigation." With his hands on his hips, he returned a derisive gaze. "Is she all right?"

"Shaken up, but otherwise fine." Allison sighed. "I can't say as much for the guy who had her."

"Travis Varney. Allison, did you kill him?"

"No. The woman who worked at the liquor store, she saved our lives. She deserves a damn medal." Allison sat down on the sofa. "What happens now? Schoeman's going to be pissed."

"You think?" Cooper grunted as he sat on the side chair. "This just went from bad to worse and we're going to have to re-think tomorrow…tonight's plan."

"I want to get this guy, Detective. I know how that sounds, but he took my daughter. His guy tried to kill my best friend and me. We know where he kept Micah. The Winthrop Group owns the damn building. That has to be enough to arrest Schoeman."

"First of all, you didn't bring this on. Okay, maybe part of it, you did. But this is Terry Hart's deal. He pulled all you into his friggin' nightmare and this is where we're at. Secondly, I expect someone, maybe you, maybe Terry, I don't know, but someone's going to be getting a call from Gus Schoeman. So, I want to track the calls your family receives. I can make that happen in the next hour. He'll want to change the drop location, no doubt about that. He knows you found his office and he won't underestimate you again."

"To be honest, I'm not sure exactly what he knows," Allison began. "I can't say 100 percent that we avoided their security cameras, but I'm pretty sure we did. Micah escaped on her own. He obviously didn't expect to leave her to her own devices long enough to figure out how to get free. So, I'm not sure what Schoeman knows or doesn't know."

"If you're right and he thinks Micah got out on her own, we stand a chance he'll keep to his original plan. He won't show up himself, of course, but we'll nab whoever he sends. We get that person to talk and we're golden."

"You have an eyewitness. Terry knows who took him. We know where Micah was held. My God, what more do you need to arrest this man?" Allison pleaded.

"Unless you want your daughter and father-in-law to end up in Witsec, we keep to the plan and get Schoeman on charges unrelated to your family." Cooper leaned in. "I understand your frustration. I really do. But the Brunetti family protects their own unless it can come back to bite them in the ass. That's what I want on Gus Schoeman. Charges that will stick and that have the possibility of shining a light on the family. They'll back off so quick, your head will spin. Trust me, I've talked to the detectives who've been involved with this family. I need to get Schoeman on charges related to Terry Hart so that no one knows anything about your family."

Allison held his gaze, studying him to figure out if he had another agenda. Because if there was one thing she banked on, it was that everyone had their own agenda. "Fine. I'll let you take your shot. You'd better hope it works."

19

T he sun still ascended in the sky. The world went on no matter that Allison had almost lost her life and her daughter had been taken. Now, having slept only a restless sleep, Allison stood outside and watched Micah reverse out of the driveway. Letting her go again was the hardest part, but it was for her own safety. Grief at Micah's departure swelled in her chest and she fought to push it down. Micah didn't need to see weakness, only strength.

This was supposed to be a time for the two of them to continue to heal. Leo's wedding had prompted Micah's change of heart and they'd continued to rebuild their once-strained relationship.

Nolan had been kept in the dark and Allison intended on keeping it that way no matter what. If he knew what had happened to Micah, he would have been on the next flight home. She didn't want to do that to him. It was just Allison now; Allison and her team to see this through.

Just as she was about to turn away and return inside, Shane's car pulled up onto the driveway. After making the call at nearly

3am, she'd insisted he wait until morning to come over. With reluctance, he had agreed.

Shane stepped out of his car and made his way to Allison as she stood on her front porch. She offered a tender smile. "Hi. You want some coffee?"

"Love some." Shane walked inside with his shoulders low and his face sullen. "I talked to Cooper after you called. He filled me in on the rest of the situation regarding tonight."

Allison grabbed a mug from the cabinet. "The good news is that I haven't heard from Schoeman, so I guess Charlie and I are in the clear."

Shane pulled up a stool. "I wouldn't go that far. He obviously knows Micah escaped. He'll find a way to retaliate, Allison."

She offered him the mug. "I did what I had to do."

He regarded her. "I wanted to be angry with you for what you and Charlie did, but I couldn't. I don't have kids, but I do understand that you'd do anything for yours."

"Some things I have to take care of on my own," Allison continued. "You're my boyfriend, not my savior."

"I'm a cop first. I could've helped, not come to your rescue." He glanced at his mug and held it between the palms of his hands. "It's over now. Cooper did his job and I'm just grateful as hell you and Charlie are okay. And Micah. I can't imagine how that must've felt for you."

"Thank you. Now the real work begins."

"You mean tonight?" He sipped on his brew.

"No. Cooper made it clear that I was to stay far away from that operation, and I intend to. You two have the means to handle it and it has nothing to do with me, not since I got my daughter back. No, I'm talking about ending this man, Gus Schoeman. Ending him and whoever else he's involved with. I've already made inroads. I just need some more time."

"Do you want me to speak as a cop now or as your boyfriend?" he asked.

Allison eyed him. "Well, that depends on what you plan to say."

"How about, you understand that if this drop goes well, we'll have Schoeman dead to rights. So I don't get why you feel the need to pursue other avenues."

"If I thought this was a slam dunk, I'd reconsider," Allison replied. "I told Cooper I'd get out of his way, but I'm not finished with this man."

Shane sighed and returned a gentle gaze. "I'm not going to try to convince you otherwise, but honestly, I don't know what I would do if something happened to you. You know I love you, right?"

Allison lowered her head. The unexpected words caught her off guard. "I know."

———

It was 7:30 in the morning when Allison walked into the office to find her partners already at work. "Charlie, you didn't have to rush in here this morning. Neither of you did."

Charlie, wearing her black-rimmed reading glasses, peered at Allison. "Yes, I did. It wasn't my kid who was taken, but I'll be damned if I don't feel like she's mine. I don't care what happened to me, I'm just glad Micah's okay. And we have a lot of work to do."

"That means a lot to me. And just so you know, Micah left. She's starting an internship soon and will be staying with a friend until then. Detective Cooper is making sure she'll be protected."

"I thought that was what he did before," Lucy replied.

"That makes two of us." Allison walked to her desk. "As far as

I know, nothing's changed for tonight, so what we did, I don't think Schoeman knows. He hasn't called for a change in venue, or anything else."

"What happens now, Alli?" Charlie asked.

"We continue with our plan. Are you ready to head back to the racetrack this morning? I have the money for you to place another bet. It's time we raise your profile."

"I can't keep losing your money. No offense, but I know you aren't exactly flush with cash right now," Charlie replied.

"Like I said, don't worry about that. It'll all work out in the end, but we need to move. We'll get Santos to give us something on Schoeman. We need to pile on as much as we can so Cooper can build a solid case. With the friends Schoeman has, I don't want to take any chances. I don't want to leave it up to depending on whoever they might arrest tonight to turn on him."

"If this is what needs to be done, then okay, let's make our move now." Charlie stood from her desk. "I'm ready when you are."

Allison looked at Lucy. "You ready?"

"As ever."

"Good." She swiped her keys from her desk and headed toward the door.

The shock hadn't yet worn off Allison. She was pretty sure it hadn't worn off Charlie yet either. She felt like she was operating on autopilot with a single objective—getting to Gus Schoeman. The proof that there had been an arrangement between Santos and Schoeman was nonexistent at the moment, but Allison relied on her gut. These two worked together on scamming the clients at the racetrack and her best guess was that this was all happening under the noses of the Brunetti family, yet they weren't in on it.

They made it to the racetrack just as it had opened. Sitting in her car in the parking lot, Allison turned to Charlie, who sat in the passenger seat. "Same as yesterday—before we faced down a gunman, okay?"

"I got it. I still don't know how the hell you scrounged up two grand to make this happen. Maybe I don't want to know. I just hope your plan works," she replied.

"It'll work," Allison said.

Charlie opened her door and stepped out under the blue sky and oppressive heat. "Just do what you did yesterday," she mouthed to herself. A quick glance and she watched as Allison and Lucy pulled away. They would park elsewhere and, just as before, Lucy would stay close enough to have eyes on her. With the high-dollar wagers, she hoped to draw the attention of Lou Santos.

Inside the cool building, Charlie made her way upstairs to the desk and took a picture of the upcoming races. Lucy's friend, once again, replied with the best way to lose all that money. Charlie shuddered at the idea. But with the bets placed, she walked out into the stands and prepared to play the part of a desperate woman.

Inside of fifteen minutes, the money was gone. Every penny of the two grand—lost. This time, however, Charlie had to make a case for herself. It was time to step this up and ask for a line of credit. If that didn't get Santos's attention, nothing else would.

"Excuse me." Charlie approached the desk. "May I speak with someone about lines of credit?"

"I'm afraid we don't do that, ma'am," the attendant replied.

"My credit is excellent. I just need a little bit more so I can get back what I started with," Charlie pleaded.

"Like I said, ma'am, I wish I could help. It's just not possible."

"There may be something I can do for you, ma'am." Santos meandered toward her as if he hadn't a care in the world.

"You can? That would be wonderful." Her tone of encouragement sounded convincing, even to herself.

"Why don't we step into my office and discuss the situation." He led the way.

Charlie glanced back in search of Lucy but couldn't see her. *You'll be fine. You can do this.*

The manager closed the door. "Take a seat, Ms..."

"Anderson. Charlie Anderson. And you are?"

"Lou Santos. I manage track operations, including customer service. Can I ask you, Ms. Anderson, are you a horse lover?"

"Not particularly. I don't dislike them, but to be honest, look at me. If I ever tried to mount a horse, I'd roll right off. I'm built like a Weeble."

He chuckled. "Oh, I doubt that. So do you enjoy the excitement of betting? That's a big draw for a lot of people. The idea of winning all that money." His bug eyes widened as if he'd just won a sizeable bet himself.

"The winning part is what interests me, Mr. Santos. As for the rest of it, I've seen my share of excitement. I don't care to see any more." That was the truth. "You mentioned you know how I might continue with my new favorite pastime? As I said to your attendant, my credit is excellent, and I pay my debts."

"I have no doubt, Ms. Anderson. While my employee is correct in that the track doesn't extend credit on a regular basis, it does leave it up to my discretion."

"Then I've come to the right place after all," Charlie replied.

He pressed together the tips of his fingers. "Yes and no. The track has tightened its criteria. That said, all is not lost, Ms. Anderson. I do know of a source that could offer assistance. Mind you, there's always a little extra cost in doing business that way, but you strike me as a woman who already knows that."

Why wouldn't he offer her the line of credit as he had to

Terry? This didn't appear to be going to plan. "I do know how these things work," Charlie added. "Tell me what I can do to expedite this potential solution." She paused a moment for dramatic effect. "I must find a way to make myself whole again, Mr. Santos. Financially and otherwise."

————

THE FIRST THING Shane noticed was that she hadn't said it back. Allison hadn't returned with the all-important "I love you, too." Okay, so maybe it hadn't been the best timing. After what had happened the night before, she was bound to be preoccupied, tense, upset. And he'd done his damnedest not to lose it over the idea she could've been killed. He'd known her long enough to realize Allison was going to do what she wanted to do to accomplish her goal. Last night, that goal was to get back her daughter, and she did just that. It would've been admirable, were it not so completely reckless.

What was done was done and it hadn't yet snowballed, but Shane had just arrived back at the station. He was about to find out whether there was a snowball and whether it was rolling out of control. "Cooper, you get any word yet about tonight?"

The detective peered up from his desk. "I spoke with the son, Leo. He said Terry hadn't received a call or visit. He also claimed his dad was shocked by what had happened to his granddaughter and far too distraught to come here himself today. Funny, the girl's father was just as distraught and yet, he seemed determined to make this happen tonight. Anyway, I guess your girl got lucky she didn't throw off the plan or end up dead."

"She's not..."

"Spare me," Cooper cut in. "I don't give a shit; I just need to know what I'm up against. I like you, Sully. I've heard good things about you from the guys upstairs. But if you're emotionally invested in this, then you need to step aside."

"I've spent too much time already learning about Schoeman and his connection to the Brunetti family. I understand the way he works. I need to be in on this. Regarding Terry Hart? I don't give a shit about him. I care about what happens to his grandkids, and yeah, I care about Allison. If you think that'll prevent me from doing my job, then I guess I'll step aside. It's your call."

Cooper studied him. "What do you know about Schoeman's ties to the family and how will it help us make an arrest?"

"I know he wants to get in tighter with them. The Winthrop Group is a small and distant arm of the family's business dealings. He wants a bigger slice of the pie. More influence. It means he'll be looking to prove his muscle. I think the threats against Terry Hart, the kidnapping of his granddaughter, it all ties together."

Cooper nodded. "That could be why we haven't heard from his people about changing the terms of the deal. Schoeman may not want the higher-ups to know his boy screwed up last night. But that could also mean he knows exactly who was there too. Allison and her partner, Charlie Wells. If that's the case, he could have something extra special in store for them to save face."

Shane appeared unyielding. "Then I want to do what it takes to make sure that doesn't happen."

———

ALLISON WAS RELIEVED when she spotted Charlie emerge from the building. "There she is." A moment later, Lucy trailed behind. It had been more than an hour and she'd grown concerned after Lucy texted saying Charlie had gone inside the manager's office.

Charlie opened the passenger door and slipped onto the seat.

"Looks like it went well." Allison waited for Lucy to step in. "Good job, Lucy."

"It wasn't me. Charlie did all the work." Lucy slipped onto the backseat.

"I have to say, I did put on one hell of an act," Charlie replied. "The manager said he wants to introduce me to a friend of his, who works for the Winthrop Group. He said he could offer a bridge loan to get me through until I recover my losses. There is something else, though. He mentioned the track was pulling back on its lending criteria. Makes me think upper management might've picked up on what Santos is doing. I don't know, but I think it helped put us in touch directly with the man responsible for all of this—Gus Schoeman."

"And the catch?" Allison asked.

"A paltry fee payable to the Winthrop Group. And when I asked what was in it for him, he said it was the customer satisfaction."

"He actually said that? Wow. Did you press him on it?" Allison continued.

"I didn't think it was a good idea. It's too early in the game. All I need is whatever paperwork they have from the Winthrop Group. The terms and such. That'll go a long way into helping us tie the two people together."

"Then, when you pay back the money..." Allison began.

Charlie shot her a look. "Wait. I'm paying it back?"

"You have to. You think I want Schoeman coming after you for payment? Not a chance. That was never part of the plan."

"Then, please, fill me in," Charlie added. "And then I'd like to know where all this money is coming from. Did you win the lottery and forget to tell your partners?"

"No, I didn't win the lottery. The money is mine. I told you not to worry about that. Going back to the plan. Once the deal is made and you get the loan from Schoeman's people, that's where I come in."

Lucy pulled up from the backseat. "How so? You already said Schoeman's seen you. He knows who you are and that's even more likely after last night."

"Terry's going to help me," Allison replied.

Charlie scoffed. "Good luck with that. Based on what I've seen, that man only cares about himself. And I don't even know him that well."

"We have an arrangement. Terry is going to meet with Santos at a set time and place, away from his office. I'll slip inside and plant a bug. The rest will be a piece of cake." She noticed the look on their faces. "What? I can't get into the man's computer or his files. How else do I figure out what he's doing?"

"Okay, so you're going to break the law and risk your P.I. license in order to catch a guy who may or may not be getting kick-backs?" Charlie asked. "A sound plan if there ever was one."

"This isn't really about Santos. I want to stop this guy, sure. But more importantly, we need to know what he's telling Schoeman or his associates."

"You won't be able to get a warrant based on what amounts to an illegal wiretap, Allison," Lucy said. "How can you get around that to use it as evidence?"

"I won't need to use it in court," Allison replied. "Schoeman's going to have a lot of pressure on him after tonight. I'll get what I need from the recordings, hopefully, and take it to him myself. I'll tell him that the Brunetti family might not be too happy if they knew what he was doing without offering them a cut of his take."

"Oh, I get it now. You want to get yourself killed," Charlie said. "Because a stunt like that will ensure it."

"The deal will be that he leaves the Hart family alone. All of us. Or I'll take the recording to the Brunetti family."

Charlie appeared deflated. "Cripes, Alli, you are too far out over your skis on this one. I love you and you know that, but this? This is crazy. You should let the Tampa police handle the drop and see how that plays out. You could be putting yourself in danger for nothing."

"Charlie's right," Lucy cut in. "This is too much."

"Maybe so. Maybe Detective Cooper will manage to get his man. But if not, and I have to keep looking over my shoulder along with my kids? Then the plan stays."

20

Terry Hart had kept a low profile while his family suffered the consequences of his actions. It wasn't supposed to work out like this, but it had. Now, he was finished standing on the sidelines of a problem he caused. What happened to Micah was the last straw. Everyone saw him for who he really was, and he knew it, too, when he looked in the mirror. But there was still something he could do to right this wrong.

The moment Allison told him what had happened to Micah, Terry could see she wasn't finished with him or the people with which he associated. So when she proposed a plan that would require him to get Lou Santos out of his office for a while, he agreed. It was then that he realized it was best not to underestimate Allison Hart. She had already had a hunch that Santos and Schoeman were working together with clients from the track, which included him. She was right.

Terry walked into Bayside Downs and headed straight for Santos's office. It was time for him to step up and finally take some responsibility. "Knock, knock."

Santos glanced up. "Terry. Wow. It's been—what, 3 or 4 days since you were in? I thought you'd given up your vice and changed your ways."

"Fat chance." He shuffled inside wearing his usual Hawaiian shirt and khaki shorts. "I wanted to have a word outside these walls if you can spare the time."

Santos's brow knitted. "What's wrong with my office? You know you can speak freely in here."

"Do I?" Terry replied. "Look, with all the shit that's gone down lately, and I know you know what I'm talking about, I figure it's best we step away from prying eyes and ears. How about we grab a late lunch? You hungry?"

Santos checked the time. "Come to think of it, I haven't eaten all day." He pushed off the chair. "Sure. Why not?"

"Good. How about The Wharf down the street? We can be in and out in a flash," Terry replied.

"Fine by me." The manager snatched his keys from the desk and dropped his phone into the pocket of his pants. "You've piqued my interest now. I'm anxious to hear what's on your mind."

Terry shuffled out of the office, and both headed outside to his car. "I'll drive."

"Sorry, no offense, Terry, but I'd feel better driving if it's all the same to you," Santos replied.

"Even better. Saves me the gas." Terry followed him to his car and slipped onto the passenger seat with a bit of a moan.

Santos turned the engine. "I think this is the first time you've offered to buy me lunch."

Terry glanced at him. "Oh, I'm paying for this? I'm joshing you. I got it."

Within minutes, they'd arrived at The Wharf, which wasn't much more than a white building with blue trim and some fishnet thrown haphazardly around for effect. The 4-foot tall lighthouse at the entrance was a nice touch.

Santos opened the door. "After you, sir."

Terry walked inside and approached the host desk. "Two please."

"Of course. Right this way." A young man wearing a white polo shirt and navy pants grabbed two menus and started toward the back of the restaurant. He gestured to a booth that overlooked the parking lot. "Will this do?"

"Just fine. Thank you," Terry replied.

As they both took their seats, the host handed over the menus. "Your server will be with you in a moment."

"Appreciate it." Terry slipped on his reading glasses and opened the menu.

Santos appeared cagey as he watched Terry. "Do you want to get to the reason why I'm really here, or do you plan on keeping up this farce that we're friends or something?"

―――――

THERE WAS a way to bring down the operation Lou Santos and Gus Schoeman had in place. Allison wasn't oblivious to the dangers, as Charlie and Lucy had so clearly pointed out. However, she had help from an unexpected source. Terry wanted to make up for what happened to Micah. Nothing could ever come close to making up for something like that, but Allison decided to use him to get what she needed. While Gus Schoeman was the real target, the relationship between Santos and him was what she'd wanted to expose. Santos was easier to get to.

Gathering audio to determine the scope of the arrangement and who else among the racetrack's clientele had been targeted was the goal. And the notion stood that it would only be used to ensure Schoeman backed off the Hart family. Any other use would place Allison's business in jeopardy.

Rarely did Allison rely on her looks to get what she wanted. In her younger years, sure, but not anymore. Aging might've had something to do with that too. While heads still turned for her, they tended to be more of the gray-haired variety. The realization of that fact grew clearer when she approached the customer service desk and spied the young, attractive man behind it, who hadn't taken much notice of her. "Hi, there."

He had a pointed chin, almond-shaped eyes, and wore his hair to his shoulders. "Yes, how can I help you, ma'am?"

"I'm Allison Lynch and I was looking for the manager, Mr. Santos. Is he around by any chance?" With her middle finger, she tucked behind her ear a strand of blonde hair that had fallen out of her bun. A move she'd learned a long time ago that used to work wonders. Her toned and tanned bare shoulder raised slightly. Yeah, it was all coming back to her now, though she'd begun to feel her efforts were in vain.

"He went out for a little while. Is there anything I can help you with?"

She was scrapping the ploy. It wasn't working on the young Millennial. Time to come up with something else. "Actually, it's kind of personal. Would it be possible for me to jot down a note and leave it for him in his office? It would only take a minute."

He wore a mild scowl as his gaze vacillated between the manager's office and her.

Allison leaned in closer to him and raised her brows. "It's just that I don't think he'd want anyone to know I was here, if you know what I mean. I can keep it quiet, but I sort of need your help to do that."

He pulled back, appearing ready to pass judgment. "Oh. I

wouldn't want it to come to all that. His office is right over there. Just be quick."

"Absolutely. I'll be sure and let him know just how very helpful you've been today." She spun on her heel and her pleasant demeanor vanished.

The office door was just ahead and she walked inside. The eyes of the kid at customer service burrowed into the back of her head and Allison wasn't about to press her luck. Get in and get out.

Santos's desk was littered with papers. He was not an organized man and that was a good thing. Allison scoped out the best location for the device that was as near to his voice as possible. That meant it would be somewhere around this heap on his desk. He didn't have a desk lamp, though if he had, it might've been too obvious a choice. The flat screen computer monitor wouldn't work well either. Then she figured it out.

Allison walked around his desk and pulled out the pencil drawer. A quick glance into the hall and it appeared no one could see her from where she stood. Now was her chance. She reached inside her bag and retrieved the recording device, a small piece of electronics that looked like a USB drive with a sticky base. She affixed it to the bottom of the pencil drawer and double-checked that it didn't catch on the drawer guides. "Perfect."

Allison pulled upright and tugged on her white sleeveless blouse before sliding her purse strap over her shoulder again. Wearing a pleasant grin, she walked out and looked over at the customer service desk. The young man eyed her, and Allison winked at him before making her way downstairs. When she stepped outside, she took in a breath as though she'd been underwater for the past five minutes. "Just get the hell out of here."

———

TERRY SET down his glass of water. "The part about buying you lunch is true. But there is more, which was why I wanted to talk away from the track." He peered out for a moment into the parking lot. "I need your help, Lou."

Santos sighed. "What is it now? You owe the big man still? I thought that was all worked out?"

"It was—for a while. Look, I don't know what to do. I gotta come up with 16k."

"16 grand? What the hell, Terry?" Santos replied.

"It's a long story. Can you help me or not?" Terry pressed on.

"A long story, my ass. What the hell did you get yourself into, huh? You think I can bail you out? What am I, a magician?"

"I just need you to talk to Gus for me. Vouch for me, yeah? Can you do that? Can you assure him I'm good for it?"

Santos set down his fork. "Are you, Terry? Because I'm not seeing it. I'm seeing a washed-up, old gambler always grasping at straws looking to make one final bet to reclaim his losses and strike it rich. I can't help you. I'm not sure anyone can."

Terry shoved his BLT into his mouth and took a bite. As he chewed, he dabbed the corners of his mouth with a napkin. When he finally swallowed, he laced together his fingers and eyed the manager. "I was really hoping you'd go with me on this, Lou. I consider you a friend, despite what you might think." He cleared his throat. "Did I mention to you that my daughter-in-law is a P.I.?"

Santos regarded him. "No, I don't think you did. In fact, I didn't think your son was married.

"Technically, she's my ex-daughter-in-law. Beautiful woman. Smart as a whip. Knows when shit stinks."

"What the hell are you getting at, Terry?" he asked.

"I'm just saying, she picks up on things real fast. Things that maybe she shouldn't, you know what I'm talking about?"

Santos pulled back his shoulders in defiance. "No, I don't think I do. Maybe you need to spell it out for me because what I'm hearing you say is that our deal isn't working for you anymore. Maybe you're looking for some kind of retribution. That's what I'm hearing. Is that what you're saying?"

Terry shrugged. "Who knows? I'm just putting it out there." He eyed Santos's plate of food. "Finish your lunch. It's good food."

The rest of the meal was shrouded in silence except for the low chatter of other diners. Terry couldn't be sure if the threat sunk in or if Santos was just going to blow him off. Of course, the money was covered thanks to the Tampa Police, but Terry needed Santos in his pocket for the next time. He needed to know if the man would have his back. Guess he got his answer.

Terry paid the bill, as promised, and returned his wallet to his shorts' pocket. "We should probably head on out. What do you say?"

"That's probably best. I need to get back to work." Santos tossed his napkin onto his plate. "Appreciate the lunch, Terry."

"My pleasure." He slid out of the narrow booth and trailed the manager outside.

They continued to Santos's car and both stepped in. Terry glanced at him from the passenger seat. "Look, man, about earlier..."

He turned the ignition. "Are you gonna say you didn't mean it? That you were just scared because you don't want Schoeman breathing down your neck?" Santos pulled out of the lot and headed down the road. "Because I sure as shit don't like being threatened, Terry."

"I'm just telling you like it is. I wish it wasn't, but I gotta look after myself and my interests. I know you'd do the same."

Santos nodded and drove on. "Whatever, man."

When they passed by the racetrack, Terry eyed him. "Where the hell you going? You missed the turn."

Santos said nothing.

"Hey. I'm talking to you," Terry insisted. "Oh, what are you taking me to see Schoeman like a good little soldier? You think his people can't find me or something? They took me two days ago."

Santos still refused to speak and only drove on.

"What are you, deaf?" Terry shouted. "You don't have to take me to him. He knows I owe him money." Several more minutes went by when Santos finally stopped the car on the side of the road. "Finally. Christ, man, what the hell's wrong with you?"

Santos reached down to his feet and retrieved a gun.

"Whoa! What the hell, man?" Terry instinctively raised his hands. "Look, I got no beef with you, Lou. You know that."

"You threatened to turn me in. Actually, you said your daughter-in-law would do it."

"She's not..."

"I don't give a shit." He cocked the gun. "You screwed up, Terry. I gave you chance after chance. Gus gave you chance after chance. You just couldn't stop, could you? You dragged your family into this shit. Who does that?"

"Look, I spoke out of turn earlier..."

"You think?" Santos replied.

"Yeah, and I'm sorry, okay? No one's going to say nothing about nothing. I swear it."

Santos revealed a crooked smile. "You addicts are all the same. I don't care if it's drugs, alcohol, or gambling. You're all the same pathetic pieces of shit who use everyone and take responsibility for nothing."

"Man, you know Schoeman's gonna be pissed if you do this, right?" Terry pleaded. "He's counting on me paying back the 16k."

Santos scoffed. "Like you could ever do that."

Terry considered spilling his guts on the drop tonight. Telling him that the cops would be there, and they'd arrest whoever Schoeman sent to pick up the cash. It was the only way out of this. "Look, man, here's the deal…"

The gun fired. Terry's eyes widened and his lips parted. He looked down at his chest and watched the blood soak through his yellow Hawaiian shirt. It ran down to his khaki shorts and then he felt the warmth on his leg. He returned his gaze to Santos.

"Sorry, man. I can't risk it. But thanks for telling me all about your daughter-in-law."

Terry slumped over.

21

The drop was scheduled for tonight and it had reached early evening already. The duffle bag containing $16,000 sat on Detective Cooper's desk and Shane waited with him for word on Terry's whereabouts.

Leo hurried toward them. "I can't find him. I called his cell phone. He's not answering. I don't know where he is."

Cooper rubbed his smooth, but aged face. "God damn it. I knew I should've brought him down earlier."

"Have you talked to him today?" Shane asked.

"This morning. After Leo and I spoke about whether Schoeman reached out to Terry or not, I made the call to speak with him myself. I needed a level of comfort that he wasn't going to flake."

"And yet it appears he did," Shane replied. "What the hell are we going to do now?"

Allison had arrived at the station because she'd wanted to be there when Terry prepared to make the drop. She had to let him know that he had done a good thing today and she did what she needed to do. But on her arrival, she caught up to Detective Cooper at his desk and noticed something wasn't right. "What's going on? Where's Terry?"

"Good question," Cooper replied. "We can't seem to get hold of him."

"I can go to his apartment and see if he's there," Allison said.

Cooper swiped his keys from his desk. "Let me."

After he disappeared into the hall, Allison walked to Leo. "You haven't talked to him today?"

"Not since this morning. Alli, what the hell are we going to do? I should've expected something like this from him. He hasn't changed at all."

"Just give him the benefit of the doubt. I'm sure he's scared out of his mind about all this."

"Yeah, we all are," Leo replied.

Shane touched Allison's shoulder and she spun around. "You don't need to be here, and especially after what happened..."

"I want to be. I want to see this to the end," she replied. "I talked to Terry a few hours ago. He seemed fine."

"Wait, you talked to him?" Shane pressed on.

"Must've been around 2 or 3 o'clock, I think." She knew damn well when she spoke to him and knew exactly what he'd planned on doing to clear Santos from his office. "I do know where he was going around that time."

"Where?" Leo asked.

"Lunch with a friend from the racetrack. That's what he told me," she replied.

"Allison, did he say where he was going for lunch?" Shane continued.

"No, but I'm sure the man he was with could tell you. He was having lunch with the manager from the racetrack." Her mind raced as to what had happened. Had Terry gotten cold feet after talking with Santos? What if he warned him? What if Santos knew everything and Terry went into hiding? She wouldn't be safe if he called her out. Maybe he wasn't a changed man after all.

"Hang on," Shane began. "Lou Santos, the same guy you suspect has a less than kosher business relationship with Gus Schoeman."

"Yes. I don't have proof, but it's a hunch. I'm pretty sure he was with Terry a few hours ago. He might know where he is now."

"No point in waiting," Leo said. "Let's go there now. It'll take ten minutes."

Allison couldn't show her face there again, not after pretending to be the manager's mistress. The guy at Customer Service would point her out in a heartbeat. "I don't think we all need to go. Shane, do you think Leo could handle that? We can wait to see what Cooper learns at Terry's apartment and have Leo call when he finds out where the two had lunch. You and I can make a run to the last place he was seen and go from there."

"Agreed." Shane turned to Leo. "Probably best not to have the police show up asking questions about Terry anyway. Go see what the manager has to say and get back to me asap."

"You got it." With a nod, Leo headed out.

"I don't have a good feeling about this, Allison," Shane said. "I think your ex-father-in-law got cold feet and bailed on us. If that's the case, we're screwed."

"I really didn't think he would do that," she replied.

"Why not? You know him better than I do. He let your kid get wrapped up in this. Why would you think he'd care about anyone other than himself? Even Leo believes that." Shane reached for his phone as a call came in. "It's Cooper." With the phone at his ear, he answered. "You find him?"

"No luck. His car isn't here. From the outside, the apartment looks dark. I think he's gone," Cooper replied.

"We have four hours before the scheduled drop. What the hell are we going to do?" Shane's attention was drawn to an approaching officer. He lowered the phone for a moment. "Yeah?"

"Detective Sully, a call just came in about a body found on the side of Brooker Creek Boulevard opposite the retention pond. Officer Talbert's on scene."

Shane's brow creased. "That's pretty close to the racetrack. I'll head out there now."

Allison paced a small circle. "Oh my God."

"Just hang on. We don't know anything right now." He returned to the call with Cooper. "We have a potential problem. Meet me at Brooker Creek Boulevard."

Allison stopped on a dime. "I'm coming with you."

———

THE POKER ROOM and surrounding bars were packed at the racetrack. Leo walked into the crowd and through to the pavilion where the bets were placed. A customer service desk was on the left side, and he approached. "Evening. Can I speak to the manager, please?"

"And you are?" the man asked.

"He's a friend of my father and as I understand it, the two met for lunch earlier today. I'd like to talk to him about that," Leo replied.

"Mr. Santos has gone home for the evening. Our second shift manager is in his office if you'd like to have a word."

"Thank you, no. I needed to speak to Mr. Santos. I appreciate your time." Leo turned and headed back out again. The lights in the parking lot burned as he made his way back to his car. He stopped a moment, unable to recall the row in which he'd parked and surveyed the lot. That was when he spotted it. "What the hell?" Leo hurried to Terry's car and peered inside. He picked up his phone. "Alli, it's me. Dad's car is here. He's not and neither is Lou Santos."

Allison was in the passenger seat of Shane's car. "Leo, listen, Shane and I are heading out to Brooker Creek Boulevard, near the track."

"Okay, why?" Leo asked.

"I don't know how to say this exactly..."

"Oh, God. Alli, what's wrong?"

"I don't know yet. Maybe nothing. We're almost there," she replied.

"I'm on my way." He ended the call and scrambled for his keys in his pocket while he rushed to his car. He recognized her tone, having heard it whenever something bad happened to one of the kids. Maybe deep inside, he already knew what she couldn't bring herself to say. Terry's car was in the parking lot of the track. No one had heard from him since Allison spoke to him earlier in the afternoon. The deck was stacked against him.

Leo drove straight on toward Brooker Creek Boulevard. Within minutes, he arrived, and the flashing red and blue lights were a good indicator that he was in the right spot. Leo parked behind one of the three patrol cars and steadied himself for what was to come. The only way out was through. He'd heard that somewhere.

He stepped out of his car and the scene took him by surprise. Officers were in the process of cordoning off the area. Flashes from cameras went off everywhere. And when a shadowed figure approached him, it took a minute for him to see that it was her. "Alli. Is it him? Is it my dad?"

"I'm so sorry, Leo."

"Oh, God." He hunched over as if he'd been punched in the gut. When he caught his breath again, he returned upright. "What happened to him?"

Allison appeared at a loss for words and so when Shane approached, she deferred to him.

"Leo, I'm truly sorry for your loss," he said.

"Please tell me what happened to him," Leo replied.

"Terry sustained a gunshot wound to his chest. Point blank. It took him quickly."

Leo walked into the road with his hands on his hips. He stopped and turned back. "Who the hell did this? Was it that Gus Schoeman? Why would he do that when Dad was about to pay him?"

"There's no indication it was Schoeman," Shane began. "The drop is still scheduled for 11pm. We don't have much time to make that happen."

"Wait. We're going through with it?" Leo asked.

"We have to see this through. Schoeman may not know Terry's gone," Shane replied.

Leo's face masked in confusion. "Then who the hell killed my father?"

"The last man who was with him. Lou Santos," Allison cut in. "As far as we know, he was with Terry this afternoon. And you checked the track. He wasn't there."

"No." Leo shoved his hands into his pockets. "One of his staff said he'd already gone home. I didn't ask questions. I didn't know I needed to." He lowered his head and closed his eyes.

Allison placed her arm around his shoulders. "I'm so sorry, Leo. I'm so very sorry."

Shane stepped away from the intimate family moment.

"The drop has to happen, Leo," Allison said. "It's our best

chance at pinning something on Schoeman's people. It could help us get to the man, himself."

Leo pulled in a deep breath and wiped his eyes before the tears spilled. "But you don't think Schoeman had anything to do with Terry's death?" Leo asked.

"Honestly, I don't know. I think it might have something to do with Lou Santos. Your dad and he might've had a deal or something. I can't really say, but it seems suspicious that Santos had lunch with Terry, then Terry ends up dead."

"And Dad's car was at the racetrack," Leo added.

"It was? You saw it yourself?" she pressed on.

"I did, then you called. Alli, you could be right about Santos."

"Hang on." Allison spun around and hurried toward Shane, who had been speaking to the responding officer. "Detective Sully?"

Shane peered over his shoulder at her and turned back to the officer. "Excuse me for a moment." He followed her as she started back to Leo. "What is it?"

"Leo says he saw Terry's car at the racetrack." She nodded for Leo to continue.

"Right, then Alli called and, well, everything sort of went fuzzy for a minute. When I got here, I forgot to tell you."

"Shit." Shane thrust his hands on his hips as he appeared to consider his next move. "Okay, so the manager's gone home, according to his staff. Terry's car is sitting in the racetrack parking lot, and the two were slated to have lunch. We're left to assume Terry got into Santos's car. No one heard from him after that. And we'll get Ballistics back soon enough on the bullet. If it's from a registered gun, we'll know." He peered at Leo. "Santos. We need to bring him in for questioning ASAP."

Allison checked the time. "Cooper should be here any minute. What about the drop? You said it has to happen."

Shane nodded. "We have to keep to the plan. The coroner is on his way. There's nothing more we can do for your dad right now, Leo. But we will find whoever did this to him. In the meantime, I don't want to lose focus on the man who we're certain ordered your daughter to be kidnapped."

Detective Cooper's car rolled up behind them. He jumped out and headed over. "Is it him?"

Shane nodded.

Cooper closed his eyes. "Damn it. What are we going to do about tonight?" He turned to Leo. "I don't mean to sound heartless. I'm sorry for your loss."

"It's okay, thank you," Leo replied.

Cooper returned a reassuring nod. "Who's doing the drop then, if not Terry?"

"Me," Leo cut in. "It has to be me."

"What? No way," Allison replied. "This doesn't have anything to do with you."

"Or you, Alli," Leo cut in. "Look, I'm his son. I will take care of this. It's that, or we'll have to worry about Schoeman trying to collect another way. Dead or not, he's going to want the money Terry owed him. And then we put the son of a bitch in jail. Him and his buddy, Santos."

"It's the right call, Allison." Shane looked at Leo. "We have two hours. Schoeman may or may not know about Terry. My guess is, he doesn't. If there is some sort of deal between Santos and Schoeman, then I have a feeling Santos acted on his own. There's no reason to take out Terry Hart when the man was about to repay his debt."

"Unless Terry let slip that the plan was about to go down," Cooper replied. "I'm not ruling out anything right now. But we do need to go on as if nothing's changed."

Allison regarded Leo. "I trust these guys to keep you safe. I don't want you to have to do this, but I'm not sure there's a choice. We have to think about the kids and what it could mean for them if we don't follow through with this."

"I know, babe—uh, Alli. Sorry." He turned to Shane "So, what do I do?"

"We head back to the station. We have the cash, and the team is getting ready now. Detective Cooper and I can fill you in on the way. If you're good with it, I'll have one of the officers drive your car back and you go with us. We need as much time as possible to make sure this goes off smoothly." He turned to Allison. "You head home. There's nothing more for you to do tonight. It's our turn to see this through."

"I'd feel better if I waited at the station. I'll have Charlie stay with me for moral support."

"Fair enough." Shane started ahead. "We should head back now."

————

CHARLIE RUSHED inside the station and headed straight to Detective Cooper's desk to find Leo and Allison standing nearby. "Leo, I'm so sorry about your dad."

"Thanks, Charlie," he replied.

She turned to Allison. "How are you holding up?"

"Hey, Charlie. Thanks for coming down. I'm doing okay," she replied.

Shane made his way to them. "Okay, Leo, you know the plan. We have the cash. It's time to move out." He turned to Detective Cooper. "Is the team ready?"

"They're ready. Let's get this show on the road. Leo, are you sure you're ready for this?"

"I am," he replied.

"Then it's time." Cooper turned on his heel.

"Leo, wait." Allison pressed her hand against his shoulder. "Just do exactly what these guys say, okay? Don't veer off the plan. Your kids need you, you understand?"

"I understand. Everything will be fine. I'm going to make sure the people who took Micah get what they deserve."

22

The coffee at the station came from an old machine and tasted a little too earthy for Allison's liking, but it gave her something to hold onto besides her phone. Willing it to ring with an update hadn't been working. The team had been gone for only half an hour, but it felt like an eternity.

"Did Shane send someone to pick up Lou Santos?" Charlie sipped on her own stale brew.

"Yes, Detective Lopez, I think? Of course, I'd be surprised if Santos stuck around waiting to be picked up by the police for murder."

"What about the bug? Did you tell Shane about it?"

"No." Allison cast down her gaze. "It all happened so fast."

"And the recordings? Can you access them? If Santos went back to his office after doing what we all think he did, and made calls, you might have a confession on those recordings. You could have it all on tape."

"I didn't think about checking it. I can access the audio

remotely, but I don't have my laptop." Allison scanned the bullpen. "I need a computer."

"Let's check up front. Carol's still here. She might be able to help." Charlie started toward the lobby and when Allison didn't follow, she turned back. "Alli? Are you coming or not?"

"Yeah, I'm coming."

Charlie reached the front desk. "Hey, Carol, Allison has a question for you."

"Allison, what's going on?" she asked.

"I need access to a computer. Any computer. Can you help me out?"

"Sure. We have a guest office. You can use the computer in there." Carol slipped out from behind the desk and glanced to a colleague. "Hold down the fort? I'll be right back." She turned back to Allison. "Follow me. I'll get you signed on."

"Thanks, I appreciate it."

"Don't sweat it. Are you working on a case?" she asked.

"Uh, yeah. I am. We are, actually. Charlie and I have something in the fire," Allison replied.

"Cool." The officer opened the door. "In here. We keep an office open for visiting officials and outside law enforcement. I'll get you logged in and you can have at it. Oh, but you should know, the websites are monitored. Sorry. It's the rules."

"No problem. I understand," Allison replied.

The officer punched in the keys and the screen illuminated. "Here you go. All set. Just log out when you're finished."

"Great. Thanks so much, Carol," Allison replied.

"Anytime. I'll leave you both to it." She closed the door behind her.

Charlie hovered over Allison's shoulder. "What if Santos called someone and confessed?"

"I don't think he's dumb enough to do that, but I've been

wrong before." She clicked the commands and retrieved the website. "I'm logged in. We're about to find out if he spilled his guts."

"And if he did?" Charlie asked. "It'll be an illegally obtained confession."

Allison glanced at her. "Let's deal with one thing at a time." She opened the audio files and pressed play. Shuffling paperwork and background noise were all that could be heard for the first couple of minutes.

"He's doing something. Packing up and preparing to leave town, maybe?" Charlie asked.

"Hard to say. This was recorded at around 3 o'clock, so we know he went back to his office after it happened," Allison replied.

"It's me..." a voice began.

"That's him," Allison said. "I recognize the voice."

"I screwed up—big time. I need your help," he continued. *"I don't want to say over the phone. Can I meet you? It has to be now. I'll explain everything."*

More shuffling sounded before the man spoke again. *"They'll be coming for me soon. If you can't help me, they'll come for you too. No, man, it's not a threat. It's just the way it is."*

They traded glances as both appeared to wait for the magic words.

"I put an end to a threat, okay? That's all I can say. Look, man, you gotta come through for me on this. I'm out of time. Fine. Yeah. I'll meet you there in twenty minutes."

They waited for more, but only background noise sounded.

Allison peered at her. "I think he ended the call."

"We don't know who he was talking to," Charlie added. "This doesn't help us at all."

"It does. He all but admitted to killing Terry, Charlie. Didn't you hear what he said?"

Charlie stepped away from her. "I heard a guy talking and not saying a whole lot except that he was in trouble. What the hell good does it do us? We don't know the other party on that call."

Allison pulled out a flash drive from her purse. "I'm going to download this. We have to give it to Lopez. It could help her when she questions Santos."

"Assuming she finds him. And remember, she won't be able to use the recording against him," Charlie replied.

"I'm aware."

"And when she asks how you got this information?" Charlie pressed on.

"It fell into our laps," Allison replied.

"What about the rest of it? The part where I'm supposed to get a loan from the Winthrop Group. That was how we were going to get Schoeman. How do we get him now? What about all that money you lost? Look, Lou Santos just dug his own grave. I'm not sure we should give up what we have here. Lopez will pull the manager's cell phone records. She'll find out who he was talking to on that call. The evidence will point to Santos. I'm sure of it."

"What are you saying, Charlie?"

"I'm saying, we use what's on this audio file. We keep to the plan, and I meet with Schoeman. He won't want the Brunetti family knowing what he's done behind their backs. Not cutting them in on the deal. Alli, we have to push forward. With this? We're closer than ever to ensuring Schoeman pays for what he did to Micah. And isn't that what you wanted?"

———

LEO WAS in the front seat of Detective Cooper's car as they sat a block away from the drop location.

"You're sure you can do this? It's not too late to back out," Cooper said.

"Yes, it is. I think we all know that," Leo replied. "It'll destroy any case you thought you had or could build. I'm not in the same business as Alli, but she does talk to me. I know this is the kind of stuff she has to deal with. Can't say I'm happy about it, but I get it now. I understand and I'm ready to do this."

Shane was in the backseat and pulled up. "We'll have eyes on you the entire time, you got it? It's a simple case of drop the bag and walk away. That's the extent of your part in this."

"I got it, Shane. And you'll arrest the man who picks up the bag, right?" Leo asked.

"That's the plan," Cooper replied. "I have three of my guys surrounding the area. This building is empty, so there are lots of hiding places. As soon as he picks up the cash, we close in. Easy peasy." Cooper checked the time. "This is it, Mr. Hart. This is for your daughter and for your pop."

Leo opened the door to step out. "So long as you catch the bastards, I don't care what happens to me."

"Nothing's going to happen to you," Shane said as Leo closed the door. He peered at Cooper. "I swear to God, nothing better happen to him."

Leo walked toward the front of the high-rise that was still under construction. The bay glistened beside him under the bright light of a full moon. The sound of boats swaying and lines hitting the docks offered familiarity and comfort. He held the suitcase stuffed with $16,000 and his palm sweated on the handle. It wasn't a lot of cash in the grand scheme of things, but it was more than he'd ever held onto in his life. Thoughts of Terry drifted in and out. Some good, some bad. There would be a time to properly mourn him, but that time was not now, not when Allison needed him the most. Jenny hadn't known about any of this. She knew it was supposed to happen tonight, but she hadn't known what happened to Terry. Leo figured it was best to keep her safe from knowing more than she needed to. And it would only cause her to worry—and get angry with him. Rightly so, he imagined. But this was something he had to do. Terry had been a thorn in his side pretty much since the beginning. Why would the fact that he was dead be any different?

The spot was just ahead. A signpost without a sign near the entrance. That was where he was to leave the cash. From there, he would just continue down the walkway back toward the parking lot. The lot was empty. Shane and Detective Cooper waited down the block. Where were these so-called "eyes" that were supposed to be on him? He glanced around as if he could spot them. Maybe that wasn't the best idea. It occurred to him Schoeman's people were also probably out there somewhere, watching; making sure no cops were around. And here Leo was, practically searching for them. "Just keep your cool, man," he whispered.

A quick check of the time on his watch. "One minute." Leo reached the signpost and set down the suitcase. All he had to do now was leave, but the voice startled him.

"Buddy? You got ears or what? I been calling out to you." A heavy-set bald man with a cigarette hanging from his lips emerged from the darkness.

Leo spun around. "Huh?"

"Who the hell are you?" the man asked. "You ain't Terry."

———

ALL THEY HAD WAS radio contact. The detectives waited in the car a block away while Cooper's team kept eyes on the drop.

The radio came to life. "Cooper, we have a problem."

He reached for the receiver. "What is it?"

"They're talking. Hart was supposed to drop the bag and leave, but the guy picking it up stopped him. I don't know what they're saying, but Hart looks nervous. What do you want us to do?"

"Has the guy picked up the bag?" Cooper asked.

"Not yet."

"Shit." He peered at Shane. "Then they know Leo isn't Terry."

"They have to move in," Shane demanded. "Get Leo the hell out of there now."

"We can't arrest the man if he doesn't pick up the money, Sully. You know that. We have to let Hart play this out." Cooper pressed the receiver. "Be ready. If you see a gun, shoot him before he shoots Hart, you hear me?"

"Copy that."

"Christ." Shane looked out the passenger window. "I need to get over there. Leo's a damn P.E. teacher, not an undercover cop. He doesn't know what the hell he's doing. He's going to get himself killed." Shane opened the door.

"Stop," Cooper said. "If he sees you or if Schoeman has anybody else watching, and I have no doubt he does, you'll be signing Hart's death warrant. You got me, Sully? My team's on this. They'll take him out if anything starts to go south."

"I think we're beyond that now," Shane replied. "I think Schoeman's here, himself. He's watching this go down. He must know what happened to Terry Hart, which means, he knows we're in on this. I'm telling you, Cooper, it's time to pull the plug."

––––––––

LEO STOOD FROZEN in place while his mind raced to find the words. The man before him, beady-eyed, and grizzled, looked ready to cut him down and if Leo didn't talk fast, he wouldn't be talking at all. "I'm not Terry. He was my father. Someone killed him today. You wouldn't know anything about that, would you?" Sweat beaded on the back of his neck and at the top of his hairline. Had this guy noticed the fear in Leo's eyes, yet?

The man scoffed. "No, man. I'm sorry for your loss." There was no sentiment behind his words. "If he's dead, why bother with the drop? It was Terry who owed, not you."

"I didn't want anyone coming after my family again, like they did my daughter," Leo replied. "Terry was a son of a bitch most of the time. I don't want to have to worry about paying off his associates for the rest of my life."

The man nodded. "What do you know about that? About what went down the other night?"

"Just that my daughter was left alone and she found a way out. She's safe and far away from here. And anyone who comes near her again will have to go through me first," Leo replied.

The man chuckled before he glanced at the duffle bag. "Is it all there?"

"Yes. Now your boss has no reason to come at us again. None." Leo waited for a response. "Are you going to keep to the deal, or what? I got better things to do."

The man raised a brow. "You got yourself a pretty big set on you, huh?" He glanced at the bag, then toward the building.

Leo narrowed his eyes for only a moment, considering that there were other people here working for Schoeman. Just like there were other cops here, too. Who outnumbered who, and was this about to be a shootout? He quickly surveyed the grounds in search of safety should gunfire erupt. Maybe he'd seen too many movies, but then again, this whole situation felt like he was in a Dirty Harry movie.

The man stepped toward the bag and glanced at Leo. "You should probably go now, friend."

Leo's heart dropped into his stomach as he turned on his heel and started walking away. The idea he'd be shot in the back loomed large and his pace quickened. When were they going to close in on this guy? Where was Cooper's team?

———

THE RADIO SOUNDED AGAIN in Cooper's car. "He picked up the cash. We're ready on your command."

Cooper pressed the button on the receiver. "Where's Hart? Is he clear?"

"About 100-odd feet and he'll be clear. Give us the word, Detective."

Shane peered at him. "What are you waiting for?"

"I need to know Hart's far enough away. Schoeman isn't stupid. He'll have his people out there, same as we do. In fact, they might already know we have a team waiting. If Hart's anywhere near when shit goes south, they'll burn him."

Shane knew he was right, but the longer they waited, the better chance Schoeman's man had of getting away. Then all of this would have been for nothing. "He has to be clear now. It's time to move, Cooper."

The team leader's voice sounded again. "Cooper, he's leaving, man. What's the word?"

"Is Hart clear?" he asked.

"100 percent."

Cooper turned the engine. "Go." He pulled the gearshift into Drive and pressed on the gas. A hard right, and he was on the street backing up to the building. Leo was supposed to head to that rear lot. "Jesus, do you see Hart?"

Shane peered into the dark, empty parking lot with wide eyes. "Where are you, Leo? Come on."

Cooper slammed on the brakes and opened his door. "You

hear that? It's going down. I gotta get the hell over there. Find Hart!"

Shane jumped out of the passenger side and brandished his gun. "Leo? Where the hell are you?" Cooper was already heading to the front of the building where raised voices sounded, but he had to find him. "Leo?" he shouted.

The chaos grew as more voices yelled out. There must've been half a dozen or more people by the sound of it. "Leo?" Shane called out again. "Come on man, where are you?" He pressed on near the back of the empty building.

Gunfire erupted. Shane stopped in his tracks. "Cooper!" He ran toward the front where the shots had been fired. "Cooper!" When he reached the front of the building, Shane looked on. "Holy shit."

23

Detective Cooper stood over what appeared to be the lifeless body of an unidentified man. The only known factor was that this man had worked for Schoeman. He had been the designated pick-up for the cash. Now, he was dead. The others in Schoeman's crew, gone.

Shane jogged toward him. "What the hell happened?"

"It's like they were waiting for us. Like they knew we would be here," Cooper replied. "The other two took off. Didn't even try to return fire."

"Who fired the first shot?" Shane pressed on.

"I did, sir." An officer in tactical gear approached them. "I saw this guy was reaching for something. I couldn't take the chance. Our man was just outside range, but I couldn't risk it."

Cooper kicked the gun a few inches from the dead man's hands. "He was right. The guy was armed. It would've been him or us." He surveyed the grounds. "Where the hell is Hart?"

"I don't know. I called out to him in the back where he was supposed to meet us," Shane replied.

"He must be hiding somewhere, not that I blame him." Cooper turned to his team leader. "Go find him, would you?"

"Copy that." The officer gathered the rest of his team and started ahead.

"What the hell are we supposed to do now?" Shane asked. "We needed this guy to leverage Schoeman."

"I'm aware," Cooper said. "You heard from Lopez yet on Lou Santos? He should be in the station being questioned by now."

Shane retrieved his phone. "Shit. Missed call." He pressed the contact button. "Hey, Lopez, it's Sully. What's the word on Lou Santos? You bring him in?" Shane's brow knitted as the detective spoke on the other end of the line. "God damn it." He peered at Cooper. "He wasn't home. His wife said she hadn't seen him or heard from him since around noon." Shane returned his attention to the call. "Okay. We'll be in soon and we'll have to get a warrant issued and a BOLO. Yeah, got it. Thanks, Lopez." Shane ended the call. "Gives us a pretty damn good idea who killed Terry Hart. This dead guy here isn't going to help us get to Schoeman. If Allison's right and Santos has some sort of arrangement with Schoeman, that might be our in."

Cooper eyed him. "Then we'd sure as hell better find him."

———

ALLISON AND CHARLIE hadn't heard anything from Shane or Detective Cooper. The drop was scheduled to go down more than 30 minutes ago. Allison peered at her phone. "I should call him."

"Shane?" Charlie asked as they waited at Cooper's desk.

"No. Leo. I should've heard from him by now. Something's wrong, Charlie. I can feel it."

"Nothing's wrong. You would've heard from one of them if it was. What concerns me more is that Lopez hasn't returned."

"We have to face it, Charlie. Santos is gone." Allison's concern over Leo weighed on her mind, even more so than bringing in the man suspected of murdering Leo's father. He wasn't cut out for this kind of thing. Most people weren't, not even Allison, herself. But he'd volunteered anyway and now she considered the possibility that something could've happened to him. Allison shook her head. "No."

Charlie looked back. "What's that?"

"Nothing."

Charlie offered a reassuring hand. "Leo's fine. Shane's fine. You have to trust that the detectives know what they're doing."

Allison nodded. "You're right."

The partners headed back to the lobby when Charlie approached Carol at the front desk. "Hey, thanks for helping us out with the computer access earlier. I don't suppose you've gotten word on Detective Lopez's return. We're hoping she's bringing in the man they think is responsible for the murder of Allison's father-in-law."

"Right, I'm so sorry about that. Last I heard, Detective Lopez was on her way back, empty-handed. The next step is usually issuing a warrant for his arrest and a BOLO on his vehicle." She regarded Allison. "Is there anything I can do to help you?"

"I don't think so but thank you. We appreciate the heads up." Allison started back toward the bullpen.

Charlie hurried to catch up to Allison. "Alli, wait."

She stopped at Cooper's desk. "This whole thing has spun out of control."

"There's nothing you could've done to stop what happened to Terry today," Charlie replied.

"Of course there was. I was the one who asked him to get Santos out of his office so I could plant a bug. My God, Charlie, he's dead because of me. And now his killer is missing. I haven't heard from Leo. God knows what happened at the drop. How did this spiral so quickly?"

"Okay, Alli, I know you think this is on you, but it's not. I'm sorry to say, this is on Terry. I know I shouldn't speak ill of the dead, but all you did was try to help. No way could you have known that man was going to kill him." Charlie ushered her to a chair near the detective's desk. "Just sit down a minute and let's think this through. Lopez will track down Santos. That's her job. I wish we knew what was happening with Leo right now, but I..." Charlie's attention was diverted. "They're back."

The detectives walked into the bullpen and Allison leapt from the chair. "Where's Leo? Where's Leo?"

"I'm right here." He emerged from behind them. "I'm okay."

"Oh, thank God." Allison threw her arms around his broad shoulders. "Why didn't you call? I've been worried sick. Are you okay?"

"I'm fine. These guys made sure of that."

Shane cleared his throat. "He did great, Allison. Exactly what he was supposed to do."

Cooper continued to his desk. "We need to get with Lopez and get an update. Right now, Schoeman's going to be on edge. Another one of his worker bees is dead. The drop was a bust. He won't be able to keep that quiet. It'll reach the Brunetti family. When it does, they'll want to know what the hell he's been up to."

"One of his men is dead?" Allison asked.

"The guy picking up the money," Cooper began. "Shit went downhill pretty fast. He reached for a gun. Our guys took him out. He had two others with him, but they fled the scene. They'll be the ones to give the news to Schoeman. So, he's lost the cash. The man who owed him that cash is dead. He's going to be scrambling. The time is now to connect the dots and take him down, along with Santos. Sully explained your thoughts on a connection between the two."

"I suspected he was using people like Terry Hart in a way that made him money. Getting them to take out lines of credits and loans with the Winthrop Group," she began. "I don't have proof, but I was working on getting it."

"How so?" Shane asked.

"We put Charlie in front of Lou Santos to see what happened. He set up a meeting with the Winthrop Group. That's the extent of it, but it led us to believe the connection between the two exists and that each was benefiting off the racetrack clientele." Allison left out the bit where, of course, Charlie had planned to meet Schoeman. "Then, earlier this morning, Terry and I hatched a plan whereby he would get Santos out of his office for a short while so I could get in and plant a recording device to gather evidence and learn what kind of partnership the two had. Terry agreed to take Santos to lunch."

"You know you can't use illegal recordings in court," Shane interjected. "And I don't even want to think about the danger you put yourself in."

"I do know the rules on unauthorized recordings," Allison continued. "I had no intention of using it in court. It was going to be my insurance. Shane, my daughter was kidnapped. If you thought for one second I was going to sit back and let him get away with that..."

Cooper scratched at his full head of hair and raised his brows. "Well, Allison, I gotta say, that's one hell of a plan. And it might've worked."

"Instead, Santos killed Terry. I had no idea that was even a remote possibility." She glanced at Leo. "I'm so sorry, Leo. He's gone because of me."

Leo held her gaze. "No. My dad was a lot of things. He pissed off a lot of people. Consider it his special talent. This isn't on you, Alli. Terry's lifestyle finally caught up to him. I'm just sorry he pulled all of us into it."

"Look, I think we're all missing the bigger picture here," Cooper began. "What happened with Terry Hart wasn't anyone's fault but the man who pulled the trigger. That said, we have a bug in Lou Santos's office, and we need to hear what you have right now."

———

It was 1 o'clock in the morning and Lou Santos had dug himself a deep grave, so he turned to the only man he thought could help. That man sat across from him now and didn't look happy about it. But this wasn't the worst thing that had happened to Gus Schoeman tonight.

His office door opened, and two men walked inside. The smell of anxiety and fear oozed from their pores. "Jesus H. Christ, I can smell you two from here. Get in and close the door."

"Mr. Schoeman, it wasn't supposed to go down like that," one of the men pleaded.

"No shit. Brewer's dead. Whose fault is that?" Schoeman asked.

"The cops surrounded us. Came out of nowhere," the other guy said. "Brewer panicked. Reached for his gun. Cops took him down just like that." He snapped his fingers to make his point. "We took off. I still don't know how we got away."

"And the money?"

The larger of the two men folded his hands in front of him and lowered his gaze. "We didn't get it, Mr. Schoeman."

Schoeman turned to Santos. "So now I got another dead employee, and the man who owes me 16k is also dead. You're the one who killed him. What the hell am I supposed to do now?"

"I can make this up to you, Gus. That older lady I sent your way? We got her hook, line, and sinker. She'll be in for it deep. You didn't see her. She reeked of desperation."

"Do you really think I can keep playing this game? Do you have any idea the shitstorm you all created for me? The family won't let this go." He pulled back. "Someone's going to have to pay for this. And it sure as hell won't be me."

"I'll have to leave town for a while," Santos began. "But I can still keep my end of the deal."

"The hell you can," Schoeman replied. "You're right about one thing. You will be leaving town. If you draw more heat on me than is already coming my way, I'll be the one to take you out myself." He turned to the other men. "As far as Brewer goes, he was working alone. You got me? Went out and decided to make a deal and it went tits up. Cost him his life. No one in the family is going to make the connection to Terry Hart or his son. We'll deal with the cops when the time comes. They got nothing on me and that's the way it's going to stay."

"What should we do?" the man asked. "They don't know who we are. I think we're in the clear."

Schoeman eyed them. "Dump your phones. They'll have Brewer's, no doubt, and will pull his phone records to find his part-ners. I'll have to trash my burner, too. They can't trace him back to me. So what I want from you two is to track down Terry's son, Leo Hart. Don't do anything to him. Find him and bring me the infor-mation on his whereabouts. That's all. Nothing more, you got me?"

"Yes, sir," the man replied.

"Then get the hell out of my face." After they walked out, he turned to Santos. "So what the hell to do with you, huh?"

"Like I said, I'll leave town. Keep a low profile. No one knows I was with Terry."

"You sure about that?" Schoeman asked. "You drove him in your car, isn't that right?"

"Uh, yeah, I did."

Schoeman nodded. "And no one saw Terry get into your car?"

Santos appeared to think for a moment. "No."

"Uh, huh. What about the goddam security cameras in the parking lot, you asshole. You think the cops won't check that and see you and Terry Hart drove off together? Did you think about that, you stupid idiot?"

"I can go to the track right now and pull the files. I can erase them," he replied.

Schoeman stood from his chair and turned around to peer through his office window at the skyline. "You really didn't think this through, did you, you smarmy little shit."

"Like I said, Terry threatened to go to the cops about our arrangement. I was protecting you."

Schoeman spun around. "Protecting me? Oh, I don't think so. You don't think about anyone but yourself. And this time, it's going to bite you in the ass." He leaned over his desk and pressed his palms against the top. "Now, you listen to me. Here's what you're going to do. You're going to go see Mr. Brunetti. You're going to tell him this whole thing was your doing. The ransom, the murder of Terry Hart. It was all because you were trying to skim off me. My people, who are in turn, their people, are dead because of you."

Santos scoffed. "If I do that, they'll kill me where I stand."

"You aren't worth the trouble to them. They'll leave you to Tampa's finest. But if they suspect for one second that I was in on it, you won't have to worry about them. You'll only have to worry about me."

———

ALLISON LOGGED into the cloud to access the recording device in Santos's office. Nothing new had been recorded, which meant that Santos hadn't returned to the track. The detectives, including Lopez, were now working to issue the various calls to find Santos. And it appeared that Detective Cooper was the only one in Allison's corner.

"There's nothing more you can do tonight, Allison," Shane began. "We'll get a search warrant for the racetrack and execute it first thing this morning. Lopez got the BOLO out on Santos's car. You should go home. You, Charlie, and Leo."

"Can I talk to you for a minute?" She led him into the corridor and looked at him squarely in the eye. "I did what I had to do to get the evidence needed to hurt the man responsible for taking Micah."

"Allison, I know that's what you thought you were doing. You know this could cost you your license, right?"

"I thought about that, and it could be argued that Santos's office was considered a public space. I can legally record anything in a public space." Allison had fallen back on Lucy's suggested line of defense. "His door was always open because he was also the head of Customer Service. It's a legitimate argument, assuming someone decides to file an ethics complaint against me. Detective Cooper didn't seem all that concerned about it."

"That's because it's not his license on the line. It's yours." Shane appeared to consider her idea. "Allison, I know how what happened to Micah messed with your head. I get that. But you, of all people, know right from wrong in your line of work."

"I had no intention of bringing the recording to anyone other than Schoeman's attention. I had to find a way to protect my children. I'm not asking you to lie for me, Shane. I did what I did, and

I'll suffer the consequences should they come to pass. But I do know when there's gray area. This is gray area. And nothing of any use was recorded, so it doesn't matter anymore."

"You picked up Santos talking to someone about helping him get away with something," Shane replied.

"Yes, but no names. And frankly, his phone records will be the first thing Detective Lopez pulls up. She'll see who he talked to." Allison took his hands into hers. "I know you think I take unnecessary risks, Shane, but I worked within the system to get to the truth. Did I bend the rules? Yes. Did I break them? I don't see it that way. I'm sorry if you do."

24

It was going to be up to Leo to smooth things over with his new wife. Not only was it outside of Allison's purview, but she also had far greater concerns. If he had still been married to her, she would've understood, but then again, it had involved Micah. Jenny might see things differently.

Now, at the top of her mind was the fact that Terry's killer remained free, and Allison suspected Gus Schoeman would see his way to aiding in Santos's plight. The entire ordeal tonight had done nothing to bring them closer to arresting Gus Schoeman.

Detective Cooper had a team staking out the racetrack in the event Santos reared his head. But no one seemed to care that Schoeman was still out there operating as though nothing had happened. Not a care in the world. Proof, Cooper said, was what he needed to bring in Schoeman. That proof, such as it was, died with Terry Hart.

As far as the plan Allison had to catch Schoeman in the act, as it were, by having Charlie agree to take a loan from him, well, going through with that now seemed insane.

She still had some of the money, a cool $5000 to play with. Of course, that left her $3000 in the hole. And the person who'd lent her that money would eventually want it back. That situation would come back to haunt her, but not tonight.

Allison was pulled from her own worrisome thoughts as she sat curled up on the sofa when the knock on her door sounded. A smile played on her lips because while she wasn't expecting anyone in the wee hours of the night, she knew who stood on the other side.

And on opening the door, her instincts were spot on. "How'd I know you'd be standing here?"

"Because I'm your best friend." Charlie walked inside. "And this isn't over yet, so what do we plan on doing about all this?"

"You think I have a plan?" Allison closed the door behind her. "It's 2:30 in the morning. I'm exhausted. Terry's dead. I almost lost Leo. My boyfriend is angry that I'm risking my fledgling P.I. career." She padded back into the living room. "And you think I've had time to come up with another plan to get Gus Schoeman?"

"Um, yeah. And I'm here because if you think I'm letting you do any of this alone, you're crazier than I look."

"Well, then, I guess I should put on some coffee." Allison turned sharply and walked to the kitchen.

Charlie watched as Allison passed her by and followed behind. "That's my girl. So listen, as far as we know, Detective Cooper will have the warrants to search both the racetrack and Santos's home first thing in the morning. I don't know what you had in mind, but my two cents? While they're busy finding the man who killed Terry, I move up the meeting with Schoeman to this morning before all hell breaks loose."

Allison put on the coffee. "Hell broke loose a few hours ago, Charlie. I don't think any of that matters at this point. Santos will be found, and he will be arrested for murdering Terry. Schoeman will be scrambling to keep quiet about what happened with the drop tonight. Another man died. It'll be hard for him to mop that up."

"It still matters that we find a way to put an end to him, Alli. I know Cooper thinks Santos will open up about his arrangement once he's in custody, but come on. If he did that, he'd be as good as dead once he stepped foot in prison. You and Leo can't worry about what Schoeman might do to the kids. This is our shot to get hard evidence on Schoeman that he's part of a conspiracy to commit bookmaking. That's a felony charge. And who knows what else I can find once I meet with him and see the terms of the deal. I have no doubt he'll be charging exorbitant interest on the loans to desperate gamblers. Look, we didn't get him on trafficking stolen goods..."

"Because he didn't steal the goods. Terry handed them over," Allison replied.

"Exactly, but this? The Brunetti family would be very interested to know what he's had going on the side and not giving them a cut. Not to mention Schoeman's use of extreme tactics to get his money back. Kidnapping, extortion. Last I checked, that was against the law, too. Once he goes down, the rest of the dominos will fall, and his people will do whatever it takes to save their own butts. I can help prove it. And that's what I'm going to do."

Allison handed her a cup of coffee. "I can see I'm not going to change your mind. So, I'll play along. You and I will arrive at the Winthrop Group's office at 8am." She checked the time. "Five hours or so from now."

"Piece of cake," Charlie replied. "I'll get in and make the deal with him that he's expecting."

"This all has to happen before 9am because I expect Lopez, Cooper, and Shane will move fast. Once word reaches Schoeman that they're searching Santos's property and his office, he'll get nervous, not knowing what kind of records Santos kept on their arrangement."

"Got it," Charlie said. "There's one other thing. While I'm handling Schoeman, you'll be meeting with the Brunetti family."

Allison reared back in surprise. "What?"

"You shouldn't be there with me. Schoeman knows who you are. You set the stage and let the family in on Schoeman's scheme. Then, when the crap hits the fan and Schoeman starts turning to anyone who can help him avoid the charges, the family won't be the ones to do it. They'll let him rot in prison for ordering Micah's kidnapping because he stabbed them in the back."

"You've watched too many episodes of 'The Sopranos,' Charlie."

"Maybe, but that's beside the point. If you tell them the truth; that Schoeman came after your family when they had nothing to do with Terry Hart, I think they'll see reason. You learned of their guy's actions and are looking to get him off your back."

Allison set down her cup of coffee. "This is crazy. We're both risking our lives by doing this. I'm okay with risking mine, but not yours, Charlie."

"It has to be this way for you and your family to be safe. Simple as that," she replied.

Allison sighed. "Fine. We need someone to get me in the door with the family, and there's only one person I know who can do that."

———

A HEAVY-EYED MILO NASH opened the door of his Queen Anne Revival home in Tampa's historic district to find Allison and Charlie standing on his porch. The fifty-something man with a substantial paunch wore his robe tied at the middle. His thinning dark hair was slightly disheveled; a look he would've likely preferred to avoid, but it was nearly 4 o'clock in the morning. "My, my, my, if it isn't the daring duo from ACL Investigative Services. While I am usually pleased as punch to receive a call from you, Allison, you'll forgive me for my less than eager disposition at present."

Allison cracked a smile. "You're the same as always, Milo. I'm so sorry to bring this to your doorstep, but Charlie and I have a situation."

"I did have an inkling. Please come in before the neighbors see me in this state." He waited for them to walk inside and quickly closed the door. "I'll offer you coffee, but it does appear as though you both are fully caffeinated."

"You're not wrong," Charlie began. "But I'll take another cup."

"Yes, indeed." Milo started into his kitchen and turned on the light.

"We wouldn't be here if there was any other way, Milo," Allison replied.

He poured two mugs to the brim with fresh black coffee. "Oh, I suspected as much."

"Milo, we don't have much time," Charlie cut in. "The past few days have seen Alli and me held at gunpoint, Micah kidnapped, and Alli's former father-in-law shot dead."

He handed Charlie a mug. "What on earth? Well, by all means, let's not squander another moment with pleasantries."

Allison locked eyes with him as she turned serious. "Are you familiar with the Brunetti family?"

He chuckled a moment, but then looked at Allison and his smile faded. "You're serious? Well, of course I have. My office has worked many a case involving their organization's shenanigans. To no avail, I might add. They do know how to protect themselves and have been doing just that for many, many years now. Please don't tell me this involves them."

"To a degree, yes," Allison replied.

"A small degree, I hope. Miniscule, would be better," he replied.

"We're after a man who has ties to the family. Distant, but as we understand it, he had been working to gain a larger slice of their pie," Charlie added. "It's too long a story to get into now, but we're here because we would like to understand how to go about getting their help in going after Gus Schoeman. He runs the..."

"Winthrop Group," Milo interrupted. "I am all too familiar with that group and Mr. Schoeman. To be honest, I would love nothing more than to see that man spend the better part of his remaining years in prison. I assume that is also your goal?"

"We believe he ordered Micah's kidnapping," Allison said. "The family, as far as we know, has no idea about the deals Schoeman has had in place. Deals that didn't include the family."

"I see. If it involves the almighty dollar, they won't be happy to learn that," Milo replied.

"That's what we're counting on," Allison added. "Charlie and I thought you might have a connection inside the family. You know a lot of people in this town, Milo. In the D.A.'s office, we figured you'd come across an associate or two of the family."

"You figured right. You need me to get you in and keep you safe once you're in."

"Yes," Allison replied. "We need to convince them that Schoeman is working against their interests, working deals behind their backs, and that it's time he pays the price for his betrayal."

"Allison will be taking the lead from that standpoint. Me?" Charlie added. "I'll be meeting with Schoeman on the pretense of another deal. When I get word that the family agrees to get Schoeman to fold, I let him know. He won't touch me after that."

Milo shook his head. "I wouldn't be too sure of that, Charlie. I can understand why you and Allison planned this out as you have, but Schoeman would see the writing on the wall. He might not be so willing to go with what the family requests. I say that's just too dangerous a proposition."

"I said the same thing," Allison replied. "So what's the solution?"

Milo eyed them. "I can tell you the family will likely agree to see you rather than anyone from law enforcement. That part, as I said, I believe I can arrange. Charlie, I do understand your concern about Mr. Schoeman. That man's slicker than a stripper pole."

Allison and Charlie smirked.

"I apologize if I offend, though I doubt I did. So ensuring he doesn't fly the coop is understandable. However, I think the solution here is for Charlie to perhaps wait it out."

"How do you mean?" Charlie asked.

"I can easily get you the details of the car Schoeman drives," Milo began. "My suggestion would be for you to stand watch and follow, from a safe distance of course, if he chooses to leave after the family informs him of their position on the matter of his unauthorized dealings. That would be a far safer alternative than being face to face with a man who will most certainly not like what he will hear from the family. That way, I would feel infinitely better knowing you and Allison were safe and you will still get your man. If it appears he might be leaving altogether, then you should be able to get the law to detain him, in the short term. If I know the Brunetti family, and I think I do, they'll give up Schoeman in a New York minute and the Tampa police will be able to build a solid case against him. And for harming Micah? Well, I'd make extra sure he was prosecuted to the fullest extent of the law."

———

THE SUN HAD BEGUN its climb in the eastern sky. Neither Allison nor Charlie had slept in more than 24 hours. The search warrant at the racetrack would be served in less than two hours. The trail to catch Lou Santos might be a long one, but it was one Allison and Charlie could not follow. It was in the hands of the fine Tampa detectives. Their jobs? Well, the covert operation was about to begin.

No doubt there had been an element of danger to the plan, but it was much less so than Allison and Charlie's original incarnation. Milo was about to come through, as he always had.

"I still don't agree with Milo's idea that I sit and wait at Schoeman's car," Charlie began.

"It's the safest way to keep eyes on him, you know that." Allison grabbed a bottle of water from the fridge. "I don't think I can stomach any more coffee. You?"

"God no. I'll be on the crapper for the next two hours if I have another cup," Charlie replied. "I trust Milo and I'm sure he knows the family far better than we do. But we're trusting that Schoeman won't see that he's reached the end of his rope and just take off, consequences be damned."

"That could still happen. But I don't think the family will let him get very far. Milo says their reach extends across most of the state. Schoeman must know that," Allison replied. "We can only do what we can do."

"And you'll be satisfied if Schoeman doesn't take the fall for Micah's kidnapping? You'll just wash your hands of the whole thing? Because, somehow, I don't see you doing that, Alli."

"We'll just have to wait and see how this pans out." She checked the time. "I'm going to make a call to Leo and see how he's doing. He'll be up. In fact, I doubt he's slept at all."

"How's Shane been with all this?" Charlie asked.

With her phone in her hand, she glanced at Charlie. "How do you mean?"

"I mean with Leo. I saw how you were with him when you thought something had happened. I also saw Shane's reaction," Charlie replied.

"He's my kids' father, Charlie. I couldn't bear it if anything happened to him."

"Oh, I know. But maybe you should help Shane see it that way too."

"I can't worry about that now." Allison made the call. "Leo, it's me. How you holding up?" She stepped away and lowered her tone. "No, it's good here. Charlie's with me. Neither of us has slept. We're just waiting to see how it goes this morning with the search warrants." Allison nodded. "So, she's angry, huh? I can't blame her."

Charlie tried to keep her ear on the conversation, but as Allison walked into the living room, her voice faded. She took another drink of water and waited.

Several moments later, Allison returned.

"Well, how's he doing?" Charlie asked.

"Not great. Jenny's angry over what he did. He unleashed hell on her. Started talking about what I found concerning her old boyfriend. Sounds like it was a verbal bloodbath. She left him, Charlie."

"Holy crap. She left him after his dad was just murdered? Does he want to see you?"

"No. I think he wants to be alone for a while. He said Detective Cooper promised to keep him updated on their progress. I didn't tell him what we had planned."

"Oh, Alli, I'm so sorry about all of this."

"Leo never did handle stressful situations well. Lashing out was always kind of his thing."

"He'll come to his senses when all this is over," Charlie said.

25

Detective Lopez pounded on the door of Lou Santos's home as the sun peeked over the horizon. His wife, still in her pajamas opened it wearing fear in her eyes. "I told you, he's not here."

"We have a warrant to search the premises." Lopez handed her the document. "It's best if you step aside and let my team do their job, Mrs. Santos." The hardened detective, who had worked undercover with the Brunetti family years earlier, had been pulled into the murder investigation of Terry Hart. With her hand on the butt of her gun, she walked inside. "Find the computer, laptop, phones, tablets. Anything electronic." She turned to Mrs. Santos again. "Your husband hasn't called you? Don't lie to me because we can pull your phone records and you'll be charged with aiding and abetting." Lopez's sharp features and dark hair that was pulled back in a tight ponytail reinforced her words.

"No. I promise you, he hasn't called me. I don't know where he is," Mrs. Santos replied.

Lopez motioned for her team to continue. "Fine. I still have a job to do."

———

BAYSIDE DOWNS PREPARED to open their doors. Shane and Detective Cooper waited outside with a team of three others who were ready to search the property. As Shane stood outside under a bright sun, he had begun to regret the way he left things with Allison last night. He wondered why he'd been so hard on her, when in the past, before they became a couple, he would've scoffed at her technique, but supported her anyway. Instead, he'd admonished her for doing the job she thought she needed to do. He was never a black and white person and yet, he'd behaved as such. Of course there was grey area. There was always grey area. And who would bring charges against her for bugging the office of a murderer? The man guilty of murder? Maybe Cooper had been right. Maybe Shane was too close to work on this investigation. Last night's drop had been a disaster and now they were hunting the man who killed Allison's ex-father-in-law.

"Are you ready to go inside?" Cooper asked. "They just unlocked the doors. Let's see if the manager left us a present, yeah?"

"Yeah." Shane joined him as they reached the entrance. "We'll get copies of the CCTV footage too. We can start putting together a precise timeline."

"Agreed." He made his way to the information desk and held out his badge. "Detective Cooper, Detective Sullivan. Tampa PD. We have a warrant to search Lou Santos's office and surrounding areas."

"Um, of course. I just need to get in touch with the owner if you can give me a minute." The man picked up the phone and made the call.

"One minute." Cooper held up his index finger to make his point. He turned to Shane and in a whisper continued. "First thing we do is get the bug Hart planted. We need to make it disappear."

"Yeah, thanks man," Shane replied.

"Thanks for what? She's not a cop, but as far as I'm concerned, she's working for the greater good, same as us. What she did wasn't exactly kosher, but she's not going down for it, I'll tell you that much."

So this detective, who hardly knew Allison at all, had her back more than Shane had. He needed to rethink what was important.

"Detectives? The owner asked that I get a copy of the warrant and send it to him before you get started. He's out of town today, I'm afraid."

Cooper turned back to him. "I'll tell you what, I'll give you a copy because you're entitled to that. You do whatever the hell you want to do with it. In the meantime, we're going to do our jobs. Your boss has a problem with that, he can take it up with the brass, yeah?"

"She, sir. My boss is a she."

"Thanks for the clarification," Cooper replied sarcastically. "Now, tell me where to find Santos's office."

"Upstairs and to your left. The office marked "Customer Service.""

"Thank you for your cooperation." Cooper patted Shane on the back. "Let's go, compadre." He turned to the other officers standing behind him. "Check with this fine gentleman about the server room. We'll want copies of Santos's files from their hard drives."

Upstairs was where the betting took place. Several cashier

stations lined the back wall with TV monitors above. It was quiet. A couple patrons, mostly older men, milled about and appeared to wait for the first race.

Cooper surveyed the floor. "Lookey there. The door marked Customer Service." He started ahead when a man called out.

"Uh, excuse me, can I help you?" he asked.

"Tampa PD," Shane began. "We have a warrant to search this office. Do you know Lou Santos?"

"Of course I do. He basically runs the place," the man said, "In fact, he should've arrived already."

"I'm pretty sure he's not here because he knows we're looking for him," Cooper cut in. "You'll have to see the guy downstairs if you want a copy of the warrant. We have a job to do." He started ahead and grabbed the door handle. "Hey, we're going to need a key over here."

The man reached under his desk and retrieved his keys. "Lou usually opens up. I'm sorry about that. Can I ask what's going on? Is he in trouble?"

Cooper pushed open the door. "You could say that. He's wanted for questioning in connection with a murder. Do you know where he was late yesterday afternoon?"

The man appeared to search his memory. "Um, he said he was having lunch with a client. Terry Hart—a regular. My God, is it Mr. Hart? Is he dead?"

"Yes, sir, he is," Shane jumped in. "We'll be taking Santos's computer and files, so if you know anything, now would be the time to tell us."

———

ALLISON SAT in her car in the parking lot of Paramount Developers. They were the second largest developer in the state and according to Milo, was the home of the supposed legitimate side of the Brunetti family. He'd arranged a meeting for 9am with Frank Lucenz. Frank was high enough on the family tree, but not so high that Allison would be on the family's radar. It was a favor he'd called in and Milo knew that someday, he'd have to repay that favor. Now, it was in Allison's hands to convince Frank Lucenz that Gus Schoeman had an arrangement and kept his earnings from that arrangement quiet. More importantly, he'd picked up a side gig of kidnapping to ensure his loans were repaid.

Allison stepped out of her new car, the initial enthusiasm seeming unimportant now. She trusted that Milo wasn't sending her into the lion's den unless she was carrying a big juicy steak. The situation was precarious, but Milo insisted this was the best possible plan of action that would ensure the safety of the ACL team.

Inside the lavish building with sleek, modern finishes, Allison made her way to the reception desk. "Good morning. Allison Hart. I have a 9am appointment with Mr. Frank Lucenz."

"Of course. I'll let him know you're here." The woman made the call.

Allison let her gaze roam around the lobby where expensive-looking art hung beneath soft spotlights. Sofas faced each other at the seating area to the right. And to the left was a small café with self-serve coffee.

"Ma'am?"

Allison returned her attention to the receptionist. "Mr. Ballentine will show you to Mr. Lucenz's office."

A large man in a dark suit appeared before her seemingly from nowhere. "Right this way, ma'am."

Allison followed Ballentine and stepped into the elevator with him. Her slender frame appeared even smaller as she stood next to him. Her thoughts turned to Charlie, knowing her partner probably just arrived at Schoeman's office. It was going to be her job to keep eyes out for his car and follow him if he leaves. Lucy was at the office keeping track of their locations through GPS in the event something went awry. But what could go wrong at a meeting with a member of a crime syndicate, and keeping tabs on a kidnapper who may or may not be in contact with a killer? In Allison's experience, a whole lot.

The elevator doors opened and Ballentine stepped out. "Right this way, ma'am."

Milo already set the stage, she just had to finish the act. "Thank you." She followed him down what seemed to be an infinite corridor until he stopped at the end.

"This is Mr. Lucenz's office." Ballentine opened the door. "Excuse me, sir? Ms. Allison Hart is here to see you."

"Please show her in, Ballentine." He stood from his black high-back leather chair and extended his hand. "Ms. Hart."

"Mr. Lucenz. Thank you for agreeing to see me." She took his hand and returned a firm shake.

"When the D.A.'s office calls, I tend to answer." He looked at Ballentine. "That'll be all. Thank you."

"Yes, sir." Ballentine closed the door on his way out.

"So, Ms. Hart, I am aware of why you're here, but I wouldn't mind a little insight if you'd be so kind." He returned to his chair. "Oh, may I get you some water or coffee?"

"No, thank you." Allison cleared her throat as she prepared to relay the words she'd practiced for the past few hours. The man before her was polished. Nothing like she expected. Maybe it was her who'd watched Tony Soprano one too many times. He wore an expensive suit. No tie. His dark hair was perfectly coifed and parted on the side. Likely around 40, with white teeth, a slight tan, and dimples in his cheeks. He wasn't attractive so much as he was drop-dead gorgeous.

"So, tell me then, how can I help?" He laced together his fingers and lay his hands on top of his desk. "Aside from what Mr. Nash has requested, I'd like to hear from you how you came to be sitting in my office now."

Despite his appearance, this man was still a criminal. One who had, to date, gotten away with his crimes. Allison couldn't let herself be disarmed by his obvious allure. She was here to make sure Gus Schoeman would never have the opportunity to come near anyone in her family again.

"Well, Mr. Lucenz..."

"Call me Frank. Please."

She nodded. "Frank. Milo gave you the rundown, so I'll give you the specifics. Gus Schoeman, head of the Winthrop Group, is working against you and your company. His dealings have, unfortunately, caused my family members harm, along with harm that I only narrowly escaped."

He nodded. "I see. That is a problem."

"Yes, sir. I see that as a problem too." Allison continued to relay the details, leaving out the specifics about the names and things that happened to her family members. The last thing she wanted was for this man to know about Micah, Nolan, or Leo, let alone Charlie and Lucy.

When she finished with the incredible tale, his gaze narrowed, his chin raised, and Frank Lucenz appeared to consider whether Allison Hart was a friend, foe, or something in between.

"Ms. Hart..."

"Allison," she replied.

"Allison. I have no doubt Milo Nash offered you insight about my organization."

"Yes, some."

"So you'll understand why I will answer your questions in as vague and obscure a way as humanly possible. I must still protect my interests."

"I understand," Allison replied.

He studied her and paused a moment. "Are you the Allison Hart responsible for what happened to the city mayor about a year ago?"

Tread lightly, Allison, she thought. "Responsible for it? I wouldn't say that so much as aided in the efforts of the Tampa Police."

He laughed. "What a very delicate and diplomatic answer, Allison."

She smiled in response but refused to show the fear that lingered behind that smile. "I want justice for what happened to my family, Frank. Nothing more. I hope I have made that point crystal clear."

"I believe you have, Allison. I believe you have." He continued to peer at her for too long before he pulled up at his desk. "I'll tell you what, consider the matter resolved. Gus Schoeman is no longer a concern for you, your associates, or your family. You have my word."

Relief swept over her as her lips raised into a grin. "Thank you, Frank. I can't tell you how much I appreciate your help."

"Hmmm." He nodded. "There is one thing I'd like for you to consider as you leave my office today."

Her smile faltered. "Yes?"

"Allison, you are clearly an intelligent woman, very beautiful, and intuitive. That said, I'm sure you understand that nothing in this life is free."

She swallowed down the lump in her throat. "I do understand that, Frank. Very much, as a matter of fact."

"That's good to hear. I'll take care of everything. There's

nothing more you need to concern yourself with regarding Gus Schoeman. Is that understood?"

"Of course. Thank you, Frank. Your assistance is very much appreciated." Allison stood and extended her hand. "It was a pleasure meeting you."

He stood and took her hand. "The pleasure was all mine, Allison."

When he held on longer than necessary, Allison's nerves stood on end.

"Enjoy the rest of your day." He finally released his grip.

"And you." Allison spun on her black stiletto heel and headed to the door again.

"One more thing, Allison."

"Yes?" She closed her eyes but quickly turned around again.

"Would you like to have dinner with me Friday night?"

There it was. Nothing in this life was free. He'd just made that clear. But how to turn down a man like this without doing damage? "That's a very kind offer, Frank, but I'm afraid I'm already spoken for."

"Is that so?" he asked. "Not that I should be surprised. As I said, your beauty is unmatched as far as I can see."

"Again, that's kind of you."

"Is it the detective?" he asked.

Her heart jumped into her throat, though her gaze remained steadfast. "I'm sorry?"

"Unless I'm misinformed, you're friends with one of the Tampa Police detectives. Maybe more than friends?"

"In my line of work, I have a lot of friends in law enforcement. It goes with the territory." She turned around again.

"He's a lucky man, Allison."

She continued to open the door, but Ballentine beat her to it.

"Oh, excuse me, Ms. Hart." He looked beyond her. "Mr. Lucenz, you have a visitor."

"I didn't think I had another appointment this morning, Ballentine."

"No, sir. He said you'd want to see him right away."

"Then please show him in. Oh, but would you allow Ms. Hart to go first, please."

"Of course." Ballentine held open the door for Allison as she walked through. Her heart still raced. How had he known about Shane? How could he have possibly known? As Allison walked on, she stopped in her tracks when another man approached.

He continued walking by her without any acknowledgment, but she knew exactly who he was.

Ballentine's booming voice sounded behind her. "Mr. Santos, Mr. Lucenz has cleared his schedule for you."

26

When Allison arrived at her car, she slipped behind the wheel and grabbed her phone. She'd just come face to face with Terry's killer and he hadn't recognized her. This was the man being hunted at this very moment.

Allison made the call to Charlie. "Hey, it's me. The meeting's over. Is Schoeman still at his office?"

"I've been sitting in my car for almost an hour and my face is melting, but yeah, Schoeman's still here. Are you doing okay? What happened at the meeting?" Charlie asked. "I had thought for a second that Milo might not have the influence he thinks he does."

"Milo was on point," Allison replied. "I got Lucenz to agree to take care of Schoeman. I didn't ask how he intended to do it. He was interested in the scheme with Santos, and that was before I saw him as I was leaving."

"What?" Charlie cut in. "You saw Santos? Cripes, Alli, did you call Detective Cooper? They can arrest him now."

"Not yet. I just saw him 2 minutes ago. He was about to meet with Lucenz. Apparently, it was an unscheduled arrival."

"Well, you have to call them now before he leaves. Alli, get the hell out of there and call Shane, call Cooper. Call someone who can come pick that guy up."

"If I do that, Charlie, Lucenz will know it was me. He might renege on the deal about Schoeman, or worse."

"What do you mean, 'or worse'?" Charlie pressed on.

"He knew I was seeing Shane. You didn't see the look on his face, Charlie. He's not a man to screw around with."

"Then what? Do we let Santos walk? He's probably going there to arrange some sort of escape."

"Lucenz didn't know about the deal Schoeman had with Santos. He seemed a little surprised when I told him. I don't think that's going to help Santos's cause," Allison replied.

"What are you saying? He's going to take care of Santos too? And by taking care of, I mean..."

"I know what you mean. And I don't know what he'll do." Allison peered through the windshield at the building ahead. "I have to get out of here. Listen, I'll talk to Shane now. You're right in that they have to know Santos is here. But maybe, all things considered, they'll follow him out of here and make the arrest somewhere else. That would be the safest bet. After what I just agreed to, no way will Frank Lucenz follow through if the cops show up here now."

———

INSIDE THE MANAGER'S OFFICE, Detective Cooper pulled the plug on the desktop computer. Shane searched the file cabinet and retrieved whatever files appeared relevant, tossing them into a box.

"Sully, I think I found it." Cooper had his hand under the

pencil drawer. "Yep. This is it." He tucked the recording device in his pants pocket. "We'll just hang onto that."

"Appreciate it."

"No need, brother. This ain't worth the hassle." Cooper continued to pack up the manager's belongings when his phone rang. "It's Lopez." He answered. "Cooper here. Yeah, what'd you find? Damn. I'd still bring in the wife and get a statement from her. She has to know something." He nodded and creased his brow. "Sully and I are still at his office collecting whatever we can. We'll huddle up back at the station and see what we have. No word on the BOLO?" He shook his head. "All right. We just have to keep plugging away. Catch up with you soon." He ended the call.

"Nothing?" Shane asked.

"Not much. Not nothing, but not much. We'll meet with Lopez back at the station. She's bringing in the wife. Not sure what we'll get out of her."

"Uh, excuse me." The man from behind the betting desk knocked on the door frame. "I don't mean to interrupt, but guests are beginning to ask questions. Are you two about finished in here?"

"Almost," Cooper peered at him a moment. "What can you tell us about your boss?"

"Me? Uh, well, I don't know. He came into work, did his job, I guess. There's not much else to tell. Oh well, except for maybe he's kind of a dirtbag, I guess."

"What's that now?" Cooper asked.

"I mean, just yesterday a woman came up to me looking for him. She was like, super pretty. A little too old for me, but if I was into cougars..."

"What about her?" Shane asked, already knowing who the guy was talking about.

"She asked if he was here. I said no. But she wanted to leave a note for him or something. I said she could slip inside and leave him a note. I don't know, I guess she didn't want to call him or whatever. She made it seem like they were a thing. He's married."

"We're aware," Cooper said. "Did this woman give a name?"

"Allison something or other. I can't remember her last name," he replied. "She was only in here for a minute or two. I've never seen her before."

So that was how she gained access. Shane recalled Allison feeling the guilt for Terry's death because she claimed he'd helped her by getting Santos out of his office. But why would the man have killed Terry? It didn't make sense. "Word has it your boss was introducing people to outside loan companies. Apparently, to help them keep up with their gambling habits, and then getting some sort of kickbacks for it. Do you know anything about that?"

The young man shrugged. "I don't know. It was none of my business. I know he went to lunch with Terry Hart. He's just an old guy with a gambling problem. He was always in here asking for help. I tried to stay out of it. Not my job."

"Sure," Cooper replied. "So you don't know where they went yesterday?"

"No. I'm sorry, I don't." He surveyed the mess in the office. "You guys sure are tearing up the place. Do you think he did it? Did he kill that old man?"

"That's what we're trying to find out," Shane added. "If you can recall anything else, give me a call, would you?" He handed the man a business card.

"Yeah, of course I will." He started out but stopped and turned back. "You know, there is one thing. I don't know if it matters or not, but a while back...maybe a month or so ago...I needed to ask Lou something and I popped in. I saw something on his desk that I thought was strange."

"What'd you see?" Cooper pressed on.

"Lou's responsible for turning in the day's bets. He generates this report and hands it over to Accounting. They do something with it—I have no idea. Anyway, I remember seeing on his desk something written on one of the reports. Red pen. It was a note from Accounting. It said that the report didn't match the take for the day. And apparently, the note said it was a recurring event and that he needed to take care of it."

"What did you do when you saw it?" Shane asked.

"Nothing. Lou and I kind of locked eyes for a minute, then I went about the rest of my day. He never said anything. Neither did I." He sighed. "Maybe I should have."

————

THE BEST THING for Allison to do was to pull out of the parking lot and get the hell away from this building as quickly as possible. So she did, and started back to the ACL office where Lucy awaited her partners' return.

It wasn't too late to make the call. To get the police out to follow Santos. "Detective Cooper, It's Allison Hart. I saw him, Lou Santos. He's here."

"Where's here, Allison?"

At the mention of her name, Shane turned his attention to Cooper's call.

"I'm leaving the Paramount Developers building now. I walked right by him. He didn't recognize me, but I recognized him."

"What were you doing there? You do know who runs that place, right?" Cooper asked. "Or do I want to know?"

"It's not important, but Detective, no one there was expecting Santos. He just showed up, which makes me think..."

"He's looking for a way out," Cooper cut in.

"Charlie's keeping a look out for Schoeman's car in case he decides to go dark for a while. With Santos in the crosshairs of law enforcement, he might see this as a time to get clear of the guy. I don't know what Santos hoped to accomplish, but maybe he was looking for a way out of this mess and turned to the only people Schoeman knew would offer help."

"For a price. There's always a price." He sighed. "Okay, listen, where are you now?"

"Heading back to my office," she replied. "Detective Cooper, if you go and get him where he's at right now, there's a good chance this will come back on me. I can't risk being even remotely associated with the cops showing up at this building."

"Got it. I'll get with Sully. We're about finished with Santos's office anyway. We'll come up with something. Follow him or whatever. But it'll take us twenty minutes or more to get there. I don't know if he'll stick around for that long."

"Wait," Allison began. "I could redirect Charlie's efforts. What if I send her here and keep an eye out for Santos? She can track him until you or another officer shows up. After the meeting, I think maybe I've taken care of the Schoeman problem anyway. I don't think she needs to waste her time with him now."

"Do I want to know how you managed to do that?" Cooper asked.

"Not really," Allison replied.

"Hold up," Cooper cut in. "I have a better idea. We have a BOLO on Santos's car. With you clear of the building, let's keep your partner clear as well. I'll have a unit drive by. The guy should've known we'd get his plates out there to law enforcement. It wouldn't come back to you, Allison. I promise you that."

"Yeah, okay. I'll call Charlie back to the office. I think we've done what we can do. I'll leave the rest to you guys."

———

CHARLIE SPOTTED Gus Schoeman as he walked to his car. She slumped down below the steering wheel. Her car was parked far enough away, though, that the likelihood of Schoeman spotting her was minuscule.

Schoeman pressed the remote on his car keys and the lights of his Infinity SUV flashed. After what Alli had mentioned, that she had an agreement, of sorts, with an even more dangerous figure, maybe this was pointless. Or maybe this guy was going to try to leave town, and Charlie could alert Allison and let her plan play out. He wasn't going to get away with any of this. Terry Hart would still be alive if it weren't for his scheme. He may not have pulled the trigger, but Santos was in so deep, he clearly didn't see a way out other than to eliminate his perceived threat.

Charlie was there to make sure Schoeman didn't escape justice. Micah deserved better and she wasn't about to let him get away.

He stepped inside his SUV and the engine roared to life. With his sunglasses on, he drove out onto the frontage road. Charlie waited a moment and followed. If there was one thing she'd become an expert at, it was following people. She never thought it would be a skill to list on her resume, but she'd gotten damn good at it.

Charlie's phone buzzed with a call, and she answered. "Alli, he's leaving. I'm trailing him now."

"You are? I'm almost at the office. Listen, Charlie, I don't think you need to do this now. Cooper is going to send a unit and bring in Santos. With the agreement I made with Lucenz, there's no point in you trailing Schoeman."

"Okay, great. But that doesn't help us get Schoeman. Are you forgetting, Alli, that he took your daughter?"

"No. Not a chance, but I've made arrangements with Lucenz. He's going to take care of Schoeman. There's nothing more we can do, Charlie. Come back to the office, okay? We'll get with Lucy and just wait to see what Cooper does."

"Wait to see?" Charlie asked. "Alli, I get it, but come on. Schoeman could be going anywhere right now. He could be on his way to the airport about to leave the country. Lucenz might've told you he would take care of Schoeman, but I don't think Schoeman will go quietly." She listened as Allison remained silent. A moment later, she continued. "You know I'm right. Alli, I'll be safe. I'm keeping my distance. Just let me see where he goes. I won't approach. I'm a little crazy, but I'm not batshit crazy."

"I can't risk it, Charlie. I told Lucenz I'd stay hands-off while he takes care of things. I can't go back on that now when the ink on the deal isn't even dry yet. Just come back to the office, okay? Everything else is in the hands of Detective Cooper."

"Fine. I'm on my way." Charlie ended the call.

Allison arrived at her office and rested her head on top of the steering wheel. What had started out as a simple plan to get Schoeman to pay for taking Micah, had ballooned into Allison asking a crime family for favors. And after that call, she wasn't sure Charlie would follow through on her words. She knew the woman too well.

Her phone rang and the caller ID popped up on the screen on her dash. She answered. "Leo, how you doing?"

"Detective Cooper called me. He said they had a tip on a location for Santos."

"This is good news, Leo. Very good news," she replied, already having played a part in making that happen.

"It is good news, I know," he said. "I wanted to tell you that first, but there's something else too."

"What is it?"

"Alli, Jenny and I talked this morning."

"Okay. That's good too, right? You're going to smooth things over, just like I said."

"Yeah, I think so. But after talking, we agreed that trust had become an issue—for both of us."

"I'm sure. Especially after she had turned to her ex-boyfriend," Allison cut in.

"Right. But also because she thinks I try to turn to you too much. Alli, she thinks I might still have feelings for you."

"Well, that's just crazy. That's her being paranoid," she replied.

"I think so too, but it doesn't change the fact that's how she feels. After what happened to you and to Micah, my dad. I mean, my God, how much more can I take, you know?"

Allison was quiet for a moment as she waited for the shoe to drop.

"We agreed that we both messed up and that we both need to try to trust each other again."

"What exactly are you getting at, Leo?" Allison's tone hardened.

"I'm saying, now that the kids are grown. They're adults now. There's really no reason you and I need to see each other anymore. Well, except for things like Micah's graduation, Nolan's games. Things like that. But the way we have been? Jenny doesn't want it that way anymore."

"I see." Her tone was flat. "Is that what you want too, Leo? You want to cut me out of your life? I mean, could you have picked a worse time to lay this on me?"

"I know. I know it's a shitty thing to do. But with Terry gone, and all this crap. It's too much. It's too much for her and it's too much for me. Since you became a P.I..."

Allison shook her head. "So it's my fault because now that I'm a private investigator, I've brought all this onto our family. Never mind it was Terry who I was trying to help."

"I know you tried to help him. I asked you to, that's the bitch of it. Alli, I have to do what Jenny asks if I want to make this marriage work. I can't fail again."

Allison scoffed. "Failed. Right. Hey, you know what, Leo, do what you have to do. If your new wife can't handle our relationship, what do I care? I have my kids. I have my work and my partners."

"And Shane," Leo added.

"And Shane. So, hey, you know, good luck, Leo. I'll make sure Cooper keeps you posted on capturing the man who murdered your father." She ended the call. "Same ol' Leo. Making everything about himself. Why should I be surprised?"

27

I t was just going to be a quick detour. Charlie was going to follow Gus Schoeman long enough to get an idea of his plans. But as she tailed him and he made the turn onto Heron Avenue, the hairs on the back of her neck stood on end. She didn't have to wonder where he was headed. The answer was clear. "No. What the hell are you doing?"

She picked up her phone. "Alli, you and Lucy need to leave the office. Now!"

"What?"

"Just go. He's coming. Schoeman's coming and I don't think it's to offer condolences for Terry." Charlie's eyes remained fixed on the luxury SUV as it continued toward the ACL office. "Both of you need to leave now."

Allison was quiet for a moment. "Yeah. Okay. We'll go."

No explanation was needed. Whatever deal Allison thought she struck with Lucenz, a member of a crime family, had vanished. There was no other reason for Schoeman to go to the ACL office other than to take care of a mutual problem. And, as Charlie saw it, that problem was Allison.

It was time to get some help, so Charlie made the call. "Shane, it's Charlie. Listen, you guys need to come to the office. Send a patrol car, just get an officer over here and it has to be now."

"What the hell's going on, Charlie and where's Allison?" Shane asked.

"Doing her best to get her and Lucy the hell out of there before it's too late. I'm following Schoeman and he's headed straight to our office."

"Jesus. Why? Why is he going there? What the hell happened?"

"Shane, if I had the time, I'd explain. I'm following him now. He's almost there and I don't know if Alli and Lucy are out yet. I told them to just go." Charlie pulled into the parking lot behind him. "Cripes, Shane. I'm here. He's here. We need help." She dropped the phone and fell back so he wouldn't see her car. "Oh no." Charlie's heart jumped into her throat. Allison and Lucy emerged from the shadow of the building and ran into the parking lot.

Schoeman's SUV slowed. "No." Charlie's eyes darted back at Allison. The lights on her new Toyota flashed. They were almost there, but he saw them and sped up. "No." Charlie slammed her foot on the gas and spun her tires for a moment, drawing Schoeman's attention. A second later, she was right in front of them. "Get in. He's here!"

Allison opened the back door. "Lucy, hurry!" She closed it and jumped onto the passenger seat and turned to Charlie. "Go."

Charlie spun the wheel and turned around. "Shane's on his way, or sending someone. I don't know. We just need to get the hell out of here." She peered into the rearview mirror. "Cripes, he's closing in. Hold on to your britches, ladies." Charlie gripped the wheel and slammed the gas again as her midsize crossover struggled to gain traction and pick up speed.

Allison's eyes widened as she gazed through the passenger window. Schoeman was gaining ground. "He's coming, Charlie. Go. Go. Go!" Her hand pressed against the door as if that would somehow slow him down. "Where the hell are they? Where the hell are the cops? I don't understand what's happening."

"I do." Charlie jumped the curb of the sidewalk and made it onto the street. "Lucenz went back on his word. Schoeman's here to shut you up. To shut all of us up and I don't plan on sticking around long enough to figure out how they intend to do that." She glanced into the rearview mirror again. "Oh, crap."

Lucy looked over her shoulder. "Hurry, Charlie. Hurry!"

———

THE STREETSCAPE PASSED by in a blur as Detective Cooper drove along the highway at breakneck speeds. The radio kicked on and Dispatch sounded. "Units are on their way to the Commerce Park building. ETA 2 minutes."

"Shit, we'll be there before they will," Cooper said. "Try calling again."

Shane dialed the number. "Allison? Oh, thank God. Where are you? We're almost there. Are you guys okay?"

"He's behind us." She glanced back over her shoulder. "We're with Charlie. Shane, we need help."

"We're on the way," he replied.

"Schoeman's chasing us down Palmdale Avenue. He's in a new white Infinity SUV. We're already a mile from the office. Our best bet is to head to the nearest substation."

"That's more than five miles away. We'll reach you before

then. Stay south on Palmdale. We're less than a minute behind. Tell Charlie to keep going. Don't stop," Shane continued.

"There's a red light ahead, Alli!" Charlie shouted. "What do we do?"

Allison turned to her. Their eyes locked, then she peered ahead at the approaching intersection. "Punch it."

Charlie pushed back, bracing with her hands clinging to the steering wheel. "Lucy, hang on!"

Allison gripped the handle above the door and squeezed her eyes shut. "Oh, shit!" She dropped her phone to the floorboard and waited for the impact.

"We're through. Holy crap, we're through." Charlie looked into the rearview mirror again. "He stopped at the light. We're in the clear."

Lucy turned away from the back window. "You did it."

"Yeah, but now what?" She turned to Allison. "What do we do now?"

Allison reached down to retrieve her phone and picked it up again. "Shane?"

"I'm still here. Are you guys okay?"

"We're okay. Charlie pulled a hell of a stunt but we're okay."

"Thank God. Listen, do you hear that?" he asked.

Allison cocked her head. "Sirens."

"That's us. We're going to track down Schoeman. Go to the station and wait for us. Do not stop anywhere else."

"Okay. You have to stop him, Shane. He'll keep coming after me," Allison replied. "And if he doesn't find me, he might try to find the kids."

"That's not going to happen. We're close now. I gotta go. Stay at the station." He ended the call and turned to Cooper. "South on Palmdale."

"Are they clear?" he asked.

"They're clear. They're headed to the east side station." Shane picked up the radio. "All units near the 1800 block of South Palmdale Ave, be on the lookout for a white newer model Infinity SUV. White male, mid 40s. Possibly armed."

"Sully, that's him up ahead." Cooper peered through the windshield. "We can get him." The car's siren still blared, and traffic parted to let them through. He picked up the radio. "Suspect heading south on Palmdale. Any units in the area, please respond."

The call was answered. "We're ahead of him. We'll wait it out," the patrolman replied.

"He's not going to slip by all of us." Cooper continued to weave in and out of traffic. "What the hell was he doing coming after Allison? How the hell does he know who she is?"

"Santos must have something to do with this," Shane replied. "Shit, I think he just spotted us."

"We got him, Sully." Cooper pressed the gas and closed the gap between his Mustang and the SUV. With the lights flashing, he tailed Schoeman. "Pull over you son of a bitch." He continued riding close to the bumper and saw the eyes of Schoeman in the rearview. "That's right. Game over, pal."

Schoeman drove ahead and finally pulled off onto a side street.

Cooper stopped behind him and opened his door. "Back me up."

"You got it." Shane stepped out and pulled out his weapon, starting toward the passenger side of the SUV.

Cooper continued toward the driver's side but stayed back with his gun drawn. "Turn off the engine and toss your keys out the window. Now."

The lights still swirled from inside the Mustang, but the sirens were off. Cooper glanced at Sully before setting his sights on the sideview mirror. "Open your door and slowly step out of the vehicle."

"What's this about, Officer?" Schoeman asked while he remained inside.

"Get out of your car, sir. Now," Cooper insisted.

The driver's door opened.

"Let's see those hands," Cooper added. "Step out slowly and with your hands raised, I want your back facing me. You got it?"

"Yes, sir." Schoeman stepped out and kept his back to Cooper and his hands raised. "I still don't know what this is about, Officer."

Cooper reached for his handcuffs while keeping his gun trained on Schoeman. "Why were you going after that Chevy? Got a bad case of road rage, or something?" He approached him and snatched one of Schoeman's arms, pulling it down. He slapped the cuff on his wrist, then pulled down the other one and cuffed them together.

"I don't know what you're talking about, sir. I was just on my way to grab a bite to eat," Schoeman replied.

"I think we both know that's not true." Cooper held onto Schoeman's hands and led him back to the vehicle. "Sully, let's get one of the units here and we'll have them escort Mr. Schoeman to the station."

"Am I under arrest?" Schoeman asked, but Cooper ignored him.

Shane picked up the radio and made the call. Within moments, a patrol car arrived, and the officers stepped out to assist.

"What about Santos?" Shane asked. "I think it's now or never. He'll find out we got Schoeman, and I doubt he'll stick around after that."

Cooper nodded and approached the blonde-haired man. "I'll leave you with these fine officers and see you back at the station."

He started to walk away but turned back. "Unless you want to help yourself out and feel like talking about your friend, Lou Santos. Turns out he's in a real bind right now and last I heard, he was talking to one of those head honchos with the Brunetti family."

Schoeman turned down his lips. "Don't know who you're talking about."

"You sure? I heard you knew the guy Santos killed yesterday. Maybe you have something to say about that?"

Schoeman shrugged.

"Have it your way." Cooper waved at Shane. "Let's go round him up too. Since we know where he's at and all." He glanced back at Schoeman, who appeared unmoved.

Cooper stepped into his Mustang and waited for Shane to join him. "Damn. I thought that might actually work."

"Not where the Brunetti family is concerned," Shane began. "No one's going to cross them."

"Probably not. You should let Allison know we got him."

Shane picked up the phone. "Allison, are you at the station?"

"Yes, we're here. We're in the lobby of the east station. Did you get him?" she asked.

"We got him. He's being taken into custody now. Cooper and I are going to find Santos. Can you get to the downtown station? I think you three should stick around there until we can bring in Santos. There's no way to be sure he and Schoeman weren't working together to find you."

"We'll head there now," she replied. "Shane, Frank Lucenz is a member of the family. Milo got me in to see him this morning. We knew we had to get to the Brunetti family and tell them what Schoeman had done. I thought I'd made a deal with Lucenz, but he went back on it by the look of things. He sent Schoeman after me."

"What kind of deal? Do you know what happens to people who make deals with men like Frank Lucenz?"

"I do now." Allison ended the call and turned to Charlie and Lucy. "They got Schoeman."

Charlie sighed with relief. "Finally. What are they going to charge him with? He didn't do anything to us and as far as I know, we still don't have proof he ordered Micah's kidnapping or Terry's."

"Cooper will have to figure out a way to keep him in custody until he can bring charges. He hadn't wanted anything to come back on me or my family, but I don't see how that's possible at this point. They're going after Santos now."

"What you should be thinking about is why Frank Lucenz sent Schoeman after you in the first place," Lucy cut in. "Allison, we don't want to be on his bad side. I'm not sure how we fix this, or if it can be fixed."

It's possible Schoeman and Santos were working together to find me. I thought Santos hadn't recognized me, but maybe he had. Maybe Lucenz didn't play a role in this."

"You're giving that man too much credit," Charlie said. "I don't want to rule out any scenario right now."

Allison let her eyes roam the small substation lobby. "I should pay him another visit. Offer him something to keep him off our backs. I don't know if it was him, but I don't know it wasn't. I need to show him what I have."

"And if it was him, you're walking right toward him," Lucy said.

"And if it wasn't..." Allison considered an idea. "He should know I'm serious about what I know. He's the type of man who wants to see strength, not cowardice or fear."

"We started this to get Schoeman off the streets because of what he did to Micah," Charlie added. "We've done that."

"For how long, though, Charlie? And if Cooper can't make any charges stick? What then? Now I have Lucenz to worry about too," she replied. "I recognize that we can't bring down the Brunetti family or Frank Lucenz."

Lucy narrowed her gaze. "No, it would be crazy to think that. But there could be something else." She looked at Allison. "Like the proof you will need if you step foot in Lucenz's office again."

"What's on your mind, kiddo?" Charlie asked.

"Allison, the device I gave you to put in Santos's office..."

"What about it?" she replied.

"You can still access it through the cloud server. We know it recorded a conversation with who we think was with Schoeman." Lucy peered at them. "What if we can prove it? Who can get us access to Santos's phone records quickly?"

"Shane, I assume," Allison replied. "He's a little preoccupied at the moment."

"Right, but what I'm getting at is using the calls to Schoeman as proof to offer Lucenz. Proof that Schoeman was tied in with Santos. You told him that was the case, but he doesn't know you have proof. That was evidenced by the fact that he may have sent someone after you. He didn't believe you, Allison."

"But if we can prove it, like you say," Charlie cut in. "He might be more apt to listen to what Allison has to say. He might be more willing to ensure Schoeman pays for the kidnapping and Santos goes down for killing Terry..."

"Leaving Lucenz, and more importantly, the Brunetti family, off the hook," Allison replied. "I'm not sure I have any other choice right now."

28

The Brunetti family hadn't survived this long, weathering political and financial storms for decades, without the use of strategic pressure. Such pressure had been placed on loyal followers and adversaries alike. So when Lou Santos waltzed into Frank Lucenz's office to confess he'd been the one who devised the scheme with Schoeman, Lucenz figured he'd gotten it right when he sent Schoeman after the lady P.I. That man was, and would always be, a soldier. Santos was no one, as far as Lucenz was concerned.

"I appreciate you taking time out of your day to let me set things straight," Santos said. "This is on me and Schoeman was trying to help me out."

Lucenz sat behind his desk. "He got something out of it too, though. So, not entirely on you." He clasped his hands together and rested them on his desk. "The problem I see is that you brought a shiny spotlight right on top of my head. No way you're getting clear of this murder rap. I only thank God Gus saw that the right thing to do was to have you come to me and bring this to my attention. Helps me to get ahead of the problem, you know what I'm saying?"

"Yes, sir," Santos replied. "But despite what you've been told, I was simply defending myself against Terry Hart. The man owed Gus a lot of money. I was helping him to collect. Things got out of control."

"No shit," Lucenz replied. "You killed an old man, and you want to claim self-defense? Good luck with that." He stood and peered through his office window into the parking lot. "I'll tell you what, Mr. Santos, if I were you, I'd get the hell out of this city. Cops are after you and if they come here, we're going to have ourselves a problem. You understand?"

"Yes, sir. I won't take up any more of your time. I just wanted to clear the air as far as Gus Schoeman was concerned. I hope you'll take to heart my sincere apologies for exposing even a hint of trouble for you, sir." He turned on his heel and started through the door.

"I'd walk faster than that, Mr. Santos," Lucenz shouted before glancing at Ballentine. It only took a slight nod for the man to know exactly what his boss wanted him to do. Lou Santos wasn't going to be a problem for Schoeman or Lucenz for much longer.

———

DETECTIVE COOPER's Mustang rolled up to the parking lot of the building that had been home to the supposed legit side of the Brunetti family, Paramount Developers. Law enforcement had been unable to prove otherwise. "If he's still here, he's not as smart as he thinks."

Shane nodded. "Given where we are, I'm inclined to think if he is here, he may not be breathing or he's on his way to the waterside with his ankles tied to a masonry block."

"Dark. I like it." Cooper drove slowly through the lot. "What time was it when Allison called to tell us he was here?"

Shane checked his phone. "A solid 25 minutes. We should've had a unit run by."

"I'd planned to until we got caught up with Schoeman." His eyes narrowed as he peered through the windshield. "Hold on, Sully. We might be in luck. See that guy who just walked out of the building?"

Shane eyed the man. "Yeah. Could be him. Too far away to know for sure. Oh, hang on. Someone else is coming out."

"Following," Cooper added. "And keeping his distance. That's not good."

"Not for Santos, if that's him," Shane replied. "What do you want to do? We roll up now, we could be interrupting something."

"If we wait, chances are these guys will drive out of here. That's Santos, for sure. I say we follow and see what happens." He peered at Shane. "Nothing's going to happen to Santos on this property."

"But if we grab him now, it's over. He'll be charged with Terry Hart's murder." Shane turned to him. "What is it you're really trying to do here, Cooper? Because it's starting to look like a career-making play to me."

"So what if it is? Don't we want the same thing? To gut organized crime in this city? How far are you willing to go, Sully? You're here with me. If we're witness to an attempted hit..."

"Assuming we stop it in time," Shane cut in.

"Which we will, then we'll be able to follow the trail all the way back to the top floor of this building. Santos will still go to prison for murder. Schoeman will serve time for kidnapping. And we'll get a shot at Lucenz, maybe those above him too. Maybe Brunetti, himself."

Shane was already one of the oldest so-called "rookie" detectives in Major Crimes. And at nearly 41-years-old, he should've been a veteran by now. Even a captain. Could Cooper be right? Was this the way to move up quickly?

"What do you say, Sully? You want to go for it, or you want the safe bet?" Cooper asked. "It's time to make the call or we'll lose them both."

Santos continued toward his car and the man, who was clearly the designated muscle, followed behind. A hit was about to go down. Shane looked on. "Yeah, okay. Let's shadow them and see what happens."

———

THE PLAN SEEMED simple enough but it would mean going against what Shane suggested, which was for them to wait it out at the Downtown station. But Shane hadn't known exactly why Lucenz turned on Allison. She hadn't even known herself, if that was the case.

"Allison, what do you want to do?" Charlie regarded her. "I have no doubt that Shane and Detective Cooper will find Santos and bring him in. Schoeman's already on his way in. These are the guys we were after. But now..."

"Lucenz has me on his radar and might have tried to get Schoeman to fix the problem," she replied. "Making Lucenz my problem."

"Exactly. We don't know if he'll follow through on anything, especially after Schoeman is charged, but I'd prefer a safety net. Lucy's idea gives us that," Charlie said.

"And if Lucenz sees it as a threat?" Allison continued. "Will I get out of there alive?"

"We'll make sure of that," Lucy added. "No one gets left behind. Charlie and I will be there, ready to jump when you say."

"No one's keeping us here, Alli," Charlie said. "This is about you, us, and the safety of our families. I think you know where I stand."

Allison nodded. "Yeah, I think I do. Let's go. Now's the time so we can impress upon Lucenz that his man is in police custody, and we can help end this for him."

———

It was still early in the afternoon when Shane and Cooper trailed what was to be a possible hit job. With Schoeman off the street and Santos in plain sight, Shane felt that Allison and the team were safe. And while he hadn't known what played out between Allison and Frank Lucenz, he assumed whatever was about to happen now would make the mid-level member of the Brunetti family clam up pretty quickly.

"Any idea where the hell Santos is going?" Shane asked.

"Not home. Not work. Right now, I have no idea," Cooper replied. "But he's still being followed by the muscle." He glanced at Shane. "Having second thoughts?"

"No. I just want this to be over. None of this should've ever involved Allison Hart and her family. We have to find a way to make the charges against Schoeman stick. He ordered the kidnapping of Allison's daughter, and he took Terry Hart too."

"Unfortunately, Sully, we don't have proof of that yet. But we'll get it. I have a feeling if this goes down the way we need it to, the pieces will fall into place because Lucenz will make it so. We still have the dead guy from the botched drop. Schoeman won't get out of this without serving time, and plenty of it."

"I hope you're right," Shane replied.

"You must care for Allison a lot." Cooper kept his eyes on the road.

"She's a hell of a P.I. and a good person. I don't want to see anything more happen to her."

"Well, we'll do our best to see to it she gets the justice she deserves." Cooper narrowed his gaze. "He's slowing down."

Shane pulled up at attention. "We're near the industrial park. What the hell business does Santos have here?"

"I don't know, but it's a damn good place to make someone disappear," Cooper replied. "Lucenz's man is dropping back too. We need to do the same. Ok, here we go, man. This is about to happen." Cooper stopped on the curb of the adjacent street while Ballentine followed Santos into the parking lot.

Santos stopped the car.

"Should we get out now?" Shane asked. "I don't want to wait too long."

"Give me a minute. We need to see this play out before we know what the end result will be. If we jump the gun, we're screwed."

The detectives watched as Ballentine stepped out of his car and approached Santos still sitting in his.

"We can't see clearly enough from here," Shane began. "We need to move in."

"Shit, you're right." Cooper opened his door slowly and stepped out. "Stay low, man."

Shane followed, keeping low to the ground, and caught up to Cooper. They made their way to the thin line of shrubs that would give them some cover as they moved closer to the empty parking lot.

"Why is no one here?" Shane asked.

"I don't know. Looks like the place is shut down or something. Why here? Why would Santos come here? It's like he wants to be..." Cooper's eyes widened as he turned to Shane. "Get back in the car, Sully. Now."

"What? Why?"

"It's a goddam ambush. They know we're here. Get in the car!"

———

CHARLIE PULLED to a stop in front of the building. "So, this is where the biggest crime family in the state run their operations, huh?"

"That's what I hear. Their legitimate operations, anyway," Allison replied. "I'll go in now. You two stay here, near the entrance if possible."

"You're not going in there alone, Alli. Are you serious?" Charlie asked. "I'm coming in with you."

"So am I," Lucy said. "And if you tell me I should wait here because I'm just a kid..."

Allison regarded her partners. "No, you're right. Both of you should come in. They aren't going to do anything to us."

"Not here." Charlie opened her door. "Let's go."

The partners stepped out of the Chevy crossover and walked to the lobby where Allison thought she'd struck a deal earlier. Turned out, the joke may have been on her. Now she was coming back with proof that Schoeman and Santos were working together, and it wouldn't be too hard to get either one of them to turn on Lucenz to save their own skins, or so she hoped.

Allison didn't get the phone records, but she still had a copy of the recording from Santos's office. It would have to be enough. "Stay here. I have to go up there alone."

"I agree," Charlie replied. "We'll hang tight here. But if you're not back in 30 minutes, we're coming up to get you."

Allison smiled. "Thanks, Charlie." She turned to Lucy. "Don't let this one wander off, okay?"

"Not a chance. This will work, Allison."

"Fingers crossed." She turned toward the elevator and started up to the top floor, not bothering to stop at the lobby. No one paid her any attention. She took in a deep breath and when the doors parted, she stepped into the corridor back to the office of Frank Lucenz. Back to tell him he'd miscalculated. Sure. Piece of cake.

As she walked along the hall, a man in a suit approached ahead. "Excuse me, ma'am. May I help you?"

This one was different from the first, larger man in a suit. "I'm here to see Mr. Lucenz again. Just to have a quick word."

"Is he expecting you?" the man asked.

"No, but I promise not to take up more than a few minutes of his time." Allison batted her eyes and wore a seductive smile. She hated to resort to using her looks, but hey, desperate times and all that.

"Let me see if he can spare a moment." The man turned back around.

He disappeared and Allison stood in the hall, waiting and looking a little lost. When the man reappeared wearing a pleasant smile, Allison felt that she was in the clear.

"Mr. Lucenz will see you now. Follow me, please." He continued toward the office and opened the door. "Allison Hart, sir."

He stood from his desk. "Allison. I'm surprised to see you back here. I thought we finished our conversation earlier."

"So did I." She walked in. "I didn't think you were a man who went back on his word, Frank."

"Excuse me?" He raised his brow.

"I thought we had an agreement, but since I was almost run down earlier today by someone we both know, I may have come away from our meeting with a different understanding."

He walked around his desk. "Please, Allison, sit down."

Lucenz perched on the edge in front of Allison. "If there was a misunderstanding, then it was mine. You see, I thought we mutually agreed upon an outcome to ensure justice and safety for your family. Instead, I found myself wondering why it was that you sent the police to my office."

"I didn't," she replied.

"No? That is a misunderstanding then, but they showed up, nonetheless. I saw them with my own eyes. So when you say we had a deal, I thought we did too. I wonder why it is that you're here then, Allison."

"I can assure you that I didn't send the police." She thought Shane understood to wait. Who had arrived then, if not him? Someone screwed up and now she had to wriggle out of the bind. "They are out looking for Santos since he murdered my father-in-law. It's my understanding they have his license plate number and know what car he drives. Isn't it possible he was tracked here?"

"It's possible. But that doesn't answer my question. Why are *you* here?" He pointed at her with a firm finger.

"Because I'm not sure I made entirely clear the proof I have of a connection between the two men who seem to have become a thorn in both our sides. That connection could very easily be drawn back to you. I'm here to negotiate a deal and I hope this time we are in full agreement and that there will be no room for misinterpretation."

He smiled out of one corner of his mouth. "Well, Allison. I'm all ears."

29

In retrospect, considering using what amounted to blackmail against a member of a crime family may have been the wrong path toward Allison's goals. She relayed the details of her proof to Frank Lucenz and while he examined it, reading his face was impossible.

"I didn't want to let things get this far, Frank. I do understand the risk I've taken. But I ask that you understand this has now involved my family, my children. I don't know if you have children of your own, but I suspect you would do whatever it took to ensure their safety." Allison swallowed down the fear that threatened to fracture her voice.

His eyes were downturned onto the USB he held in his hand. When they raised up, he captured her gaze. "Allison." He shook his head. "I'm not sure I've met anyone—anyone not in the business—who would put themselves in a position such as this. I do have children and I can empathize. However, coming to me with this..." he took in a deep breath.

Her pulse quickened as she listened to him. "I only want my family to be safe just like I said before."

Lucenz pulled straight back in his chair. "I've never been one to underestimate people, Allison. I imagine you've taken steps to ensure this audio conversation isn't the only copy."

"I have," she replied.

He nodded. "Good thing. It doesn't say much, but as far as I'm concerned, it's enough." He stood up. "I'll tell you what, Allison Hart. You lose this recording. Lose the video you have showing Gus's people taking the boxes from your father-in-law, then I think we can come to an understanding. I'll keep your family safe. No one, and I mean, no one, will come after you or anyone you know. Can we agree?"

This sounded like something out of *"The Godfather,"* but she was in this now and there was no turning back. "Agreed."

———

SHANE GRIPPED the side of the car door while Cooper pressed hard on the gas. Smoke billowed from the Mustang's tires as they spun under the weight of the engine's torque. He watched as Santos and a man he hadn't known rush back to their cars, apparently ready to follow. "You gotta go, man."

"You think?" Cooper straightened the wheel, and the tires gripped the asphalt.

As Shane peered through the rear window, he noticed the men weren't driving toward them. "Hey, they're not moving. They're not coming for us."

Cooper had already turned around the car and looked into the rearview mirror. "Wait, what the hell?"

"They aren't coming, man. What the hell's going on?" Shane demanded.

Cooper didn't answer and only shook his head as he kept his sights fixed on the mirror. His gaze widened. "Oh shit."

Shane gripped the back of the seat as he continued to peer through the back window. "Oh my God. What the hell is happening right now?"

"This is it, man. He's going to put a bullet in Santos right now. He's getting out of his car and not coming this way."

"We have to stop it. Stop the car. Go back. It was a ploy to expose Santos. They weren't coming for us." Shane opened his car door.

"Holy shit, Sully!" The detective slammed on his brakes.

Shane jumped out with his gun at the ready and ran back toward the men. "Stop! Drop your weapon!"

Cooper jumped out and followed. "Son of a bitch." With his weapon drawn, he took cover behind his door. "Sully, get back! Take cover!"

Shane heard him call out, but he was transfixed on the event about to unfold a couple hundred feet ahead of him. "Put your gun down, now!"

"Drop back, Sully!" Cooper insisted.

Ballentine held his gun at the chest of Lou Santos, who stood only feet from him. Santos had his hands raised. "Come on, man. Don't do this. Frank said we were square."

"Yeah, well I just got a call from him. When Mr. Lucenz gives an order, I follow it," Ballentine replied.

"These cops will gun you down if you shoot me," Santos replied.

"I guess that's the price I gotta pay, then."

Santos scoffed. "You're crazy, man." He looked at Shane and in a raised voice, shouted. "He's crazy. He's going to kill me."

Shane was still 100 feet away with his gun ready. "You need to throw down your weapon or you'll leave us with no choice, brother. Don't let it end like this."

Santos eyed Ballentine. "He's talking to you. Listen to him."

Ballentine revealed a wide smile before he raised his arms high. His right hand still held the gun.

"Drop it, man," Cooper said as he caught up to Shane.

Ballentine bent over and set it on the ground before slowly pulling up again with his hands raised. "Done. Okay? It's done." He turned his gaze to Santos and smiled. "I don't need to get you here. It'll be easier on the inside anyway."

———

FRANK LUCENZ ROSE from his chair. "It's done. And as long as you keep your end of the deal, you won't see or hear from anyone who works for me." He eyed Allison. "Not that you aren't something spectacular to look at, but I hope I don't see you again, Allison Hart."

She stood from the chair and offered her hand. "I feel exactly the same, Frank." Allison turned on her heel and walked out of the office. As she entered the hall, her hands trembled, and her knees felt weak. She'd held her own against Frank Lucenz. It was over. Finally and truly over.

Allison returned to the lobby to find Charlie and Lucy waiting nearby. Charlie hurried toward her. "It was almost 30 minutes. I thought we were going to have to call the cops."

Allison grabbed onto Charlie's arm to steady herself.

"Are you okay?" Lucy rushed to her side.

"I'm okay. I just want to get out of here."

"You got it." Charlie took the lead and helped Allison outside. "Where to?"

"The station," Allison replied. "We'll go back there and wait. Has anyone heard from Shane? Detective Cooper?"

"Neither of us have, right Charlie?" Lucy asked.

"We have no idea what's going on, so let's get back to the station and get some answers."

They returned to Charlie's car and Allison stepped onto the passenger seat. She closed her eyes and took in a breath while the other two got in.

Charlie pressed the starter button. "Alli, you don't look so good."

"I wasn't sure I could stand my ground..."

"But you did," Lucy cut in. "And you got the result you wanted. Right?"

Allison peered back at her. "I did. No one from the Brunetti family will ever bother us again."

Charlie glanced at her as she drove out of the lot. "And did he take his pound of flesh?"

Allison peered through the passenger window. "In a manner of speaking."

THE DRIVE back to the Downtown station was quiet. Allison considered what she would tell Shane, but then was quick to realize none of that mattered now. What mattered was that Micah and Nolan were safe. Her partners were safe, and she was safe. She cared about Shane, but no one could ever stop her from putting her family first. He would have to understand that, or they weren't going to have much of a future.

Allison hadn't told the girls about Leo and how he'd managed to abandon her, yet again. She hadn't understood how he could let Jenny dictate the terms of his relationship with the mother of his children. But even that held little weight in light of what had tran-spired today.

Charlie parked up and they walked inside the station. It was sometime after lunch, but Allison hadn't paid much attention. It could've been midnight were the sun not shining to say differently.

Inside, Carol was at the front desk and noticed the partners enter. "Well, look who's here. Decided you couldn't stay away, huh?"

"What can we say?" Allison began. "We like the action."

Carol laughed. "There's plenty of that here today. I think Sully's at his desk if you're looking for him."

"Thanks, Carol." Allison nodded and the partners continued through the corridor.

Detective Cooper was at his desk and caught up to them before they reached the stairs. "Allison? There you are. Jesus, where the hell you been?"

She turned back. "It's a long story. Are they here?"

"Our friendly neighborhood bookies? Yes, they're here. We brought in another of Lucenz's men. He held Santos at gunpoint when Sully and I were there to arrest Santos."

"Oh my God. What happened?" Charlie asked.

"Long story," Cooper replied. "I'm sure Sully will fill you in." He reached for Allison's arm. "Leo Hart is on his way down. He knows we caught his father's killer."

"Thank you," Allison replied.

Cooper eyed her. "Hey, can I talk to you for a minute?"

"Um, sure." Allison stepped away from Charlie and Lucy. "What's wrong?"

Cooper retrieved the bug. "I figured you'd want this back."

Allison took it from him. "I appreciate it. I only wish Shane was on the same page about this whole thing."

"He'll come around. Seems to me he's just looking out for you.

He's okay in my book. And it's pretty clear how he feels about you."

Allison wore an uncertain smile. "Sometimes I wonder."

"Don't." He glanced away. "Hey, I got a shit ton of paperwork to sort through. Go on upstairs. I know Sully's waiting to talk to you. And Allison, listen, these guys? Frank Lucenz, the Brunetti family, and all that—don't sweat it, yeah? We got your back."

He turned away and Allison returned to the girls. "Let's head upstairs and see Shane."

"Sure, but maybe Lucy and I should wait for Leo to show, huh? We can keep him company while he's giving his statement," Charlie replied. "I'm sure he'll appreciate the support."

"I'm not as sure as you are, but thank you. That's a good idea." Allison started upstairs.

Lucy nudged Charlie. "What was that about?"

Charlie shook her head. "No idea."

Allison reached the second floor and headed toward Major Crimes. She spotted Shane at his desk and caught his gaze. "Hey."

He regarded her. "Hey. I thought you three were sticking around here till we brought in Santos and Schoeman?"

"I had some things to take care of," Allison replied.

"And did you?" Shane asked.

"I think so." It was clear he wanted to know more but he didn't push her. Allison was certain her expression said it all. "When did you bring in Santos?"

"Just a little while ago. It took time to track him down, but Cooper and I made the arrest." He didn't mention all that happened when they arrested Santos.

"You did it, then. You got the guy who killed Terry."

"And arrested the man who was responsible for taking Micah. That's all I really wanted, Allison," he replied.

"I know, and I thank you for that." She managed a tender

smile. "Is there anything you need from me or the girls? We've been up since yesterday afternoon, and I know we're all exhausted."

"Uh, no. I don't think so. Your part in all this is done. Isn't it?"

"Oh yeah. Our hands are clean of this mess," she replied.

"Good. Yeah, so you guys should go home. I've got a few more hours to stick around and we actually just got a lead on the murder case I have on the fire, so fingers crossed, we get a real break in that case."

"I have no doubt you will." She held his gaze for a moment. "After every case I've had, I feel like, the next one has to be better, you know? Easier."

He chuckled. "Yeah."

"But I'm starting to think this is the job and somedays are just harder than others. And some cases are just harder than others. I didn't know that when I got into this game," Allison said.

"No one does. Same for me here."

"But I do know one thing, Shane. I know at the end of the day, you'll always have my back. Even if you don't like the decisions I make, you won't leave me hanging out to dry."

He locked eyes with her. "Never, Allison. Never."

She started to turn away but stopped short and turned back. "Oh, there was one other thing." Allison stepped closer and leaned into his ear. "I love you too." She pulled back and smiled before walking away.

As Allison disappeared down the steps, Shane smiled wide and tucked his hands into his pants pockets. "Well, there you go."

THE END

ABOUT THE AUTHOR

Robin Mahle has published more than 30 crime fiction novels, many, of which, topped the Amazon charts in the US, Canada, and the UK. And most recently, she has delved into the world of psychological thrillers.

Also a screenwriter, she has adapted some of her works into teleplays, which have gone on to place in film festivals nationwide.

From detectives to federal agents, and from killers to corruption, her page-turning tales grab hold and refuse to let go. Throw in tense action and thrilling twists, and it becomes clear why her readers come back for more.

Robin lives in Coastal Virginia with her husband and two children.

If you enjoyed Ms. Mahle's work, please share your experience by leaving a review on <u>Amazon.</u>

ALSO BY ROBIN MAHLE

The Kate Reid FBI Thriller Series (17 books)

The Chef (stand-alone psych thriller)

The Man in My Attic (stand-alone psych thriller)

The Compound (standalone psych thriller)

The Remy Fontaine Fugitive Hunter Thrillers (4 books)

The Det. Rebecca Ellis Thrillers (5 books)

The Allison Hart PI Thrillers (5 Books)

The Lacy Merrick Thrillers (4 books)

**Visit robinmahle.com and sign up to receive Robin's Newsletter so you can stay up to date on her new releases, events, contests and even exclusive new material!